The Dinner Lady

Hannah Hendy lives in a small town in South Wales with her brand new wife (Covid wedding!) and two rescue cats. A professional chef by trade, she started writing to fill the time on boring night shifts. She is the author of *The Dinner Lady Detectives*, which is her first novel but definitely not her last!

The Dinner Lady Detectives

HANNAH HENDY

San Diego, California

Canelo US
An imprint of Printers Row Publishing Group
9717 Pacific Heights Blvd, San Diego, CA 92121
www.canelobooksus.com

Printers Row Publishing Group is a division of Readerlink Distribution Services, LLC. Canelo US is a registered trademark of Readerlink Distribution Services, LLC.

This edition originally published in the United Kingdom in 2021 by Canelo.

Published in partnership with Canelo.

Correspondence regarding the content of this book should be sent to Canelo US, Editorial Department, at the above address. Author inquiries should be sent to Canelo, Unit 9, 5th Floor, Cargo Works, 1–2 Hatfields, London SE1 9PG, United Kingdom, www.canelo.co.

Publisher: Peter Norton • Associate Publisher: Ana Parker
Art Director: Charles McStravick
Senior Developmental Editor: April Graham
Production Team: Beno Chan, Julie Greene, Rusty von Dyl

Library of Congress Control Number: 2022933871

ISBN: 978-1-6672-0224-2

Printed in India

26 25 24 23 22   1 2 3 4 5

In memory of my Grampie, Les Carter.
You'll never walk alone.

Prologue

The sky outside was grey and miserable, a damp kind of darkness that sucked any remnants of joy from the tidy cul-de-sac on Seymour Road. Another dull Sunday evening, Margery thought to herself as she tended to her knitting in front of the imitation fireplace. The small television in the corner hummed the *Antiques Roadshow* theme, and soon they would be guessing the price of heirlooms.

'Who says women can't multitask?' Clementine said. She chuckled whilst finishing the *Times* cryptic crossword she did every Sunday. Margery laughed back in what she hoped were the right places, even now as she struggled to knit a particularly difficult sleeve, the wool almost certainly getting the better of her. They had lived together at number twenty-two for more than thirty years, and the routine had barely changed. Margery sometimes could not believe how fast the time had gone.

Today was different. There was a soft knock on the door followed by a rapping on the letter box. Though the mystery guest only tapped lightly at their brass door knocker, it was so quiet in the room that it had shattered the peace completely. The ball of wool slipped from Margery's fingers and bounced under the coffee table

I

as the two women sat silently, staring at each other for what felt like an age. Clementine's big brown eyes were wide with surprise, her white eyebrows rising high on her wrinkled forehead.

'Who the devil could that be?' Clementine finally said. The next knock made Clementine reluctantly lower her crossword. 'Margery,' she hissed, 'get the door!'

Margery got up dutifully from her comfortable seat in the cosy living room and made her way out into the cold hallway. She peered through the peephole.

'It's Seren!' Margery said. 'Hide the Quality Street!'

Clementine jumped to attention and ran over to the coffee table where the large, colourful tin had sat since Christmas. Margery and Clementine were treating themselves to a sweet a night.

'It's okay!' Clementine said. 'We've only toffee pennies left, she's welcome to those.'

Margery breathed a sigh of relief and opened the door. 'Hello, Seren. To what do we owe this pleasure?'

'Good evening, Margery,' Seren said, forever out of breath. She bent to stub her cigarette out in the large terracotta plant pot on the doorstep. 'So sorry to bother you at this ungodly hour.' Margery looked up at the carriage clock in the hallway and saw that it said five thirty. 'But you know I wouldn't have come if it wasn't of high importance. May I come in?'

'Oh, of course,' said Margery, and swung the door back to usher her in, sighing in dismay at the cigarette butt now nestled next to her favourite succulent. Seren lumbered past her, almost knocking over the small hallway bookcase that housed Clementine's 'Books I may read again'. She sat down in the pink floral armchair Margery had just vacated, helping herself to a toffee penny. As she took off her huge, dirty coat and hung it on the side of the chair, several lumps of rolling tobacco fell onto the floor out of its front pocket. Margery noted Seren's yellow fingernails, making a mental note to get the chair cover dry-cleaned at the earliest convenience.

As Margery pottered about the kitchen putting together the tea things, she pondered on what Seren could be here to tell them. A social visit from her was unheard of. Until very recently Seren had refused to go out at all in the evenings, and it was strange to see her looking so normal outside of the work clothes they usually saw her in. Well… almost normal.

Margery felt bad for thinking it, but there was just no denying that Seren was not known for looking after herself. It was even worse now that Seren lived alone. Today her unwashed hair was pulled back tightly in a scrunchie, and what looked to be several days' worth of foundation had created a tidemark across her jawline. Though she was not overweight, the selection of dirty, oversized anoraks and saggy old leggings she exclusively wore outside of work did nothing for her.

Poor Seren, Margery thought. She shook her head. Poor, poor Seren. She brought in the pot of tea on the wheeled trolley, and felt embarrassed by Clementine's blatantly disgusted look at Seren's appearance.

'So… what was it you wanted to talk to us about, dear?' Margery said, trying to snap Clementine out of staring as

3

she helped herself to a cup of tea and sat down on the arm of the armchair. 'Help yourself to a toffee penny, or can I get you something a little more substantial?'

'Thanks, but no thank you,' Seren said, opening her third sweet. 'You've put out a fine array of crudités already, and I shan't keep you long.'

Margery frowned confusedly at the small finger bowl of Twiglets and the saucer of party rings she had put out on the coffee table next to the Quality Street. There was not a vegetable in sight.

'Unfortunately, this is not a social visit. I've come here on very dire business indeed.'

'Well, spit it out woman. We haven't got all night.' Clementine said, a little too impatiently for Margery's liking.

Seren leaned forward, conspiratorially 'There's been a death!'

Margery dropped her teacup in shock. 'Good God!'

'Margery, please don't swear!' Clementine said, turning to Seren who was nodding her head vigorously as though she was a person of great importance. As though no one had ever caught her eating profiteroles in the school kitchen's walk-in freezer. 'What do you mean Seren, who's died?'

'It was a terrible accident! Well, that's what they're saying down at the leisure centre,' Seren said, still nodding. 'I wouldn't have believed it myself, but accidents do happen. You know, just last week I broke my back tooth eating a Cadbury mini egg.' Margery and Clementine exchanged a look. 'Anyway, she was one of our own. Our kitchen manager, Mrs Hughes!'

'Mrs Hughes?' Margery said, struggling to find her voice. 'You can't mean Caroline Hughes?'

'Unfortunately, I do, and I have it straight from the mouth of the man who found her! Gary Matthews. Do you know him, works on security? Found her dead Friday night.' She picked the teacup off the floor and handed it back to Margery. 'Do you know the worst bit about it?' Seren paused dramatically. Margery and Clementine shook their heads, enraptured. 'She didn't even get to deliver her last batch of Avon!'

Margery gasped and dropped the teacup again.

'I don't know how many people know already. You're first on my rounds, and I'm not too sure on the fine details because I don't like to pry. I'm not a busybody, you know that!' Seren paused to reach for another toffee penny from the bowl. 'I just thought you should know before work tomorrow.'

It was a lot to take in, Margery thought. Especially in the whirlwind of a way Seren had rushed out the news. 'Gosh, Seren,' she finally said. 'A death like that, and it's hardly been a year since, well…' She stopped, not wanting to upset the woman sitting across from her.

'I know,' said Seren. 'I'm… well… I'd still rather not talk about that if it's all the same to you.'

Clementine and Margery nodded in sympathy.

Seren hadn't really had an easy time of it recently. Margery made a mental note to drop a Tupperware of homemade lamb cawl or shepherd's pie off at her house.

'Well, I'd better be off. Thank you for your hospitality.' Seren dragged herself up and out of the chair in a flurry of falling toffee penny wrappers, grasping her dirty coat that Margery was sure she just sprayed with deodorant instead of washing. Margery saw her out, feeling ashamed of her relief when they were rid of the smell of the woman's clothes.

'Can you believe that, Clem?' Margery tentatively perched back down onto the chair. 'Caroline dead. Avon undelivered. That just doesn't happen here.'

Clementine had remained in her seat, and she picked up the cryptic crossword again. 'No, things like that don't happen in Dewstow.' After a minute, she sighed and threw the newspaper down on the coffee table in defeat, letting her reading glasses fall onto the cord they were attached to so she could rub her eyes. 'We should get a good night's sleep. Who knows what awaits us tomorrow.'

Chapter One

The next morning, sat in their usual seats on the number five bus, Margery and Clementine listened intently to the gossip that surrounded them.

'Oh, Margery! Clem! You knew her, didn't you?' said Mrs Mugglethwaite, the lady who worked at the post office. Everyone in the bus turned and stared.

Margery smiled back grimly, glancing nervously at Clementine.

Clementine sighed dramatically, in the manner of a woman who has had an extraordinary burden placed upon her shoulders. 'We did know her, we worked with her for years. Such a shame!'

The ladies of the number five all nodded agreeably.

'Such a glamorous woman. She'd been to London, you know!' Clementine said, proudly. There was much oohing at that, and Margery was sure she even heard Mrs Melon, the greengrocer, gasp out loud.

The bus lurched onward, the engine whining as it struggled to pull itself up Dewstow Hill. It was a cold morning, the kind that made you want to stay in bed, and Margery rather wished that they had. She snuck a glance at Clementine, who was drawing small patterns in the early morning fog clouding the bus window distractedly, and wondered what she was thinking. She knew Clem was more upset about Caroline than she had let on to Seren. Clem had tossed and turned in the bed next to her, keeping them both awake all night. Margery's eyes burned with exhaustion. It was going to be a long day.

Breakfast itself had been a stilted affair. They hadn't spoken much, both wrapped up in their own thoughts and the shock of the news, Margery supposed, as she stared past Clementine's glum face and out of the window at the scenery whipping past. She had always thought that Dewstow was a particularly pretty town. The town would not win any awards for excitement, but with its mostly preserved country views and the charming High Street, it was a very pleasant place to live.

She was glad that they had settled here all those years ago, in fact Margery and Clementine had worked together at Summerview Secondary School for longer than they had owned their house. Officially titled 'Education Centre Nourishment Consultants', they all preferred 'Dinner Ladies' better. Well, everyone apart from Clementine who demanded the use of their full title. She became terribly upset if it was not used, though Margery sometimes suspected that this was more because she enjoyed making a scene than anything else. As part of a team of eight, including Seren and the late Caroline Hughes, they captured the attention of the 1200 pupils, aged 11 to 16, between the hours of twelve and one o'clock every weekday.

They had a cushy role as far as cooking positions went, usually finishing well before three o'clock each day. Margery was proud to work for the school, which had a reputation for being one of the best in the area. The students were bright and interesting, and the school was consistently awarded a 'Good' Ofsted rating, though the headmaster, Mr Barrow, was always pushing for an 'Outstanding'. Apart from the time in 2004 when six sheep escaped from a neighbouring field into the playground, Caroline's death was the most exciting yet distressing thing to happen in Margery and Clementine's entire lives.

When they arrived to set up in the kitchen at eight fifteen, there was already a hubbub of activity. It was one of the biggest kitchens Margery had ever worked in personally, although it did still bear the tell-tale sign of bad planning that most catering establishments had. For one, the kitchen was on the first floor which made it much more difficult to take in deliveries, and also the room was a strange shape, as if serving food had been a complete afterthought to the architect who designed the school.

The main preparation area, where the dinner ladies spent most of their time, was just behind the serving area, and the children would queue by the till, all staring in as they served them. There was a small dishwasher towards the back of the room next to the dry store, and then down a long, narrow corridor were several tall standing fridges and the humongous walk-in freezer. The equipment was basic as catering set-ups go, you wouldn't find a sous vide machine or a blast chiller if you decided you wanted to practise a technique you had seen on MasterChef, but they made do with what they had as best they could.

The youngest 'Education Centre Nourishment Consultant', Ceri-Ann, was sat in one of the huge metal sinks, smoking a cigarette out of the open window while furiously texting. Sharon was wailing uncontrollably on Karen's shoulder, and Karen continued to pat her on the back, reciting comforting clichés about death. The only person carrying on as if it was a normal day was tiny Gloria, busily unpacking all the frozen peas and mash potato from the delivery, in time for the lunch period.

'Morning ladies!' Gloria paused in her work to greet Margery and Clementine, her glasses fogged up in condensation from the frozen goods. The rest of her school-issue catering department uniform as spick and span as the day she had received it.

Margery smiled back, adorning her head with a new hairnet from the plastic dispensing box on the wall, before stepping through the doorway into the kitchen. 'Good morning, Gloria. Though there's not much good about it today, is there?'

Gloria nodded, folding the cardboard delivery boxes to take them down the fire escape to the recycling area outside. 'Yeah, terrible news about Caroline.'

Sharon wailed at the mention of Caroline and clutched Karen's arm tighter. 'Terrible business,' Karen said, shaking her head in what seemed like a well-rehearsed bit, 'but at least she is with the angels now.'

'Quite, quite,' Clementine mused. 'Does anyone know exactly what happened?'

'Not really,' Ceri-Ann said, flicking her cigarette butt out the window down to the ground a storey below, not bothering to look up from her phone. Margery noted with annoyance that Ceri-Ann was wearing her hair net as far back as she could get it, just gently covering the very roots of her hair which she had pulled into an over-sized bun. 'They've taped off the freezer, though. The policeman said we weren't allowed to go in there.'

'Why not?' Margery asked, and Gloria flapped her hands about frantically at her to get her to stop.

'Because the cleaners haven't been in to clean it up yet,' Sharon cried from where she still leaned against Karen's muscular shoulder. 'They said they don't work weekends, even for this!'

Sharon dissolved into a fresh batch of tears, and Karen patted her gingerly on the back again. 'There, there Sharon. I'm sure she didn't feel any pain, she's in a better place now. And anyway, she loved being in the freezer. She really went out with her boots on.'

'What do you mean?' Margery said, 'She died here? Oh my God... she's not still in there, is she?' she exclaimed, feeling herself leaning back against the nearest kitchen countertop, as her legs went to jelly.

Gloria shook her head. 'No, they took her body away before we all got here. You know what Barbara's like, though,' she said, then rolled her eyes at the sight of Sharon sobbing, tears pouring down her pale face. 'She'd rather eat a bag of lemons than call the cleaning team in on her day off.' She sighed, putting the last piece of folded cardboard on the floor. 'Can you and Clementine take

Mr Barrow his tea trolley this morning? The assembly is at nine, and I can't leave the delivery only partly put away. Anyway, Ceri-Ann is insisting she needs to mark herself "safe" on Facebook.'

She turned to glare at Ceri-Ann, who was engrossed in taking a very sombre-looking selfie. 'Whatever the hell that means,' Gloria mumbled. 'Sharon, can you *please* stop that incessant wailing and help me with the onions? If we're going to make the assembly on time, we need everything ready before we go!'

'Of course we can take the headmaster's trolley,' Clementine said, 'but where is Seren? That's usually her job.'

'Saw her at the newsagents this morning buying her breakfast,' Ceri-Ann said, finally jumping down from the sink and grabbing a colour-coded chopping board. 'Haven't seen her since.'

The dinner ladies knew what Seren's breakfast consisted of – half a pack of Lambert & Butler cigarettes and a chocolate chip muffin. She was never usually this late, though.

In Seren's absence, Margery and Clementine busied themselves arranging the tea trolley in the dry store. They carefully avoided the cordoned-off part of the kitchen, but Margery could see Clementine giving it occasional glances. They decided on the good biscuits from the top shelf, as today seemed as good a day as any to use them, and tried to find two similar teaspoons. Failing miserably, they settled for plastic ones.

The headmaster's office was a short walk away, and yet to Margery it seemed to take hours. Every corridor looked exactly the same, even with the different displays of children's work proudly arranged on the walls above the threadbare carpet. Though the students changed year by year, the subjects never seemed to. Margery always thought the teachers must just replace the old work with new identical pages and wondered how they managed to tell it all apart. It was fascinating how even the students' faces all blended in together after a while. Sometimes Margery and Clementine would be out doing their weekly big shop and a former student would run over to say hello, eager to greet the ladies who used to give them extra chips on a Friday. Nevertheless, Margery very rarely recognised school pupils outside of the school grounds. If she was honest with herself, she struggled when she was on the school grounds. She had taken to calling them all 'Dear'.

It occurred to her, as they made their way down each identical corridor, that they had accidentally picked the trolley with the most worn-out wheels and it was slaloming all over the hallway.

'For God's sake pull yourself together, Margery!' Clementine said, 'Yes, Caroline is dead and we're a bit short-staffed, but we've faced harder times than these. Remember when we ran out of custard for the cornflake crunch? Hmm?'

Margery rolled her eyes. 'It's not me, Clem, it's the trolley, and regardless, I think Caroline's death is slightly worse than one of the pupils breaking his tooth on a cornflake crunch!'

Clementine scoffed. 'Well, Lord help us if we ever lose the key for the vending machine again. That would be a *real* disaster.'

They finally rounded the corner and stopped outside the headmaster's office. Clementine reached out to knock on the gaudy green door, but it swung open of its own accord at the slightest pressure. Margery and Clementine exchanged a nervous look.

'Well,' Margery whispered, 'it's like you said, we must persevere and all that.'

'Yes well, after you Margery,' Clementine whispered back.

After a long staring contest, Margery finally lost the battle of wills and, with a sigh, she manoeuvred the tea trolley into the office, wobbling it behind Mr Barrow's imposing desk. He had told them all when he purchased it that he commissioned it from a local carpenter, but Ceri-Ann had seen it in the online Oak Furniture Land sale, and shown them all on her phone. The stiff wheels of the tea trolley made it hard work to put it where the headmaster liked it, and suddenly all the plastic teaspoons and self-serve sachets of Kenco coffee were all over the floor, the hot water for drinks only kept contained by sturdy catering flasks.

'Margery, do not swear!' Clementine said, as they both dropped to the floor to pick it all up, even though Margery had not uttered a word. 'We haven't failed a tea run in twenty years. We can't start now.'

By the time they had everything back on the trolley, with the good biscuits rearranged in concentric circles,

Margery was panting with the exertion of it all. She leaned on the desk for a moment to catch her breath.

'Margery!' Clementine snapped her out of her daze. She was peering at the documents lying on the head-master's desk under Margery's hands. 'Does that say what I think it does?'

'Well, that depends on what you think it says, I suppose. You don't have your reading glasses on,' Margery said, lifting the paper close to her face. She, too, did not have her reading glasses on. 'Oh my.'

Transcribed on the document she was holding were notes from the police report on Caroline's death. She tried to skim it as fast as she could. Mr Barrow was obviously trying to write an accident report for the freezer, judging by the open risk-assessment folder that had laid next to the paper on the desk. Two of the scribbled lines stood out – "Blood needs cleaning" and "Scratches on inside of freezer door".

Clementine gasped from where she was reading over Margery's shoulder. Margery was suddenly aware of the voices outside in the corridor, and she dropped the paper back on the desk as if it had burnt her, just as Mr Barrow entered the office.

'Oh, hello ladies,' he greeted, beaming at them as he entered, despite practically having to bend himself in half to get through the average-sized door frame. Although he was in his late fifties, his smile always made him seem a lot younger to Margery, along with the fact he still had a full head of red hair, darkened by the gel he used to slick it back. 'Thank you ever so much for the trolley. I'll need a few cups of coffee with the way this day is going already, though it would be nice to have something a bit stronger!'

He smiled as they moved away from his side of the desk so he could take off his three-button suit jacket, and place it firmly on the back of the IKEA chair he had told everyone was a gift from an estranged aunt who lived in Italy.

'Not a problem, Headmaster,' Clementine squeaked, and they departed the office, power-walking as fast as they could.

Margery could not imagine how to say what she was thinking. How could there possibly be scratches on the freezer door? It was a ginormous great metal thing and, in Margery's mind, completely impenetrable by anything less than a sledgehammer. What could have happened to cause something like that? And blood needed clearing up! It was almost unthinkable.

Clementine broke the silence first. 'The special assembly starts in a few minutes. I don't know why he ordered for all that coffee now. He won't even have time to drink it!' Margery sensed that Clementine was more upset about what they had read than whether the head-master drank his coffee, but she was too shocked to try and lure the conversation out of her. 'The biscuits will have gone soft by the time he gets round to eating them. The good biscuits too! What a waste!'

'It's okay,' Margery said. 'If any of them have survived when we go to clear the trolley, I'll pop them back in the box. They'll be good as new.'

When they reached the door to the canteen, Clementine stopped and took a deep breath. 'Okay…' she said, more to herself than to Margery.

Margery patted her gently on the back. 'Come on, Clem, let's gather the troops so we can get a good spot in the hall together. We don't want to end up sitting too close to any of the children!'

–

It seemed the school governors had decided against closing the school for any period of mourning. It was only one of the dinner ladies that had died, Margery thought bitterly. Though she had to admit that most of the school pupils would have no idea who thought up the menus and arranged for bake sales to happen. She was certain that Mr Barrow had arranged the assembly less as an opportunity for them to grieve together and more because he liked to talk. Usually, a week could not pass without him calling them all together so he could read a Rudyard Kipling poem at them. Most of the time he would change the words to make it school relevant, and Margery particularly dreaded the twenty-minute version of 'If' that he always brought out on GCSE results day.

What was left of the dinner lady team, sans Seren, gathered at the back of the hall close to the exit. At the very front of the massive room, facing towards the rows and rows of uncomfortable plastic chairs, sat the headmaster and the Deputy Head, Mrs Rosemary Smith, who today wore a prim ladies' skirt suit. Her hair was perfectly coiffed into its silver bob as usual, tucked behind her ears to show off a large pair of expensive-looking drop earrings.

The students piled in by form groups, and for a few minutes the screeching of chairs took precedence over the portable CD player at the front of the school hall that was blaring out 'Smoke on the Water'. As the song ended, Mr Barrow lunged up from his seat to turn it off; his long gangly limbs were almost comical in the way that they were stuffed into his too-short suit.

He clapped his hands together as silence fell over the hall and began his speech. 'Children, as some of you may know, Mrs Hughes, our catering manager... ahem... sadly passed away over the weekend.' He paused for effect, and the children began to whisper excitedly. 'Mrs Hughes was a tremendously important member of our kitchen team here at Summerview, and it has been a terrible, terrible loss to our family.' He cleared his throat. 'As you will all remember from the special assembly we held in March to celebrate our kitchen staff's birthdays, Caroline was only...' Margery could see even from her spot a fair distance away that he was trying to check something he had written on his palm. '...seventy-eight, and it is a great shame. A true shame.'

Mr Barrow insisted on holding the dinner ladies' birthday celebrations all on the same day to save time and electricity holding assemblies. Clementine was dreadfully upset last year when they had mistakenly said she was sixty-three instead of sixty-two.

'But as we all know, Caroline was a very big Deep Purple fan, and that is why I chose to play you that song today.'

Margery had never heard Caroline mention a love of rock music. She thought that maybe it was a similar situation to the one that had happened a few years ago. Karen's grandmother had died, and Karen's mother had told her that Doris Day's version of 'Que Sera, Sera' had been her grandmother's favourite song. She had treasured this precious piece of information as though the song was a dear personal possession of her grandmother's, using it to find light in a dark time. She had even gone as far as to get a large tattoo of the lyrics on her thigh. Then a year ago, Karen's mother confessed that she did not know her mother's favourite song at all. She and Karen's father had put a few age-relevant songs into a hat and played the one they pulled out of it at the funeral.

'Such a terrible waste of a life. Terrible, terrible' Mr Barrow was stalling. For a man who liked to talk so much, Margery thought, it was surprising how quickly he ran out of things to say.

'Anyway, if any of you are feeling particularly sad or upset about the departing of Mrs Hughes, please don't hesitate to talk to your form teacher about your feelings. No matter how silly you feel!' he said, gesticulating a bit too earnestly with his hands. 'Some of you may have felt this sadness before, if you have lost a pet or... umm... a grandparent.'

The Year Sevens were beginning to become restless in the two front rows. 'Would you... would you like to say anything, Mrs Smith?' Mr Barrow turned around to look desperately at his deputy head. She shook her head almost violently in her desperation not to be involved.

'Okay, well then, let's move on.' He was sweating a bit now, Margery noted in disgust as he gulped and tugged at the collar of his shirt. 'As a tribute to our wonderful Mrs Hughes, the recorder club are going to play, uh, what song is it again, Mrs Large?'

The tiny music teacher stepped forward. 'Well, we haven't had time to rehearse anything special,' she squeaked, beckoning the front row of Year Sevens to stand up. 'So, we're going to do "London's Burning" in a round.'

'"London's Burning!"' Mr Barrow exclaimed a little too enthusiastically. 'Such a fitting tribute, Mrs Hughes *had* been to London recently. Everybody, please clap for the recorder club!'

As the cacophony of Year Sevens wielding recorders began, the dinner ladies excused themselves and slipped from the hall, claiming there was custard to make and fish fingers to defrost.

Chapter Two

'That was rubbish,' Margery said as they entered the safe haven of the kitchen.

'Margery, please do not swear,' Clementine said.

'It was bloody rubbish!' Karen said. 'Caroline hated all kinds of music. "What's the point of singing? It's just talking with instruments," she used to say!'

Sharon wailed at the mention of Caroline again. They turned the gas and equipment back on and got back to their daily duties. Sharon stopped to sniff dramatically every now and then. The kitchen door burst open suddenly, and in came Seren, almost purple in the face, huffing and puffing like she was in respiratory arrest and very, very sweaty.

'Seren! Where on earth have you been?' Clementine exclaimed. 'You look awful! Come and sit down, Ceri-Ann will get you a nice glass of water,' she eyed Seren again, 'and some paper towels.'

'I'm. Sorry. I'm. So. Late,' Seren puffed. Gloria passed over her asthma inhaler. 'I've. Been. Walking. Up. Dewstow. Hill… for an hour!'

'An hour!' Karen scoffed. 'It's a five-minute walk at most!' Seren shot her a dirty look. Karen had completed a five-kilometre charity walk several years ago, and took pride in being the fittest of all the dinner ladies, often over-simplifying distances and difficulty.

'Oh, Seren. You've got to start getting the bus again,' Gloria said, dabbing gently at Seren's forehead with a napkin. 'It's been months. No one's talking about it anymore!'

'Yes, they are!' Seren wailed. 'They talk about it all the time.'

Gloria went back to making soothing noises and wiped Seren's brow. 'Ceri-Ann,' she hissed, her long braid nearly catching Seren in the face as she turned. 'Get Seren a cup of tea.'

Ceri-Ann scuttled off, phone in hand.

—

Margery thought about Seren for the rest of the day and well into the evening.

Seren had been walking Dewstow Hill to get to work for nearly a year, but she had never been that late before. It lingered in her thoughts while they ate the sausage and mash Clementine had made for dinner, and even after they had retired to the living room for a rousing card game of Piccalilli Paula.

'Do you not think, Clem, that it's all a bit weird? Seren is never late, she's usually there before we get there, and we get the earliest bus!'

Clementine turned to look at her, considering for a moment. 'You're right, it's not like her at all.' She picked up a new card from the pile and carefully slotted it into place in her hand. 'The whole thing is weird though.'

Margery wondered about the insurance claim Mr Barrow was trying to file. How could Caroline's death have been an accident when her end seemed so brutal? Maybe she was jumping to conclusions, she thought. No one had actually explained how it had happened yet.

'It's such a shame really, Caroline was in such good spirits on Friday too,' Margery said carefully, laying down her winning hand with a smile. 'Piccalilli Paula!' Clementine sighed and started to reset the game, muttering something under her breath about the deck not being shuffled very well.

'She was always in good spirits though, wasn't she?' Clementine said as she doled out the cards. 'Caroline, I mean. She was always so cheerful and lovely.'

Margery shook her head at that, taking the cards Clementine had dealt her and sneaking a peek. 'Do you not remember when Seren forgot to put the spoons out for lunch service and Caroline made her eat an entire saucepan of custard with a fork as a punishment?'

'And how we laughed, Margery!'

They lapsed back into a comfortable silence, with only the ticking of carriage clocks and slapping down of cards heard in the small cosy room.

–

Later that night, in their dark bedroom, Margery could not stop turning the strangeness of the day over and over in her head. It was one thing to know Caroline was dead,

23

another entirely to work in an environment without her. They had all become part of the wallpaper of the school. She could not think of a day where she had not seen Mrs Hughes pottering about the place unsteadily, using her walking stick to trip people.

'That must be what's upsetting me,' Margery thought out loud. She certainly had not been close friends with Caroline. She much preferred to keep her at an arm's length emotionally. It was hard enough to deal with Clementine's erratic mood swings and bossiness on a daily basis, without simultaneously inviting the often-flippant cruelty of Caroline's practical joking into her personal life.

'Margery,' Clementine hissed from across their bedroom into the darkness.

'Yes, Clem?'

'That bit of paper in Mr Barrow's office was a bit weird, wasn't it?'

Margery thought about it. 'Yes, it was. I wish there was something more we could do to find out what that was all about.'

There was a long pause and Margery suddenly wished she had never said anything. This could quickly turn into one of Clementine's 'things', which often became no more than extended wild goose chases. The last seemingly innocent Clementine-concocted adventure ended in a literal goose chase after Henry and Henrietta, the local pond's resident geese, had eaten all of the 'quack snacks' that Margery brought with them to feed the ducks. Clementine had tried, and failed, to have them both arrested for theft.

'Margery,' Clementine said. Margery could feel her sitting up to peer over at her through the darkness. 'Something's wrong with this. Seren said it was an accident, but I'm not so sure it was!'

'Well, we know literally nothing about what happened, Clem.'

'Yes, I know, but that's why we should find out more!'

They slipped back into silence. Margery stared up at the textured paint of the Artex ceiling and hoped that if she counted the bumps and ridges on it for long enough, she would be able to drift off to sleep.

'Margery!' Clementine hissed again. Margery rolled her eyes at the intrusion.

'Yes, Clem?' Though she tried, she could not keep the snap out of her voice.

'Nothing.' There was a pause, and Margery closed her eyes.

'That assembly was crap!'

'Please just go to sleep, Clementine!'

After a lot of tossing and turning, Margery did eventually manage to drift off. Her dreams were filled with horrors. She had not cooked enough chips and the children were queuing as far as the eye could see around the living room, and Caroline's big round face was screaming at her from somewhere she could not see. She woke up hours before she needed to, feeling as though she had barely slept at all.

She pondered staying in the warm bed for a bit but finally she dragged herself out of it and into her dressing gown, briefly catching a glance of herself in the gloomy morning light of their long bedroom mirror. She shook away the ghostly image of the bags under her eyes and the mess of her greying hair. Until recently it had remained the dark blonde she had been born with, but lately the years had caught up with her, though she did not look too haggard for sixty-one, she often thought.

Clementine had gone grey hilariously early in comparison, and it had been much more noticeable with her dark brown strands. Though Clementine was possibly not as vain, she had simply shrugged it off and carried on, whereas others who went grey at thirty-five might have taken up all sorts of dyes and potions to retain their youth. Clementine had always been the prettier one of the two of them, Margery supposed. Her own face was rounder and she had always been the plainer one, though part of that could be more down to Clementine's eccentricities than anything else. Margery had always found her radiant. She had, in weak moments long ago in the past, worried that Clementine might leave her for someone more interesting, but the tides of time had evened their appearances out, along with her worries.

Margery wandered downstairs to the kitchen and made a cup of tea to take into the living room, which thankfully was no longer playing the part of the school's canteen as it had in her nightmare. Instead, it was awash with early morning sunlight and the comforting ball of sleepy, purring fur that was their old lady tortoiseshell cat, Pumpkin, curled up on the arm of Margery's favourite chair. Pumpkin stretched and chirruped serenely as Margery sat down next to her.

They sat in peace for a while, Margery absent-mindedly stroking the cat as she sipped her tea and watched through the parted curtains as the day dawned outside, over their front garden and their across road neighbour number forty-four's ginormous hedge. Clementine threatened to cut it down with a chainsaw at least twice a week, more on the weeks they were due a parcel but it went to the sorting office because Dawn Simmonds of forty-four refused to take it in for them, but Margery had a soft spot for the hedge. It broke up the identical nature of the rest of the estate, and she enjoyed watching the birds that had made their home on the top of it, as did Pumpkin.

'We should have a look at where Caroline died.' Clementine appeared suddenly behind her, and Margery spilled her tea all over her dressing gown.

'For God's sake, Clem! You've got to stop doing that! I don't have my ear horn, I can't hear you sneaking around!' Margery said, dabbing at herself with the hanky she kept in the pocket of her dressing gown.

Clementine patted her knee in apology and sat down opposite her on the worn-out sofa. 'Sorry, I'll make you another cup in a minute. But you know as well as I do that this is weird, Margery!'

'I...' Margery could not deny it. 'I don't know.'

Clementine played with a loose thread on the arm of the sofa. 'I just don't think I'll be able to rest until I know what happened, you know?'

'We can't just go wandering around the crime scene. That's a silly idea. You know it is!'

27

'Hear me out,' Clementine said. 'I'm not saying that we should go poking our noses in where they're not needed.' She got up from the sofa and began pacing the room, clearly thinking up some horrible scheme to drag Margery into.

'Exactly!' Margery said. 'We shouldn't get involved, it's a matter for the police!'

'Now, now. Let's not be too hasty, Margery. We're meddlers, it's what we do!'

'You're the meddler!' Margery laughed. 'You've been getting us into trouble for literally decades.'

'Listen, Margery, we knew Caroline for years. We're *grieving*!' Clementine said the last word as if it absolved them of a multitude of sins. Margery could hear the cogs turning in Clementine's head. Clementine continued, 'So… if we *did* decide to have a little look at where Caroline died, well… how could anyone object?'

Margery shook her head. Clementine was going to win. She always did in the end.

Chapter Three

Margery and Clementine clock-watched the day away. Lunchtime had been a roaring success as it usually was, though there was a notable upswing in compliments for the dinner lady team. Complaints about lumpy custard and undercooked quiche pastry were down, and Margery could not help but think that it was a result of the wave of empathy directed towards them after Caroline's untimely departure.

Margery took charge for the time being. Someone needed to, if only to stop Karen wearing running trainers in the kitchen, and to keep Gloria from throttling Seren when she arrived late again. Being the manager was exhausting, even if it was not an official role.

She spent most of the shift begging Ceri-Ann to put her phone away, and pleading with Sharon to, 'Please, please, stop crying and start buttering bread before we all drown, for Christ's sake!' Sharon did no such thing, and the sombre tone lingered relentlessly as they worked. A much different day than usual, Margery thought. The last time the team were this miserable was the day of the Grand National sweepstake when none of them had won anything.

Usually by this time after the lunch hour, the small canteen kitchen was full of laughter as they cleaned up, but then Caroline had been the leader of most of the 'fun', Margery supposed. Though, Caroline's idea of fun was usually one horrible practical joke or another. She had constantly been filling people's home shoes with a mixture of porridge and honey, or setting someone's house keys inside a bowl of jelly. Clementine often roared with laughter at the memory of some of these pranks, but Margery, who would be the one chiselling the porridge oats from out of their shoes, did not find them so amusing.

Though she was not all bad, that was the enigma of the woman. Her sense of humour could seem so needlessly callous and flippantly cruel but then at the same time as you discovered she had glued your locker shut, you would also find that she was leaving work a little bit early to go and volunteer at the local food bank. Or that she had left extra money in the vending machine for the next person who wandered over to use it. She was constantly giving away meals to less well-off students and their families, disguising the charity as 'recipe boxes' to dissuade from embarrassment. So, really in the grand scheme of things, the occasional porridge in your shoes was mostly forgivable.

At two o'clock, Clementine offered their services in mopping the floor, and Gloria nearly bowled them over in her excitement to leave so early, throwing the cleaning-cupboard keys to Margery on her way out. Seren was hesitant to go, but eventually they shuffled her out with a thermos of premixed Angel Delight and a bag of out-of-date sandwiches from the canteen's vending machine. Margery did not know why Seren tried so hard, in all honesty. Seren had been Caroline's scapegoat for all wrongdoings, and Margery privately felt that things might improve for her now her tormentor was gone.

Margery was nervous about looking inside the freezer. She did not like Clementine's plan one bit. Clementine never had much impulse control, and the older she got the worse it seemed to become. But Margery learnt over the years, when faced with similarly outrageous schemes, that to swim against the current was to drown, and Margery intended to float.

Clementine insisted, in an almost hushed whisper, that they were not doing anything wrong by having a little look, but she simultaneously decided that they should don protective clothing. 'You know, just in case, Margery!' Clementine said, but would not give her any further details on why. Nevertheless, when Clementine handed her the goggles and gloves they usually wore when cleaning the ovens, Margery put them on obediently.

'Right, Margery,' Clementine said, pulling on her own set of rubber gloves and easing the goggles down onto her face, 'we shall have to get into Caroline's mindset and retrace her steps, what would she be doing?'

'No idea!' Margery said.

'Well…' Clementine was obviously trying to think of what the particularly robust children in an Enid Blyton novel would do. 'Let's think logically about it. Where would she have gone?'

Margery shrugged. She genuinely did not know. They spent most of their days trying to leave work early; she could not fathom why Caroline would still have been here on a Friday night.

'Well!' Clementine enthused again. 'Why was she here? How many cups of tea would she have had?'

Clementine must really be clutching at straws.

'As we both know, Caroline hasn't drunk a cup of tea since 1976,' Margery said. Clementine nodded back. It was a well-known fact amongst the dinner ladies.

'Ooh, but she did enjoy a hot chocolate though!' Clementine said. 'Good call Margery! To the water boiler!'

Two cups of off-brand Horlicks later and they were still none the wiser to Caroline's plight.

'Well,' Margery said. 'That didn't help at all.'

'No,' Clementine said, putting her empty mug in the sink. 'I feel like we're just wasting time with all this drink-making, and we've got to get in and out of here before the cleaners turn up.' She turned to Margery suddenly wide-eyed. 'I mean, not that there's anything wrong with what we're doing, Margery!' She laughed the forced chuckle of someone who had nearly been caught doing something very, very wrong indeed. Margery rolled her eyes, and turned to look back down the kitchen.

It seemed very empty now that the rest of the team had left. The preparation area seemed much more claustrophobic than it did during the daytime. Gloria had turned the gas off before she went home, and the incredibly noisy extractor fans went off with it. Without the usual roaring of the fans, the room was left in an almost deafening silence. The kitchen had become unbearably stuffy much quicker than Margery imagined it would, and the quiet clicking from the under-counter fridges was enough to make her heart race with anxiety.

'This is stupid,' Clementine said. 'We know why we're here. Let's just get on with it.' Margery nodded in agreement, as Clementine turned on her heels. They both headed past the dry store, down the corridor and towards the freezer.

They made their way under the protective police ticker tape denoting the scene and paused. The freezer door was large enough that two people could stand in the doorway and chat at the same time, as Ceri-Ann and Clementine often did when they were both trying to get out of doing any work. On its right side was an enormous door handle, which you had to pull with quite some force to open. Margery had always found it a pain when carrying trays of food to put in it. You either had to call someone over to pull the handle for you, or do a sort of balancing act — holding the tray or container under one arm and resting it on your hip as you pulled the handle quickly, before you dropped the food all over the floor. It was designed to be airtight, Margery supposed, but that never made it any less infuriating. To get out of the freezer, if someone accidentally shut you in, you simply pressed hard on the big round button on the other side of the door. The panel next to the door handle displayed the temperature, which the dinner ladies dutifully logged in the kitchen paperwork twice a day. Today it sat at a stirring minus twenty degrees centigrade.

The freezer was always a source of fun for Caroline, so this whole thing was a bit ironic really. Margery remembered the day Caroline demanded that Seren mop the freezer. Seren had complied obediently, not realising her mistake until the hot water from the mop hit the freezer floor, freezing both the mop and Seren's kitchen clogs to it simultaneously. That was Caroline's cue to fling the door open and laugh hysterically, whilst filming the entire scene on the old VHS camcorder she always carried around in her handbag.

Clementine pulled the door handle hard and it swung open easily. For a moment, as the fog swirled out and the cold air met the warmth of the kitchen, the freezer looked almost as it did the Friday before. Neat shelving units of boxed cakes, single-serve pies and paninis lining the walls, and there would be nothing else inside, Margery prayed, no other horrors to jump out. It was one thing to know that this was Caroline's final resting place and quite another to see it in person.

The fog cleared and they stepped back in shock. In the dim light, from the small bulb on the freezer ceiling, Margery saw that the freezer door was entirely coated in blood. Not just the door: the freezer floor had a line of blood smeared along it from the front to the back, as though someone had dragged themselves across it while bleeding. The emergency door button was similarly coated, where it had obviously stood useless.

'Oh…' Clementine breathed out. She looked as stunned as Margery felt. There were several long scrapes in the ice on the inside of the door, where someone had clawed at it. A chill went down Margery's spine as she imagined Caroline trying desperately to escape. She had to turn away with her hand over her mouth, trying with all her might to not be sick.

'Oh…' Clementine said again, quieter this time.

Margery turned back around: every instinct she had was telling her to run, get on the bus, go home and forget she had ever seen anything, but she forced herself to turn and look again. She had to know what happened, they had come this far.

'Clem, there's something back there! Under the shelf.' She retched and had to look away again.

'Okay.' Clementine seemed to be psyching herself up. 'Okay!' She charged into the freezer and slid on the icy floor, one of the rubber gloves flapping off in her haste.

'Careful, Clem!' Margery said, and followed her into the cold air instinctively. Margery was right. On the floor right at the back of the freezer was a clipboard. It had slipped behind the shelving unit, and was lodged between the shelving and the back wall. Clementine had to really yank it to get it up from its precarious position, but she managed it after a few strong tugs.

'It's just the stocktake paperwork,' Clementine said grimly. 'That's the mystery of what she was doing on Friday solved.'

They should have known, Margery thought. Caroline always did the stocktake on Friday nights, though they

35

were not usually there to witness it. Caroline had always seemed quite at home in the freezer the few times Margery had seen her in there, her face set determinedly as if she were about to start individually counting each frozen pea. Margery shivered and pulled the collar of her kitchen-issue polo shirt closer to her neck. Her nose was beginning to feel like it might fall off; her lungs burned as she inhaled in the cold air.

'We should put it back,' Margery said, her breath billowing out in a cloud. She was about to suggest to Clementine that they went straight home and forgot all about this, when the freezer door slammed shut, throwing them into pitch black.

'Margery!' Clementine yelped, and they both screamed in surprise. Margery made her way back to where she was sure the door was, and scrabbled around in the darkness looking for the door handle, her fingers sliding all over the icy door. She was unable to even see her own hand in front of her face. She stopped still as a wave of panic washed over her and began to rise in the back of her throat. Her only thought was to yell for help, but she knew from experience that even if the freezer was not so airtight, all the boxes piled up inside made it practically soundproof. The entire dinner lady team could be in the kitchen next to it and no one would ever hear them.

Wrapping her arms around herself as she shivered, she called to Clementine. 'Clem, do you have your phone? Get it out, it'll have a light.' She could feel herself beginning to sweat, despite the cold freezer air. 'You can call Gloria!'

'No, of course I don't have my phone!' Clementine said, as though that was the stupidest thing anyone had ever said. 'Call her on your phone!'

'I don't have a phone, remember when I went to buy one and you told me not to bother? You said we could ring from the landline!'

'I don't recall saying that.'

'You said texting was the handiwork of the devil!' Margery exasperated.

'I don't think I would have said—'

'You said if you wanted to send someone a photo, you'd print it out and post it to them!'

'That doesn't sound like me!' Clementine scoffed in the darkness, but Margery cut her off again.

'You said you'd tried to send a photo to Gloria once and the signal was so bad she didn't get it for three days so you might as well have posted it!'

'Oh… well I suppose do remember that.'

Margery could not see her, but she was sure Clementine was nodding somewhere inside the icy box in which they were trapped. Margery stamped her feet, trying to warm up her frozen toes and she put her hands in the pockets of her cardigan, which was proving useless in the artificial chill of the pitch-black room. She wished that they had worn more of the protective garments she thought so silly when Clementine convinced her to put them on.

Margery could picture Clementine's mobile phone plugged into the charger on her bedside table at home, where Clementine occasionally used the front camera as a mirror to take out her top denture. She only owned it because Ceri-Ann had found out she did not have one and forced her to take her old one as a gift.

Margery rubbed her cold arms with her hands, holding them close to her sides to try and contain her own body heat. She did not dare to reach out and try to touch anything in case her cold fingers got stuck to one of the frozen walls or shelves, or she accidently dislodged a box of frozen lasagne portions and crushed them both. It would be just her luck to die here, she thought, to die in the freezer, frozen stiff overnight in the darkness. Only being found in the morning when Gloria opened it to defrost Tuesday lunchtime's chicken Kievs. In a split second, she decided that frostbite be damned and threw caution to the wind. She screamed as loudly as she could and threw herself against the freezer door, banging her fists against it. To her surprise it swung open, and she almost lost her balance as she went plummeting forward into the arms of an unsuspecting policeman.

'Oh God, I'm so sorry!' he said, helping her upright, 'I thought I'd just see what was inside, I wasn't expecting you!' Margery just stared at him dumbfounded. Clementine had emerged from the freezer too, and was trying to catch her breath, bent over with her hands on her knees. 'Are you all right?' he said, wringing his hands together. 'What were you doing shut in there?'

'What do you mean... shut in?' Margery said. She could see Clementine judging the young officer's weedy excuse for a moustache from the corner of her eye. He was young enough to still have the remnants of teenage acne, Margery noted, his uniform slightly too baggy on his lanky figure, as if his mother had bought it a size too big for him to grow into.

'This was under the lock.' He pointed at the broom that lay innocently on the floor next to the freezer. 'It was jammed under the fridge handle and I kind of, well... I kicked it away.'

Margery just stared at him dumbfounded, rubbing her hands together to dispel the almost painful feeling of the blood rushing back into her frozen fingers. The relief of the warm kitchen air was blissful.

Another, much older, police constable rounded the corner of the kitchen, and the younger officer stood to attention at the sight of him. Margery was sure she heard him mumble, 'My Dad said I should've just become a traffic warden,' under his breath.

'Is everything all right here, Symon?' The older constable asked, his fantastically layered hedgerow of a moustache hiding any emotion on the bottom half of his face.

Symon nodded and pointed at Margery and Clementine, suddenly red-faced. 'Yeah, all fine, Officer Thomas! Like I, uh... like I told you, ladies, you can't be here!'

Officer Thomas stepped in. 'Ladies, I'm going to have to ask you to come with me,' he said, moving towards them. 'This is a protected area. You are aware it's a criminal offence to step foot in a crime scene?'

'Officer,' Clementine began. Margery didn't like where this was going. 'We were merely popping into the freezer to get some bread rolls out to defrost. The children need bread.'

The Officer looked at her and then his gaze wandered behind them, towards the blood-coated freezer door.

'I think you both know that inviting yourselves into the middle of a police investigation is a terrible idea. Bread rolls or not,' he said witheringly. Margery could feel herself shrivelling under his gaze as he turned back to look at them sternly. 'This is a sensitive conversation and I'd prefer for it to be done at the station.'

'Someone shut us in the freezer!' Margery cried, before she could help herself.

Officer Thomas stared at them both, eyebrows raised. 'What do you mean, shut you in?'

'We couldn't get out! That policeman saved us!' Clementine pointed at young Officer Symon.

He shrugged and smiled grimly at them. 'Well, they weren't really trapped. That broom handle fell down and got stuck on the door handle.'

'We're going to have to investigate this back at the station,' Officer Thomas said, shaking his head.

'Well, we aren't going with you!' Clementine cried, and started shuffling away as fast as her kitchen clogs would allow her. Margery watched as Officer Thomas looked heavenwards in exasperation and then gave chase very slowly. Young Officer Symon handcuffed her apologetically.

Chapter Four

In the interview room at the police station, Clementine swore again and again that their story was true, and they had just been concerned the children were not receiving enough wheat in their diet. But neither she nor Margery could explain why they were wearing gloves and goggles. Officer Thomas said he had no choice but to caution them both for trespassing on a crime scene. Though, he did seem genuinely concerned about how they got themselves trapped in the freezer, jotting down their statement and promising to investigate.

'A caution lasts six years, Clem!' Margery said, with her head in her hands as they rode the bus to school the next morning. 'We're criminals for six years, and that's with good behaviour. What are we going to tell the girls down at the bingo hall?'

Margery had refused to speak to Clementine all evening. She was so angry she even slept downstairs on the lumpy old sofa, rather than be within three feet of her. She was horrified at the thought that they might not have arrived back home if that young policeman had not found them, and more annoyed that Clementine downplayed the incident, compartmentalising it in her mind where she probably kept all sorts of traumas. She had obviously added, 'nearly frozen to death like an ice lolly', to the pile and then shut the door on it again.

But then in the morning Clementine had brought in her favourite breakfast – a cup of black tea and two slices of plain toast, all served on a tray with a flower in a vase she knew Clementine had stolen from Dawn Simmonds's garden. Margery had softened like butter left under the school kitchen's heat lamp.

'Shh, Margery!' Clementine hissed back at her. 'If you're not careful you'll have to explain to all *these* ladies.'

Margery looked around the bus to check they were not being listened to. All it would take was for Mrs Mugglethwaite to overhear and the whole town would know by the end of the day. Mrs Mugglethwaite, who in her younger days had been a former 'Dewstow Town Beauty Queen' – a competition that Margery had found archaic even then – didn't just send letters at the small post office on the high street, she delivered gossip as well. They would never be able to step foot on the bus again if she found out, it would only take her a few hours and the whole town would hear about it. She chose that moment to look up and smile at them both, as if she could sense distress and a good piece of news from where she was sitting. Poor Seren had yet to step back on the bus after the events of last year, Margery thought to herself, avoiding the likes of Mrs Mugglethwaite who was not someone to be trifled with. She would sell her own mother's secrets to the devil if it got her a good story to talk about with the ladies at work.

'Anyway, it could be worse,' Clementine said matter-of-factly, bringing her back out of her thoughts.

'How could it be any worse?' Margery asked, shaking her head.

'Well… for one, we didn't die. Which is good news. And secondly, we're both in our sixties, how much more time do we really have to get into trouble with,' Clementine lowered her voice to a decibel only usually heard by bats, 'the police.' Margery sighed. 'And anyway,' Clementine said, back at normal volume, 'at least we aren't like Mrs Redburn, going to the library and photocopying her council tax bill one hundred times instead of once, and then running off and not paying the 15p for each copy!'

'That's only happened a few times!' Mrs Redburn squeaked desperately from the back of the bus as Mrs Mugglethwaite turned to smirk at her. Margery and Clementine looked at each other anxiously.

—

Margery and Clementine arrived at work early as per usual. They always liked to leave enough time to don their kitchen clogs and aprons, make a delicious cup of instant coffee and maybe even pinch a slice of toast or two when Gloria was not watching the toaster. There was a handyman in the kitchen, Margery noted immediately on their arrival. The old freezer door had been removed and he was replacing it with a new one. Inside, the freezer had been defrosted and scrubbed spotless overnight. The shelves were bare and sparkling clean, leaving no trace of what they had seen the afternoon before. The cleaners must have finally been in to sort it all out; Margery shuddered at the thought.

'Hello, ladies,' Gloria said, noticeably less cheery than usual. 'The headmaster has been in looking for you already. You'd better get over there.'

'Oh, okay,' Clementine said. 'Do we need to take a tea trolley?'

'No, he was very insistent it was just you.'

'Ooh! Someone's in trouble!' Ceri-Ann said in a sing-song voice from the other side of the room, where she was giving Sharon what looked like an unsolicited head massage.

Margery gulped. An invitation to the headmaster's office was never a good thing. The last visit came come shortly after Clementine had decided to let loose several live crickets into the school's small garden. She had insisted that she 'saved' them from being eaten by Caroline's pet snakes, but they had destroyed the place and eaten all of the vegetables the Year Sevens planted. Mr Barrow had made them retrieve each cricket personally. Margery winced at the memory.

The walk to the headmaster's office may as well be to the electric chair. Margery's hands were so sweaty she could hardly turn the handle of Mr Barrow's office door. He gestured for them to sit in the nice guest seats, in front of his beautiful Oak Furniture Land desk. He remained standing as they sat.

'Can you tell me, please,' he began slowly and quietly, and Margery could tell that he was struggling to stay calm by the vein she saw popping out of his neck, 'why I

44

got a call from the Chief Constable of Dewstow Police Station last night to tell me he had arrested, *arrested*!' he spat the word out, and Margery wiped the spittle from her cheek. 'Two of my dinner ladies!' Margery felt like she was shrinking under his gaze. 'What on earth would possess you to do what you did? Please, humour me!'

They sat in silence. Margery could not meet his eye. He shook his head at them. 'Why do you think we do CRB checks and key holder training? You are entrusted with the safety of this school, as members of it, and you have betrayed that trust entirely.' He slammed his fist down on the table, and turned away from them. 'Well. Go on,' he said, 'explain yourselves!'

There was a long, long pause. Eventually Clementine broke the silence.

'There was so much blood!' Clementine burst into tears, and Margery thought for a moment that maybe she was faking her misery to try and get out of trouble, but to her horror she saw that Clementine was sincere. She had not seen Clementine cry since her mother died several years before. Clementine was usually her rock, Margery was used to leaning on her, and it was a genuinely unsettling sight to see her so distraught.

'Caroline was one of us and she died like that, and all alone!' She put her head in her hands and began to weep. Margery gently patted her on the back. It was just like Clementine to hide her real feelings. She was like the mini egg that had broken Seren's tooth, seemingly hard and unfeeling on the outside but very much the opposite on the inside. Besides, Clementine had always got on quite well with Caroline; she had lost a friend as well as a colleague.

Mr Barrow considered them carefully, his disposition changing immediately, softening as Margery had done that morning. He reached into his desk drawer, conjured up a box of tissues and offered them to Clementine. She took one and blew her nose uproariously.

'Caroline's death… it maybe wasn't as peaceful as you thought it might have been,' he said gently, putting the box of tissues on the table in front of them, then resting his hands on the top of his chair. 'Between you and me, the police couldn't get a biohazard team here till very early this morning. I did ask our cleaning team if they would mind, but obviously given the circumstances…' his voice petered out as he realised how much information he was giving away.

'Seren said it was an accident. But it didn't look like an accident,' Margery said finally, finding her voice again.

Mr Barrow sighed. 'I don't think it was a particularly nice accident, but, and I shouldn't be telling you this really, they *do* think it was an accident. They don't suspect anyone. There's no evidence of wrongdoing. Just an unfortunate thing, I'm afraid.'

'She didn't even get to deliver her Avon!' Clementine wailed again.

Mr Barrow gave a small smile at that. He sat down opposite them, sinking deep into his chair. Margery never thought he looked completely comfortable sat down, he was so long and tall that he almost resembled a spider having its limbs contorted as someone tried to sweep it under a glass with a piece of paper.

'I always did like Caroline,' he said. 'She was fantastic fun. I used to like it when she'd freeze her false tooth in an ice cube and then put it into someone's drink at a party. "Who's got the tooth?" we'd all say!'

Margery did not think that sounded particularly fun at all, but he chuckled to himself at the memory. 'Great fun and a great shame.'

He paused, regarding them. 'I understand that you didn't think through the consequences of what you did before you went through with it. Nonetheless this is a serious offence. When the governors find out about it, it'll be a major concern. I really should at least suspend you!' Clementine sobbed again, and he passed her another tissue. 'Your only saving grace is that you both have long and exemplary service records at the school and, honestly, we don't have enough kitchen staff as it is.'

Now that one of you is dead. He didn't say the words, but they hung in the air.

Clementine and Margery nodded gravely. Mr Barrow got up and walked over to his walk-in cupboard. He took out a carrier bag and placed it on the desk in front of them.

'Tell you what, I'll deliver Caroline's Avon if you two can look after these for me. If it makes you feel any better, I think the personal items Caroline had in her locker belong with the kitchen staff really, seeing as she didn't have a family.' Margery hoped Mr Barrow would not say that the kitchen was Caroline's family. 'Though I suppose the kitchen team was her real family.' The headmaster beamed at them. 'And you were all her children!' Caroline had been very much alone since her husband died. The few times they had visited her at home she had seemed tiny in the ginormous townhouse she never downsized from.

Margery took the bag from him. 'Thank you, Mr Barrow. We appreciate it.'

'You're both on thin ice,' he said, stern again. 'There can't be anything else like this, okay?'

Margery nodded. She definitely would not be an active participant in any of Clementine's ideas for a while.

'Go on, ladies, let's all get back to work. I'm sure Gloria could use the help in the kitchen.'

–

The bus home a few hours later was a stilted affair and the walk to the house was even worse. The gossipers on the bus were still talking about the mysterious dinner-lady death, but all the fun had gone out of it now that Margery knew the truth, and worse had spent an afternoon in a police station to find it. Still, by the time they arrived home, greeted a mewing Pumpkin who was waiting for her dinner, and were on their second cup of tea, she was beginning to feel much more herself. Clementine had even snapped out of her misery long enough to toast and butter a batch of crumpets that they sat and ate at the kitchen table.

'I wish you told me you were so upset about Caroline, Clem,' Margery said through a mouthful of crumpet. 'I would have tried to talk you out of the freezer thing a bit more.'

Clementine hung her head low. 'No, I think it's better that we know. Horrible as it was.'

They fell back into peaceful silence. Margery remembered the bag the headmaster had given them and emptied the contents onto the table with buttery fingers.

'This can't be right,' she said, peering closer to have a better look.

The bag contained all the assorted junk that had been in Caroline's locker: spare socks, several pages torn from cookbooks and about sixteen ballpoint pens. But lying on the very top of the pile was a large, diamanté hoop earring. Very glitzy. Very gaudy. Caroline never would have worn it in a million years.

Clementine put her glasses on to have a look. 'Caroline never wore earrings. She always said that if she wanted to look like a pirate, she'd take to the seas wearing a jumper from Marks & Spencer's Maritime Collection.'

Margery picked up the earring and held it to the light. 'No, she never would have worn this. And there's only one. Why would she only have one?'

'Yes, Where's the other one?' Clementine said.

Chapter Five

They found themselves so busy that they had no choice but to put the mystery of the earring on hold for the rest of the week. Numerous times Margery had pondered asking around about it, but she dared not cause any sort of scene so soon after the freezer investigation incident. They both knew that they were lucky not to have been suspended. Or worse, forced into retirement. She had gone as far as to gently ask Gloria while they were peeling onions together, if she had ever seen Caroline wear any jewellery.

'Caroline never wore jewellery, you know that,' Gloria had said. 'Caroline always said jewellery reminded her of Morris dancers.'

Caroline's death was declared 'accidental' on Thursday, and by Friday Mr Barrow's secretary sent them all out personal, handwritten letters inviting them to Caroline's funeral and the following wake. No one was to wear black. Mr Barrow specifically noted that in the letter he had dictated. Instead, everyone was to wear Caroline's favourite colour, tangerine. Ceri-Ann was worriedly scouring the entire internet for something in that shade that did not look terrible, but she had had no luck so far. Margery thought it a testament to how hideous a colour it was, as Ceri-Ann was one of those tall, slender people who could usually pull off any outfit, what with her youth on her side. Margery privately thought Caroline must have included the colour choice in her will as some kind of final practical joke.

Caroline had no next of kin, so Margery assumed the headmaster had arranged the funeral himself. Caroline had lived alone in a huge old house overlooking the river, and there was a hushed murmur among the dinner ladies about what would happen to it now.

The week, though it had dragged on a bit, went quite well considering they were missing a Captain at the helm. Except for a little blip on Thursday, after Sharon and Karen had served the pupils a curry made largely from Scotch bonnets, there were no real issues. In fact, Margery thought the food seemed a bit better. Caroline could not have cared less about quality when you could have quantity. Why make a small, but fresh and delicious, amount when you could make sixty bland litres of the same thing and freeze most of it for another time, seemed to have always been her ethos.

Margery had not realised, until now, how much the food must have suffered over the years; though Jamie Oliver probably would have still scoffed in disgust at the crisps in the vending machine, it was definitely a major step in the right direction. Gloria was finally getting to put some of her delicious Filipino family recipes on the menu, and Ceri-Ann's cooking was coming along much faster in Caroline's absence, especially now she had actually started checking what ingredients were needed before she added them into things. Even Clementine began putting deliveries away properly, no longer just throwing courgettes in with cucumbers because, 'They're obviously from the same family, Margery', or labelling things in a way that she found amusing. Margery wished she had had a pound for every time she found 'baking powder' labelled as 'bacon powder' over the years.

Yes, Margery thought, they were all working together as a team for once, instead of using the kitchen as a battleground for trivial issues and conflict. There was a noticeable level of calm there had not been when Caroline was around to play practical jokes, or tell them blatantly made-up stories. Like how she had once worked for Gordon Ramsey, or how she had appeared on *Ready Steady Cook* and won with her three-ingredient dish consisting of only a jar of black olives, a dented tin of kidney beans and a bag of a supermarket's own ready-salted crisps.

'But you can't watch it anywhere because the BBC forgot to make a copy of the recording,' Caroline would say.

Still the week did seem to drag on a lot longer without any of the distractions Caroline usually caused, and Margery breathed a sigh of relief when the weekend finally rolled around.

Margery was surprised to find, however, that their Friday night game of Monopoly could not quite capture the attention it had the week before. Usually, they would both be completely engrossed; they had been playing the same game for the past two years after all, so long in fact that they had eventually needed to buy a second Monopoly set just for the extra hotels and houses, but Margery found herself asking to be excused after only an hour had passed. Margery was always the boot and Clementine was always the top hat whenever they played, though the pieces and board were beginning to show major wear and tear now, and it had been sellotaped back together one too many times. Clementine had won the game they had managed to finish two years ago, but Margery had suspected at the time she had been sneaking more hotels onto her properties when she was not looking and reading the Chance cards out incorrectly. Margery had never since been able to find the Chance card that read, 'The person with the greyest hair playing gets £500 from the bank and to also pass Go'.

Once a month, Clementine would have a case of wine delivered. She had spent a small fortune on a sommelier course a few years back, and they still enjoyed trying a different bottle or two on a Saturday afternoon and making tasting notes on them. But this week's wine was a dessert bottle and Clementine refused to drink it, reasoning that the past few days had been too bitter to ingest anything as sweet as a Sauternes. Margery could not say she disagreed, but by Sunday she found herself counting the hours down as she knitted by the fire, so distracted that she kept losing count of her stitches. By the time they finally called it a day and went to bed, she had never looked forward to a Monday so much in her life.

The day of the funeral finally arrived, and Margery felt as though she had held her breath all weekend in anticipation. Mr Barrow had managed to get everything sorted quite quickly, in time to have the funeral on the bank holiday Monday rather than close the school for the day. Very efficient of him, Margery thought. Though, it meant that most of the children and their parents did not show up, citing holidays and other general excuses. Margery did not think Caroline would have minded too much. She was never fond of children.

It was a sombre affair all in all. The church service was particularly dreary, even though they were all dressed in varying shades of orange and must have looked like a bowl of interestingly shaped satsumas to any oblivious passers-by.

The vicar kept calling Caroline 'Carolyn', at which everyone grimaced repeatedly but no one corrected him. Mr Barrow played 'Smoke on the Water' again, which Margery did not think was at all appropriate, but they all bobbed their heads along to it anyway. Then Caroline's coffin was carried back outside and plonked into the ground, and they all went back to the school for a mediocre spread of stale sandwiches and salt and vinegar Pringles, which had raised no spirits at all. Luckily there had been no rainfall, but Margery still worried about Clementine's special, 'funeral-best' wool cardigan that Margery had spent so long knitting for her.

The will reading was held immediately after the funeral service at Caroline's request, upstairs in the school's small library. It was the only place that could fit everyone invited, though Margery thought they all looked very out of place against the rows of books and educational posters.

Especially the cleaning team, who Margery never usually saw unless their day had run on much, much later than expected, or if there was a parents' evening or school play to prepare food for.

Barbara Harvey, the head cleaner and her minions, Anita and Cheryl, were not usually seen before four in the afternoon. Even when they did show up early, they would spend that time drinking the strange frothy coffee from the staff room's vending machine and smoking out on the kitchen's fire escape, occasionally popping in to say hello and steal some of the lunchtime leftovers. Barbara and her team's official job titles were 'Education Centre Sanitisation and Contamination Removal Experts', and led by Barbara they all preferred to be addressed by their full title. Everyone respected their wishes, except for Clementine, who called them 'the cleaners'.

Barbara looked up from her chair, where she sat reading a battered copy of the 'Diary of Anne Frank' and gave Margery a curt wave, her perfectly coiffed but ginormous beehive hairstyle topped off by a large orange bow that bounced slightly as she did so. Margery waved back, wondering for the millionth time how much of her wages Barbara must have to spend on hairspray, and how her hair was even staying upright in the stuffy heat of the library. Possibly the styling of the thing was one of the reasons the cleaners never seemed to be on time; Anita and Cheryl had similar hairstyles, but neither was quite as grand as Barbara's managed to be. Margery supposed that was apt on account of her position as head of the cleaning team.

They were an odd-looking crew. Cheryl and Anita were both taller and blonder than Barbara, and yet she managed to overshadow both of them in personality alone. As it was, Anita seemed to shrink into the background on every occasion Margery had met her, much too meek to compete. Cheryl fared only slightly better, though Margery thought she could probably hold her own much better than Anita could.

On the other side of the library, Karen and Sharon sat at a study table. They were wearing the exact same orange dress, and glaring at each other. Gloria was sat in between them, seemingly impervious to their fury and casually swigging squash from a plastic cup, but Margery noted that Gloria would occasionally look from Karen to Sharon and smirk in the manner of someone enjoying themselves immensely. Seren sat right at the back of the library, solemn faced, still wearing her dirty anorak, which was tucked much too tightly into the top of an orange pencil skirt that reminded Margery of struggling to remove a too-full bin bag from a bin.

'Hello? Chantelle?' Ceri-Ann hissed at full volume into her phone. 'Oh my days, yeah, we're at the will reading. Like in CSI or something.' Everyone in attendance shushed her loudly.

Mr Barrow entered pushing a bulky television and DVD player combination on a trolley, helped by a rather rotund gentleman who sported a weedy goatee and a pinstripe suit. Towering Mr Barrow nearly hit his head on top of the double doors leading into the library, but the stranger did not have such a problem. There was a good foot of air between his head and the doorframe, and Margery thought it a shame that they could not have mixed their heights and made two normal-sized people.

'Sorry about your wait, ladies,' Mr Barrow said, as he hefted the television into position and the other man began scrabbling around trying to find a plug socket.

'Are you calling us fat?' Karen demanded, and Sharon burst into tears. Mr Barrow stared at them dumbfounded for a moment, then picked up the remote from the trolley and turned to switch on the television.

'Firstly,' he said, ignoring Sharon who was still weeping, 'can anyone here who hasn't officially been invited by me please leave?' He looked behind them all pointedly, and Margery turned to see that the deputy head, Rose Smith, sat in the corner at the back by Seren. She had not even noticed her sitting there before.

Rose sighed loudly; the chair she had been sitting in caught on the linoleum and toppled over as she stood dramatically. She made a big show of pulling on her coat and checking she had her car keys in her bag, as they all waited in awkward silence. Mr Barrow checked his watch as she finally pulled them out of her handbag with a flourish. Glaring at him purposely, she pottered past them all on her high heels, clacking her way out through the library doors.

Margery wondered why the deputy head had come at all. She had been most surprised to see her at the church service. Caroline Hughes and Rose Smith had never been on particularly good terms to her knowledge, or even on speaking terms for the most part. Surely she couldn't have expected anything to be left to her in Caroline's will?

Mr Barrow cleared his throat. 'Thank you all for being here today. Mrs Hughes left me as the executor of her estate, as you are all aware, and her solicitor, Mr Tamble,' he gestured to the man standing next to him, 'is here to help me share with you Caroline's last will and testament.'

Mr Tamble nodded at them all and passed the head-master a disc from the envelope he held. Mr Barrow slid it into the DVD player and then stepped back to watch.

'Hello?' Mrs Hughes's voice rang out through the speakers but the screen showed nothing but a busily decor-ated living room. Ornamental cats littered every inch of shelf space, with even the shelves above the fireplace smothered in an abundance of them. The walls were covered in a bizarre mix of framed amateur watercolours and birthday cards, purchased mostly from National Trust sites, Margery guessed, judging by how many of them were of St Michael's Mount.

'Can you see me?' Mrs Hughes said again. There were several long seconds where the living room spun wildly, followed by a concerning number of loud bangs. Then, much too close to the screen, the deceased woman's wrinkled face appeared, forever alive in the moment of time the camera had captured.

Caroline backed away from the screen slowly, using her metal cane for support, and sat down heavily on the reclining chair in the middle of her living room, lifting her slippered feet up to rest on the pouffe in front of her. Her big oval head was just as Margery remembered it, wearing her oversized clear-framed glasses once more, her lazy eye covered with a patch, her hair blindingly white.

'Margery,' Clementine hissed at her. 'She's wearing the earring.'

She was. Margery noted with surprise. It glinted in the light from Caroline's electric fireplace. But still only one of them? Had she lost the other? Or maybe used it as collateral at her weekly poker nights? Before she had time to turn to Clementine and discuss it, Caroline Hughes cleared her throat.

Chapter Six

'Dear friends, dinner ladies...' Caroline smiled on the screen. '...fellow countrymen.' Margery rolled her eyes. 'If you are watching this...' Caroline paused for dramatic effect. Margery was sure she heard Clementine mutter something that sounded a lot like 'Show-off' under her breath. 'Then I am...' Caroline paused again, to really draw it out, '... dead!'

Sharon and Karen gasped in unison.

'And so, I am coming to you here live from my very own living room, to share with you the spectacular plunders of wealth I have gained over my many years.' Caroline raised her hands up in the air in joyous exclamation, as though she was Jesus, Margery thought wryly. Or presenting a game show.

'Well, without further ado...' Caroline leaned forward in her seat with a groan to pick up the notebook on the coffee table. The dinner ladies in the library sat waiting, enraptured. Margery thought that she could have heard a pin drop, but she supposed that was to be expected for the wealth Caroline had to give away. Her father was, for a long time, the only mechanic in town, and she had inherited a large amount of money if the rumours were true. Margery always thought that some of the diamonds Caroline had shown her from her private collection could rival the Koh-i-Noor with regards to size and carat.

'Sharon and Karen,' Caroline read aloud, Sharon looked over at Karen in excitement, the dress disaster already forgiven and forgotten. 'I leave to you my entire collection of Royal Family memorabilia.'

There was a silence as Sharon and Karen took in this new information. 'Please be aware though, dears, that you may need a hand getting it all home. The Princess Diana yearbooks are especially heavy.'

Caroline peered into her notebook and continued. 'Gloria Basa!' she said jubilantly. 'I leave you in the care of Gregory and Barty, my exotic snakes. I know they'll be very happy with you.'

Gloria sat wide-eyed at this news, the plastic cup almost slipping out of her hand. 'Oh no,' she said gravely. 'Oh no!'

'Ceri-Ann Reynolds. I thought you might like the contents of my wine cellar. Though there's not much left in there now.' Everyone ooh'd at that, except Clementine, turning to scowl nastily at Ceri-Ann, who looked upset but had finally put her phone down.

'I... I don't even drink wine.' She thought for a moment. 'I don't even have a corkscrew!'

Gloria turned to face her. 'Do you think I have anything to keep exotic snakes in? No! I've got a three-year-old. They'll probably eat her.'

Sharon stood up. 'Well, I've got a two-bedroom house and two three-year olds, for Christ's sake! Do you really think I've got any room for a bunch of Princess Diana crap?'

'So? I'm not taking it all!' Karen stood up to shout back at Sharon. 'My husband hates the Royal family. He's got a Morrissey tattoo and everything!'

'Ladies!' Margery said, trying not to snap at her colleagues and failing miserably. 'You're missing the rest of the tape.'

They all paused and turned back to Caroline on the television screen. '…and that is why you, Seren, deserve all my knitting patterns. They're from John Lewis!'

'Oh, wow Seren,' Margery said sincerely. 'Great haul.'

Seren just shrugged, stony-faced.

Mrs Hughes continued, oblivious to any drama building in the small room. 'Clem and Margery, my dear friends. For you,' she sat forward in a manner of great importance, and everyone mirrored her body language in earnest, 'my entire videotape collection. All of it!'

Caroline looked ever so pleased with herself, Margery thought. It was almost as though she had planned this.

'The original *Poldark* series. Every episode of *Coronation Street* for the past sixteen years. And the best bit of all…' Margery held her breath. 'I have tried to not record any of the adverts. It's mostly commercial free!'

Clementine swore under her breath and whispered to Margery, 'The adverts are the best bit!' Margery was suddenly glad Clementine never managed to talk her out of getting rid of the hardly used VCR player that still sat under the television in their living room.

Caroline Hughes smiled again on-screen and continued unabashed. 'Barbara and the rest of your team…' Margery turned to look over at Barbara and her team, who had all leaned forward expectantly. Cheryl, sat to Barbara's right, dropped the copy of *War and Peace* she was holding in suspense.

'To you I leave this voucher I won in the school raffle… well… I suppose it was a few years ago now, but you should be able to buy yourself a good many things with it still. It is for twenty pounds after all.' Caroline took out a piece of paper from her notepad and held it up as close as she could to the camera lens.

Margery looked over at the cleaning team, trying not to smile as the realisation that they were the proud owners of an unusable *Woolworths* voucher dawned on them.

On-screen Caroline put the notepad back down on the coffee table with a struggle, and then sat back as though considering them. 'There are a few other things, I think, the small matter of my estate for one.' She smiled. 'Though it's just the house and a few other bits and pieces, and how much could a house really be worth?' Margery saw Ceri-Ann type 'property prices my area' into her phone's search engine.

'I know that maybe you thought I would leave it to one of you, or the school or some other boring entity.' She waved her hand around flippantly at that. 'But I thought it fairer to leave it to someone who has meant the world to me recently.'

She stared down the camera lens. 'Seth. You're the absolute love of my life.'

The dinner ladies stared at the television, stunned into silence. Even Mr Barrow looked on enraptured. The only person who did not look completely surprised was Mr Tamble, the solicitor. Margery looked over at Clementine and saw the shock she felt mirrored back at her. Caroline with all her faults; her inability to manage the team, her eye patch and dodgy sense of humour, her love for running things and occasionally people over on her mobility scooter.

Caroline had taken a lover.

'I know we haven't known each other terribly long. But when you get to my age, well… you don't really have too long.' Caroline's laughter radiated through the screen. 'I know I'm an old romantic fool, and I hope that we have many more years together before this recording is needed but it's just in case.' She smiled again. This was probably the most Margery had seen her smile in years. 'You just do things to me I never thought I'd feel again.'

Clementine turned to Margery with such a look of disgust on her face that Margery had to suppress her laugh by pretending to cough. The pixels of Caroline carried on oblivious. 'I haven't felt this way since before William died, and those moments with him were few and far between really. He could be terribly boring.'

Mr Barrow led the silent chorus of nodding that followed this statement. William Hughes had been a terrible, terrible bore.

'You have my heart, Mr Thomas. You may as well have everything else, too. Anyway!' She clapped and broke the spell she had held over the library. 'That's everything I

65

believe. I do hope you all enjoy your new-to-you things, and I hope to see you on the other side,' she said and grinned. 'I'm hoping it's not too hot in hell if I end up there!'

Margery felt that if anyone deserved a porridge-filled shoe's worth of hell it was Caroline.

The next several minutes of the film were of Mrs Hughes trying to get out of the reclining chair, which, although it looked fantastically comfortable, was seemingly impossible to escape. Eventually, Mr Barrow stepped forward and turned the television off.

The room was silent. Margery looked around at the other dinner ladies' seething faces.

'Right,' Mr Barrow said. He seemed as stunned as they were, 'Well. Come along then, ladies. We'll have a bit of a send-off for Mrs Hughes and then in an hour or so, we'll go to my office so we can organise receiving your prizes... I mean... um... dear sentimental gifts from Mrs Hughes. Mr Tamble has some paperwork that you all need to sign, too, I'm sure.'

Margery and Clementine stayed perched on the uncomfortable library chairs, as the rest of the team filed out after him.

'Who the hell is S. Thomas?' Clementine said, as soon as Seren stamped through the exit in her orthopaedic trainers, the door swinging closed behind her. 'Did you even hear Caroline say anything about a new man in her life?'

'You mean Seth Thomas,' Margery corrected her. 'But no. I didn't.'

Clementine shook her head. 'It's like we never knew her at all! The Caroline I knew always said if she ever wanted to marry again to shoot her and dump her body into the sea.'

'Yes,' Margery said, 'well maybe that's why she didn't tell us.'

Clementine laughed at that, and then shook her head in disbelief. 'Seriously though, I don't want to sound greedy, but she's left the people she spent the last twenty years with a load of stuff she couldn't be arsed to take down the dump, and then her new bloke gets her house? He can't love her that much. He's not even here.'

Clementine gestured around them at the empty room, then leaned back against the plastic chair, exasperated. They sat in silence for a while.

'You know, we do know a Thomas...' Margery pondered to herself out loud. 'That officer that arrested us was a Thomas. Ooh, I wonder what his first name was.'

'Well, what are we waiting for? Let's go ask him!' Clementine had already stood up, gathering her things.

'Really? Today?' Margery said as she rushed to follow her. 'Maybe we should wait until after the wake, though?'

Clementine stopped dead at the library door and threw her hands up in exasperation. 'Really, Margery! This could be a murder investigation!'

There was a cough from the back, and Margery turned to find that Barbara and the rest of the cleaners were standing behind them.

'Hello, Barbara,' Margery said. 'Anita, Cheryl.' She nodded at each of them in acknowledgement. Anita squeaked a greeting back from where she stood, tucked behind Barbara like a loyal dog, her big, blonde bouffant topped with an oversized silver bow.

'Hello, Margery,' Barbara nodded at her. 'Clementine.'

Clementine nodded back. Margery wondered for a moment if they would now get stuck in a circle of nodding and exchanging pleasantries till all their heads fell off, but then Barbara continued.

'Could we get past, please, ladies? I think we've all had quite enough misery for today, haven't we?' Barbara smiled at them both. Margery smiled back, but secretly she always felt slightly unsettled by Barbara and her two employees who stuck to her side like limpets. They travelled the school hallways as a pack, never, ever going anywhere alone.

'Of course you can!' Clementine said cheerily. 'We were just about to join everyone.' Clementine never felt the same way about Barbara and her gang; she would often stay for a cup of coffee and a chat if she saw them at the school after hours.

'We'll see you in a minute then.' Barbara smiled at them, as she, Anita and Cheryl strode past them and out of the double doors, but Margery couldn't feel any warmth in that smile. She was actually quite surprised that Barbara had not questioned them on what they were talking about, as she was usually at the forefront of school gossip. It seemed strange that she was not interested in this, the most exciting school news in forever. She must have heard them, Margery thought. They were talking so loudly.

'Margery, are you coming?' Clementine's voice broke her from her thoughts as she swung the double doors open. Margery followed her and they made their way down the corridor towards the noise of the after-party, being held in the school hall. The cleaners had just entered the room, the doors swinging shut behind them, but Margery could still hear 'The Birdie Song' playing at full volume over the school's P.A. system. They reached the double doors to the hall's entrance, but before they could enter, it swung open again and Mr Tamble, Caroline's solicitor, wandered out and into the corridor. He was clutching a plastic cup of what Margery could smell from a mile off was sherry.

'Oh, hello ladies,' he said, slightly unsteady on his feet. 'Ever so sorry for your loss, and mine, I suppose. She was a great client.'

Margery wondered how she had not noticed before. The man was steaming drunk. He was swaying from side to side, and he had the facial flush she associated with two bottles of wine. No wonder he had not said much at the will reading. The stench of his breath would have given him away.

'Thank you, Mr Tamble,' she said. 'It was a lovely service, ah…' Margery tried to think of one of Karen's trite platitudes to take away from the awkwardness of the meeting. 'Well… at least Caroline didn't suffer.'

Mr Tamble snorted, staggering back ever so slightly, eyeing his drink as though he might find his senses in it. 'I wouldn't be so sure of that.'

'What do you mean?' Clementine asked.

He shook his head. 'Nothing, nothing.' But then he tapped his finger to the side of his nose and winked at them, leaning much too close to their faces for Margery's liking.

Inside the hall there was a loud smash, and then a loud chorus of cheers as the people inside applauded whoever had dropped their glass. Margery noted that the music changed from Seventies pop to some sort of contemporary dance music; the wake must really be in full swing by now.

'Well, if you're going to be like that, Mr Tamble, we really have to be going,' Clementine said, and gestured for him to move out of the way.

He threw his hands up in apology and staggered back from them. 'I'm sorry to be so rude, ladies. I've had a bit to drink and well… I wasn't lying when I said she was a great client. I only saw her two weeks ago when she dropped off her will.' He lost his balance and leaned back against the wall for support.

Clementine stepped back again. Margery considered him carefully. 'She only gave you her will two weeks ago?' she asked him. He stared at her, as if wishing he could take back the words he had let slip.

'Yes,' he said, nodding erratically, 'but we'd been working on it for a while before that, you know how it is…' his voice petered off.

'Just how good of friends were you, Mr Tamble?' Margery said suspiciously. The man looked sheepish suddenly, and maybe a little embarrassed.

'Please call me Ethan,' he said, blushing more than Margery thought possible, 'and well enough that I thought I'd be Mr Hughes's replacement. God, he was so boring.' Margery and Clementine nodded agreeably; William Hughes's idea of a fun night out had been vacuuming his car on the driveway.

Mr Tamble lurched forward, almost spilling his glass of sherry, and grabbed Clementine's hand with his free one. 'Listen to me,' his voice dropped to a conspiratorial whisper, 'if you love someone, let them know. You must let them know!'

Clementine pulled her hand away, forcing a smile at him. He hiccupped; his breath smelt like fruit-flavoured paint stripper.

'I'd better get back to the office,' he said, and downed the remaining sherry. He crushed the plastic cup in his hand, then searched around in the top pocket of his suit jacket till he found a crumpled business card and gave it to Margery.

'It was nice to meet you, ladies. If you ever need a will written or a divorce, give me a call.' He wobbled away, staggering down the hallway, and Margery and Clementine watched silently. Margery looked down solemnly at the bare ring finger of her left hand.

'What the hell just happened?' Clementine said. 'Caroline had two boyfriends? Caroline! *Boyfriends! Two!* She was a hundred and fifty years old. And that earring, Margery! She was wearing one earring! What kind of lunatic wears one earring?' Clementine leaned against the wall by the entrance to the school hall.

Ceri-Ann must have been kicked off her DJing spot because the dance music had stopped and they were now playing Caroline's actual favourite song, 'Private Dancer' by Tina Turner.

'I feel like if we can figure out the earring, we can work out what happened to Caroline. There's still something odd about it all.'

Margery agreed. 'Why don't we take it to show someone?' she suggested.

Clementine scoffed. 'We can't just waltz into H. Samuel with an unexplained single earring, Margery.'

'I know, Clem, but what about the antiques shop in town? Mr Fitzgerald didn't bat an eyelid when Ceri-Ann sold him her great aunt's wedding ring to buy a new iPhone.'

Clementine pondered. 'That's not a bad idea. We'll go tomorrow morning.' She slapped her hands together in excitement. 'Right. Let's go and get a glass of sherry!'

Chapter Seven

'Can't you go any faster, Margery? Good God, we might as well have taken the bus after all.'

Margery shook her head at Clementine grimly, her knuckles white, gripped tightly to the car's steering wheel as it struggled up Dewstow Hill. She thanked heavens it was automatic for the millionth time. She had not known that it was when she had bought it in the early Nineties after seeing an advert in a newsagent's window, but she was grateful for it in the hill-abundant area of the country they lived. The little car was baby blue on the outside with a white roof and a lovely ivory colour on the inside, including the seats and dashboard. At the back, it had a quaint picnic rack that they attached their bags to, the boot being full of actual picnic baskets and wellies. She mostly purchased it because she thought it was cute, though they had become something of a collector's item in the previous years. Clementine was ever so smug when she discovered that people would pay upwards of £5000 for a Nissan Figaro in half-decent condition, calling it their pension fund. Though she also said that about her Welsh love spoons and her collection of 'Victorian Women in Literature' stamps, missing

Charlotte Brontë which Clementine had accidentally sent on a postcard to her niece.

Their plan to go and find PC Thomas was derailed the moment Clementine suggested a sherry the previous afternoon. They were lucky to get up in time for work, Margery thought. The wake had gone on all evening, and they had not crawled into bed till gone nine o'clock.

'I'm sorry, Clem, but I daren't,' she said, wide-eyed. 'You know I hate this hill.'

Clementine nodded back at her, but Margery noticed she pulled her seatbelt a little tighter. If Margery was truly honest with herself, Dewstow Hill was not the only hill she hated to drive up. In fact, she only really enjoyed driving when it could be done very slowly and in very quiet places with no traffic. Her ideal drive would begin and end in a supermarket car park.

'Yes,' Clementine said, 'well, park at the top of the hill here and we'll walk the rest of the way. We have precious cargo, after all.'

Margery grimaced internally. Parking was not her forte either.

After a great deal of moving forward, then reversing, then forward again, then very slow reversing and a very near miss with a lamp post, Margery parallel parked the car in one of the short-stay spaces on Dewstow High Street. Very successfully by all accounts, she thought. Well, as well as these things usually went anyway. She had not managed to clip the curb or lose a hubcap today and she considered this a victory. She still rather wished Clementine had not demanded she get the car out of the garage that morning. She was not a confident driver at the best of times.

On numerous occasions, she had offered Clementine the loan of the car for driving lessons, but Clementine never took her up on it. Margery knew that she was completely capable of passing the test, but Dewstow's only driving instructor could only fit her in on a Thursday evening and that was when Clementine had bingo at the church hall.

'I don't drive, I get driven!' Clementine always said. Margery secretly wondered, as she could still see their house from their parking spot at the top of the hill, whether Clementine was just feeling too lazy to walk today. Or maybe Clementine just did not want to explain to the ladies on the number five bus why they were getting off two stops early. She swallowed the thought when Clem nudged her, jingling the bag with the earring jauntily.

'Come on, Margery! We'll just pop into Mr Fitzgerald's, solve this mystery, and be back at the school for a piece of toast and a cup of tea in no time.'

–

Mr Fitzgerald's Home of Antiques was a very odd shop indeed. Margery had debated ringing ahead to check if Mr Fitzgerald would actually be there, but decided at the last moment not to and that they should just try their luck. It was well known in the town that the shop's opening hours were sporadic, but no one was entirely sure why. Mrs Mugglethwaite insisted that Timothy Fitzgerald had a lover in Spain, and that was where he was on the days the shop remained locked up with the lights out, but Margery was not so sure. In any case, it was never closed for long, and never ever empty of stock. The bell above the shop door rang as Margery and Clementine entered, and Mr Fitzgerald looked up from his perch behind the counter at the back, his elderly Yorkshire terrier, Jason, on his lap. The ends of the man's long white beard sat in his cup of tea as he stroked the dog absently with long, withered fingers, gazing off into space and humming a pleasant tune to himself.

The shop was crammed full to the brim, shelving units stretching from the floor all the way up to the beamed ceilings. Each shelf was covered in unusual oddities, the ones at the very top smothered in a thick layer of dust. Amateur paintings of Princess Diana hung next to beautiful ornaments of hand-blown glass. A millefiori paperweight sat next to a jigsaw puzzle of Fred and Rose West. A Penny Black stamp in a frame was propped up against a battered game of *KerPlunk* that the sign next to it said it was '*only missing six pieces*'.

As if that were not enough, the floor was stacked up high with boxes too. There were piles and piles of broken tennis rackets, unlabelled tapes, and other assorted odds and ends in heaps strewn about the place. Margery thought Caroline would have probably liked it. It could have been a re-creation of her living room.

'Clementine and Margery!' Mr Fitzgerald clapped his hands together enthused at the sight of them, jumping up from his seat and upsetting Jason, who spilled off his lap with a yelp. 'How can I help you this fine Dewstow day? Another jigsaw perhaps?'

They shook their heads grimly. Margery thought for the first time that maybe they had made a mistake coming here. She was sure they had never done anything to deserve such an eager welcome from anyone, let alone the elderly antiques dealer. She could remember him being old when she was very young, though he had not looked quite as decrepit twenty years ago as he did now. His limbs had always been a bit too long, and he only managed to look more and more like a spider as time had gone on, Margery thought. The extensive collection of different-coloured velvet capes he wore didn't help either.

'We don't have long unfortunately, Mr Fitzgerald. We've got to get to work,' Clementine said. 'But we found something that used to belong to our dear friend Caroline Hughes, and we wondered if you could tell us anything about it.'

'Caroline?' Mr Fitzgerald said, and all the mirth seemed to go out of him as he picked up Jason again and sat back down on the chair, plopping the dog on his lap. 'Dreadful business that. It's hard to believe that something as awful as that could have happened here. Where are we for God's sake, London?' He guffawed at his own joke, though Margery didn't feel like the humour met his eyes.

'Yes, we can't either,' Clementine said, when he stopped laughing. 'In fact, we are here to talk to you about that very thing. We believe that Caroline's death was more suspicious than the police have led us to believe.'

Mr Fitzgerald stopped stroking the dog and looked at them concerned. 'My dear child,' he said. Margery and Clementine shared a look to make sure neither of them had regressed 50 years. 'What could possibly make you think that? In what way suspicious?'

Clementine sighed in a manner of great importance, Margery thought, as though she was announcing a royal pregnancy or the winner of the *Great British Bake Off*. 'We think Caroline was...' She paused for effect 'murdered!'

Mr Fitzgerald gasped and put his hands over his mouth. Jason, the dog, eyed Clementine and Margery suspiciously.

Margery waved her hands at Clementine to quiet her. 'No, we don't!'

'Yes, we do!' Clementine exclaimed back at her. She whispered ominously, 'Murdered!'

'There's absolutely no evidence for that, Clem! Don't tell people Caroline's been murdered!' Margery shouted back, 'Nothing happens here in Dewstow. It's a very safe place to live.'

'Yes, perfectly safe till you get *killed* in your very own work freezer!' Clementine said.

Mr Fitzgerald coughed from behind the counter, and they remembered where they were.

'Sorry, Mr Fitzgerald,' Margery said, embarrassed.

He smiled at her and shrugged. 'No need to apologise, ladies. I'm not sure if I can help you with Caroline, honestly, but I can try my best. I do have some emergency-planning skills. I wrote Dewstow's "Zombie apocalypse contingency plan" after all.'

'Oh, was that you?' Clementine said excitedly. 'I printed it and put it up on the fridge!'

Mr Fitzgerald nodded, his thick white fringe bouncing enthusiastically. 'Oh gosh, I spoke about it on my podcast. If I'd known you enjoyed it, I would have made you a copy of the tape recording!'

Clementine oohed at that. Margery decided to step in, so they could get back to the reason they were actually there and she would not get trapped talking about the best way to stock up for a pandemic, or what kind of torch was the best to have in the case of a nuclear war.

'Mr Fitzgerald, have you ever seen anything like this?' She raised the earring still within the bag to show him. Mr Fitzgerald looked at it for a moment.

'Hang on,' Mr Fitzgerald plopped Jason back on the floor, and put on the first pair of glasses hanging from his neck on a chain. 'No, no, these are the wrong glasses.' He picked up the other pair of glasses around his neck and put them on instead, then squinted at the bag, frowning. 'Ahh yes, just as I suspected.' He took off his glasses, picked Jason up and sat down again. 'That is an earring.'

Clementine nodded back at him in earnest.

'Yes...' Margery said, 'but we were wondering if you'd ever seen an earring like this. It was in Caroline's locker.'

Mr Fitzgerald snorted. 'My dear, Caroline *never* wore earrings! She always said they made her look like a Christmas tree.'

'We know,' Clementine nodded grimly, 'that's why it's so strange. Can't you tell us anything about it? How many carat is it?'

Mr Fitzgerald chuckled. 'Carat, ha! It's worth practically nothing, I should know...' He picked up the dog again and placed him on the counter in front of him. 'Haven't either of you noticed Jason's glamorous collar since you've been here?'

'Oh my!' Margery said, as Clementine gasped. Jason's collar was decorated in the same style as the earring, right down to the diamanté swirls.

'Where did you get that?' Clementine demanded, and Mr Fitzgerald smiled.

'I sell them. I was contacted by a very polite young lady who had started her own jewellery company, and I could hardly resist selling something so... ah... well it's just wonderful, I suppose.' Margery eyed the garish collar. 'She also sold me a few things that were obviously stolen from her aunt's house.'

'Oh my!' Margery exclaimed again. 'Who was it?' Though the realisation of who the jewellery maker was began to dawn on her as soon as she asked the question.

'I think I have one of her cards here,' Mr Fitzgerald said, rummaging around on the counter. He shuffled through the piles of bills and receipts. 'Aha! Here it is.' He handed the crumpled business card to Margery and she read it out loud to Clementine.

'Ceri-Ann's Designs and Wellness Consulting.'

Chapter Eight

'What are we going to do, Margery?' Clementine said, as Margery slowly manoeuvred the car through the school's car park.

After they saw the poorly applied diamanté of the dog collar, it became glaringly obvious to Margery who had stolen the trinkets from the Christmas crackers last year. She could still see the children's disappointed little faces as they pulled the crackers that revealed nothing but a scrap of a joke and a depressing paper hat.

'I don't know, Clem,' Margery said unsure, swerving wildly but slowly to avoid an errant crisp packet. She wished they had brought a copy of the zombie apocalypse contingency plan with them. She was sure this situation could be adapted to it.

'Anyway, just because she made the earring doesn't mean she has anything to do with this,' Margery continued as the car chugged along. 'Mr Barrow did say it was all accidental.'

'Au contraire, Margery. Accidental!' Clementine scoffed.

Karen and Sharon passed them, plodding along at a leisurely pace with matching ponytails and sports trainers on, their right wrists both adorned with a fitness watch. The girls waved at Margery and Clementine, and Clementine waved back grimly, Margery not daring to take her hands off the wheel to join her.

'Do you not think we should go to the police, Clem?' Margery said, eyeing the back of Karen's 'Race for Life 2013' T-shirt as they passed. 'Talk to that policeman we met the other day?'

'The police!' Clementine snorted. 'After that interrogation last week, we can't trust them any more than a six-day-old egg sandwich. Do you want another caution? And anyway, that officer was a right idiot. No, do you know what we need to do, Margery? We need to find out who Seth Thomas is and where the earring came from, that's all there is to it.'

Margery eased the car into the widest parking space she could see, the brakes creaking as they stopped, the front half of the car resting gently in a bush. They clambered out, Clementine narrowly avoided hitting the large white Range Rover parked next to them, as she swung the passenger side door open a bit too sharply.

'Watch the paint!' Mrs Smith's face appeared from the wound-down window of the SUV and she glared at them like an enraged bear. 'This car cost more than your house. I'd put money on it! I thought you'd have got rid of that old rust bucket by now!'

Margery unstrapped her handbag from the luggage rack and tried to ignore Mrs Smith, internally begging for Clementine to do the same. They could not afford to make a scene today. Clementine looked ready for a 'small disagreement of words' as she usually called it, but Margery saw her brow furrow as she stared at the car. Margery followed Clem's gaze to the passenger side window and locked eyes with Seren, who waved at her awkwardly with a lit cigarette between her forefingers.

'Ever so sorry, Mrs Smith!' Margery said, in a cheery voice that she hoped didn't sound too 'put on'. 'We're just running a bit late.'

'Yes, errands to run, mysteries to solve!' Clementine butted in, waving the bagged earring around. Margery stepped on her foot and Clementine yelped.

'Put that away,' Margery hissed under her breath.

Mrs Smith seemed amused, arm still draped out of the car window. It seemed to frame her short silver bob. 'Is that so?' she said, eyeing the earring. 'And what mysteries are those?'

'Oh, nothing to concern yourself about, Rose!' Clementine said a bit too briskly, and Margery watched her quickly slip the evidence away into her handbag.

Mrs Smith seemed nonplussed as she opened the car door and slid herself out from the luxurious leather seat, somehow balancing perfectly on her designer heels. Margery noted, with a twang of jealousy, that there was not even the slightest hint of a wrinkle on her smart tailored trouser suit.

Seren followed Mrs Smith from the passenger side, but not at all as gracefully. Mrs Smith snatched the cigarette from Seren's hand, flicked it on the floor and ground it out with her shoe, giving them one more withering stare as she did so.

'Well, we can't be late for work now can we, ladies? Not with certain *issues* that have arisen recently, hmmm?' It was less a question and more a pointed remark, but it was enough for Clementine and Margery to gather their things quickly.

It was lucky they arrived at the school in good time, Margery thought, because when they got to the electronic front doors, they realised that in the rush to get to the antique shop this morning neither of them brought their work pass with them. They were stranded outside the gates, meaning they had to then walk all the way around to the security office to get visitor passes. Margery could have kicked herself. She hadn't forgotten anything for work in years, but then she supposed, she was never more than five minutes late to work either. It was surprisingly freeing in a terrifying way.

'When I was in school,' Clementine began, and Margery could already tell this was going to be nonsensical and long-winded, 'we didn't even have gates. We were hardier back then. Unafraid to run from murderers and the like.' Margery made the right noises in the right places, well-practised after years of perfection. Though they were not married, Margery still sometimes really felt like they were the dictionary definition of an old married couple.

They arrived at the tiny office, an ugly cement building at the front of the school car park, and entered the small door into the hideous white-walled room with its cheap plastic chairs. Gary Matthews, the school's goliath of a security guard, was sitting behind the tiny desk. Margery noted that he could not have been wearing a smaller uniform if he tried. Several of the letters on his jumper had disappeared into the bulging vacuum of his armpits. Margery had always felt a little bit sorry for him. The students were always running him ragged, and none of them seemed to take him seriously at all.

Mr Barrow banned skateboarding from the school grounds, and the children had instead taken to skating around and around the security office as it was technically just outside the boundary. Gary had hurt his shin, bruised by an errant board after one of the students lost control of it while doing a particularly impressive kick-flip, but that was the only time Margery ever saw him complain. He always seemed happy enough, Margery thought. Gary turned and smiled at them nervously as they wandered over to the desk.

'Hello, Gary,' Clementine said.

'Hello, Ms Butcher,' Gary said, putting the book he was reading down on the desk. 'How are you today?'

'Yes, all well, thank you, Mr Matthews. Although, we have mislaid our passes and we'll need two spare ones for the day, please.'

'No problem, erm… may I see your ID, please?' Gary Matthews asked, rubbing the back of his neck.

Clementine looked at him dumbfounded. 'ID! Why would we have ID? Just give us a visitor pass.'

Gary shook his head. 'No can do, I'm afraid.'

'What?' Clementine was outraged. 'Why not? You've known us for at least two years! We've got to get into the kitchen. We can't be late.'

Gary looked like he was fighting with himself internally, after a moment chewing his lip and not looking them in the eye, he sat up stern and straight. 'Sorry, ladies, but I won't let anyone onto the premises without some form of identification anymore,' he dropped his voice low and quiet, 'not after what happened the other day.'

'You mean Caroline's death?' Margery said.

Gary had gone incredibly quiet indeed. 'Yeah, Caroline's death.' He looked as though he was about to cry. 'I won't let it happen again.'

Clementine took a seat in one of the plastic garden chairs, still eyeing him. 'What do you mean you won't let it happen?'

Gary looked at them as though gauging whether to trust them or not. 'I... I mean,' he twiddled the pencil on his desk around in his chunky fingers, agitated, 'I found her body. Mrs Hughes, I mean.' He looked as though he might cry but he held it together well, Margery thought, as she stared at him shocked. She could see Clementine from the corner of her eye mirroring her expression. 'And they said it was an accident.' His voice dropped to a whisper. 'But it was horrible.'

'Don't worry, Mr Matthews,' Clementine said, in a way Margery was sure she thought sounded sincere, but was as convincing as Pumpkin was when she was pretending she had not already been fed. 'Margery and I are on the case.'

He looked at her surprised, and Margery could tell he was trying not to smile. 'Oh! Oh, well okay, Ms Butcher... if you're on it.' He grumbled under his breath but passed them two visitor passes from under the desk.

The kitchen was a glorious hustle-bustle of activity when they finally arrived twenty minutes late. Gloria was overseeing the team as they feverishly prepared for lunchtime. The room was heavy with the hot steam rising from the dishwasher as Karen scrubbed the big metal gastronome trays in the sink next to it furiously. Laughter filled the air, supplemented by the tinny sound of music blaring from the small battery-powered radio over the main prep station. Sharon sang along, bobbing her head to the beat and chopping onions so loudly that she could have been the drummer for the band she was singing along to.

'Come on now, everyone, we only have three hours till service!' Gloria eyed Clementine and Margery suspiciously, as they tied on their aprons. 'Ladies, you are ever so late. You haven't been this late since that pigeon flew into the school hall.' She wheeled around to face them, her dark ponytail nearly flinging itself out of her hairnet at the speed of her turn. 'Good God. There isn't a pigeon in the hall again is there?'

They shook their heads and muttered apologies. Margery mumbled about how the car got the better of her, and then Clementine got straight to work opening tins of plum tomatoes and Margery jumped right into whisking up a thirty-litre batch of powdered custard.

Margery was just adding the last drop of own-brand sweetener to the mix, when she saw Clementine gesticulating at her wildly from the corner of her eye.

'Psst!' Clementine hissed. 'Margery, psst! Look, Margery! She's got a knife!'

87

Margery turned to look at where Clementine was pointing at young Ceri-Ann, standing in front of the gas hob. She was using a large plastic-handled kitchen knife to stir a pan of gravy.

'It's a kitchen, Clem. We all have knives.' She pointed at Clementine bemused. 'You're holding one too!' Clementine moved to hide the knife she was indeed holding, knocking over the tins of tomatoes she had just opened in the process. They slammed to the floor with a splat, causing Gloria to look up from where she was mashing potatoes on the other side of the kitchen.

'What's going on with you two today?' Gloria grabbed the mop and bucket from the corner of the room and stormed over. 'You haven't been this twitchy and strange since Mr Barrow came to school wearing that kilt.'

'In our defence, it *was* a tartan skirt he bought at ASDA in the January sale,' Margery said, bending down to try to scoop up some of the tomato mess from the tiled floor with the spatula from the panini machine.

'If you want to know what's going on, you should just ask Ceri-Ann!' Clementine said, oblivious to the soggy mess that was slowly seeping under the kitchen counters and around her feet. She stabbed a bony finger in Ceri-Ann's direction. '*She* killed Caroline!' There was a silence as everyone in the vicinity turned to look at Ceri-Ann in curiosity.

'No, I didn't,' Ceri-Ann said, wide-eyed and baffled. 'Don't you think they would have arrested me if I had? You bloody idiot. They've cleaned up the crime scene and everything.'

Seren stopped peeling onions at that and stepped between them 'It's not a crime scene, for Christ's sake. Caroline was about four hundred years old, and the police ruled it accidental!'

'Oh, yeah well, you'd know all about crime scenes, wouldn't you!' Ceri-Ann shouted back into Seren's face. Seren staggered backwards, hand on her heart and her mouth open in shock.

Gloria pulled Ceri-Ann back. 'Now, you know that's not fair. Seren did her community service, didn't you, Seren?' She nodded at her kindly, and the woman nodded back with tears in her eyes.

Clementine turned back to Ceri-Ann. 'Well, why was one of your hideous creations found in Caroline's locker then? Hmmm?' Margery thought fleetingly about preventing Clementine from making a scene, but there was no stopping her once she was in full flow.

Ceri-Ann just looked at her, brow furrowed. 'You mean something from my Etsy page? Did you find one of my scarfs?'

'A scarf? Lord, no,' Clementine said. Margery could not believe there was enough diamanté in the world to make something as hideous as a scarf. 'It was an earring.'

'Oh, yeah, I haven't made them for ages!' Ceri-Ann said. 'I sold a few of them. Never to Caroline though, you know what she thought about earrings.'

Seren finally had enough and turned on her heels and left, an exasperated expression on her face, not even stopping by the staff room to get her oversized anorak before pushing open the fire escape door and wandering off down the metal steps into the rain. The door slammed shut behind her.

Gloria, who was watching the exchange with great interest, said, 'You can't have sold that many? Did you keep a list of purchases?'

'Yeah, I've sold loads of them! I always include a voucher for a free health treatment if they're local. Aroma-therapy or reiki or whatever, just a little perk for them. Anyway, I'm self-taught so I've got to practise,' Ceri-Ann said, looking incredibly smug, and turning to Gloria, who was smirking. 'Anyway, I'm a businesswoman, so I keep all my finances and transactions well organised, *thanks* Gloria! Well… you know, organised enough.'

'Well, can we have a look then, please?' Margery asked. 'There might be something in them to help us find who bought her them.'

'Yeah, why not. I've got nothing to hide. You can have a look, but I need it all back by tomorrow just in case I get a big order or something.' Margery and Clementine exchanged a look at that. Ceri-Ann continued obliviously, 'Come on, I'll show you. I keep it all in the changing room.'

-

Ceri-Ann's well-organised finances turned out to be an A4 ring binder notepad, which she had triumphantly dragged out from the bottom of her locker for them. It had a unicorn motif and 'Ceri-Ann!' carefully labelled at the front with sequins.

She neatened the scrunched-up pages and handed it to Margery. 'There you go, love, the keys to my kingdom.'

Margery was sure she heard Clementine mutter something under her breath but elected to ignore her. 'Thank you, Ceri-Ann. This will be very useful. We'll get started straight away!'

'No, you won't!' Gloria said, appearing soundlessly from behind them and making Margery jump. 'Seren just ran off somewhere after Ceri-Ann's stupid comment earlier, and we all need to pull together to get lunch done.'

Clementine scoffed. 'Who died and made you the boss, Gloria?'

There was an awkward pause as they all processed the comment and Clementine realised what she had said.

'Well,' Clementine continued, 'I suppose we'll just get on with it then. Excuse me, Gloria, we have work to do.'

Clementine got stuck ladling out portions of lasagne and chips all lunch hour, and Margery ended up in the pot wash area, washing pans and dishes with Ceri-Ann. She was 'wittering inane nonsense as usual' as Clementine would have said, but Margery didn't really mind. Ceri-Ann's youthful happiness was rather cheering after the last week's events, and the lunch hour simmered along nicely. Although, she did have to repeatedly turn down Ceri-Ann's offer of something called 'ear candling', which Ceri-Ann said was very safe because she had watched a YouTube instructional video about it.

Margery sometimes wondered how Ceri-Ann had ended up here with them, and why she stayed working at the school. The work was not always particularly interesting day to day, though the children were usually quite funny. Margery thought privately that Ceri-Ann could have done much more exciting work in one of the neighbouring town's many fine dining restaurants, if her interest was merely in cooking. However, Ceri-Ann's interests all seemed to revolve around subjects that were not particularly suitable to kitchen work and, unlike Gloria, Karen and Sharon, she had no children that the daytime work hours fitted well around. Margery just had to assume that she must enjoy working with them as a team, though she did wish Ceri-Ann would stop wearing nail varnish to work. It had been a major bugbear of Caroline's ever since the headmaster had found a sliver of bright green nail in a bite of his arctic roll.

Until Ceri-Ann had arrived, Seren was the youngest dinner lady at a mere thirty-three and Caroline had delighted in having someone even younger to torture. Well… until she realised that, although Ceri-Ann had youthful-looking skin on her side, she was actually in her late twenties and was not going to be messed around by Mrs Hughes and her practical jokes.

After lunch was finished and the kitchen was relatively clean and packed away, Margery and Clementine stole themselves away to a quiet stairway and started the arduous process of sorting through Ceri-Ann's accounts.

Margery was secretly unconvinced that this would help. An out-of-place earring and a weird circumstance of death did not make for a murder case in her eyes, especially when the police had already pronounced it a closed case. But Caroline's solicitor *had* seemed suspicious, and Margery knew that if the mystery did not reveal itself immediately Clementine would get bored and give up on it. It seemed best to just go along for the ride.

For all the ugliness of Ceri-Ann's account books, they were in a surprisingly logical order and, with a highlighter pen, Margery was able to quickly sort through names, addresses and items. Clementine sat next to her on the staircase, drinking a can of Diet Coke, completely invested in not helping her at all. Margery looked over at her and sighed. She seemed to spend most of her time being Clementine's secretary.

'It's a shame she's not a little better at making the things,' Clementine said, as she took a sip. 'She could have taken the world on with her terrible designs by now. The organisation and business acumen is all here.' She waved her free hand vaguely towards Margery's workings. 'Probably.'

Margery shook her head at her in annoyance, as she continued to work through the notebook with the highlighter pen she stole from the special pen tray Caroline had kept on the top of one of the racks in the dry store, along with her still-locked toolbox of knives and a spare apron. Margery did not think Caroline would mind them borrowing her things anymore.

She reached the last page of the book and double-checked her work. 'So, if I'm right, she only sold four pairs of earrings locally, the rest were sent far and wide,' Margery said. 'Some to London!'

'Disgusting,' Clementine muttered.

Undeterred, Margery continued, 'But I think once we discredit what Ceri–Ann sold to Mr Fitzgerald, we can narrow it right down.'

Margery peered through her reading glasses at the page again. The only name she recognised did not make any sense at all. Caroline hated her when she was alive, it did not seem likely she would have bought her a gift. In fact, on the rare occasion that they had ventured into the canteen for lunch, Mrs Hughes had made herself scarce, but here it was in black and white. She sighed to herself and put the paper down on her lap.

'Hello, ladies.'

Margery looked up from her work to see Barbara and her enclave walking towards where she and Clementine were perched on the bottom step of the stairwell. Each of them had a plastic cup of vending machine coffee, and Margery could see the rectangular outline of a pack of cigarettes in the pocket of Anita's black tabard. The constant smoking was the one thing about Anita that Barbara did not seem to have a hand in; Anita seemed to enjoy it as much as Barbara did. Anita was always puffing away with the rest of the cleaners out on the kitchen's fire escape, cigarette in hand.

'Oh, hello, Barbara!' Clementine said cheerily. 'Just starting work?'

'Hello, Clementine. Hello, Margery.' Barbara smiled at them both. 'Well, we're a bit early, aren't we, girls?' Anita and Cheryl nodded in agreement.

'What are you two up to?' Cheryl asked, peering down at them. 'Looks ever so interesting.'

'Well…' Margery said, straining her mind to think of a single other reason they would be sitting in the school corridor after hours. Clementine beat her to it.

'We're solving Caroline's murder,' she chirped cheerily, putting down her drink. Margery shushed her. There was a pause as Barbara processed what Clementine had said.

'Murder now, is it?' she said finally, turning to Margery with her eyebrows raised. The look on her face was pleasant, but she looked as though she was considering something. Barbara turned to look at them, seeming to be examining them very carefully. 'There's something I've been meaning to talk to you both about, actually. Privately, I mean.'

She put her cup of coffee down on the windowsill next to the staircase and beckoned for Anita and Cheryl to leave. Margery watched them go with a mounting feeling of doom.

Barbara leaned a skinny elbow against the banister. Her wrinkled lips pursed as though she was chewing on a particularly sour piece of lemon. They stared up at her, Margery thought, like children waiting to be told off.

'Look, *ladies*.' Barbara drew out the word in a manner that was both patronising and terrifying. 'While I understand why you're both so upset, you've got to stop this nonsense about Caroline being killed. We heard you at the funeral talking about Caroline's earring or whatever silly claptrap you've both decided caused her death.' Clementine looked like she was about to make a remark, but Barbara held up a bony finger to quiet her. 'Don't try to deny it, please, Clementine. Caroline was very old, she should have retired a decade ago. If you ask me, she had it coming at her age. Yes, no one's denying it was a horrible accident,' She looked down to inspect her perfectly painted fingernails, 'but quite frankly, what you're doing is just upsetting people. I heard about Seren leaving this morning, and she didn't come back to work, did she? You can't go about being accusatory after what happened last year.'

Margery opened her mouth to apologise for inadvertently hurting Seren's feelings, but Clementine had already opened hers. 'You can't blame the dead and anyway, that's nonsense, Barbara, Caroline's death was very suspicious, and you know it!'

Barbara stepped back, eyeing them both warily. 'All I know, Clementine, is that Caroline's death has been nothing but destructive, and you of all people seem to be the biggest problem.'

'Excuse me!'

'You heard!' Barbara snapped, her big bush of carefully backcombed hair making her seem even more intimidating than normal. 'And *I* heard about your little dalliance with the police last week. We all did.'

Margery put Ceri-Ann's notebook on the stair behind her and stood up. 'We're sorry, Barbara, we' just got a bit wrapped up in... well, all of it, I suppose.' She waved her hand to try and convey the size of what they had got themselves involved in, but she was not sure it worked very well. She was more ashamed of the upset they had unintentionally caused to poor Seren. Margery was a bit embarrassed as well, truth be told. Barbara was always genuinely nice to Seren. She had kind of taken her under her wing as one of her own over the past year, another daughter to add to the menagerie she was so proud of, and Margery felt a bit selfish for not being as generous or giving with kindness.

'Compassion for everyone,' Margery's grandmother had always said. Though saying that, her grandmother had eventually shacked up with a door-to-door conman, been robbed absolutely blind and was left with just six pounds in her bank account by the end of her life. Perhaps her slogan really should have been, 'Compassion for some, a very wide arc for others.'

Barbara picked up her cup of coffee again. It must have gone freezing cold by now, Margery always wondered why she always saw Barbara microwaving her cup in the canteen and the reason must be the amount of time she spent talking. 'I'm just saying, ladies. Be very careful where you tread. You might end up following in Caroline's footsteps.' With that, she smiled at them one last time and strode off down the corridor. 'See you later, ladies!' she said as she exited.

Margery sat back down on the stairs, dumbfounded.

Clementine tutted under her breath. 'She has no capacity for silence, that woman.'

Margery turned to look at her. 'She's right though, Clem.'

Clementine snorted. 'No, she isn't! She didn't nearly get frozen to death inside a freezer, did she? And Seren has had it coming. You don't get to do what she did without some form of retribution.'

Margery reached behind them and grabbed Ceri-Ann's book again, pulling it into her lap. 'Oh, so you're admitting we nearly died now, are you?'

Clementine smirked and turned to look at the ceiling. 'Something weird is going on, Margery,' she finally said. 'We're so close to figuring out a clue. Are you really saying we should stop now?'

Margery stared down at the notebook. She was at a crossroads now, in her mind at least. It would be all too easy to give the book back to Ceri-Ann and admit defeat.

'Thing is,' she said, fidgeting with the pages of the notebook, 'I think I've already figured out the clue.'

'Oh, well done, Margery!' Clementine said, and she grabbed Margery's shoulder and beamed at her. 'How did you manage that?'

Margery smiled back. 'You'll never guess who bought the earrings, Clem!'

'Go on then, tell me,' Clementine demanded, clawing at the page as Margery lifted it up for her to see.

'Rose Smith,' Margery said.

Chapter Nine

'I'm not sure about this, Clem,' Margery said, wringing her hands together as Clementine frogmarched them towards the drama department. 'She was quite rude to us this morning. I don't think Mrs Smith will be pleased if we just turn up at her office.'

Clementine snorted. 'Rose? She's just a *drama* teacher for Christ's sake, Margery, pull yourself together. What is she going to do? Read Shakespeare at us till we fall asleep?'

'Do you not remember the time she threw an egg at you because you burnt her cheese toastie? She's not someone to be trifled with,' Margery said. 'Or the time she called you a witch because we ran out of sandwiches?'

Clementine's face soured at the memory. 'Yes, well, I must admit that I, for one, will not be in the least bit surprised when she turns out to have had something to do with all this.'

They arrived and paused outside Mrs Smith's office, which also doubled as the costume department for the drama club and storage for any excess gym equipment. Her desk was squashed against the left-hand side of the room, and on the other side and all around the desk were boxes and boxes of deflated footballs. The entire room was full of assorted school bric-a-brac, errant pool noodles that had been stolen from the leisure centre and smelly lost gym kits. Margery always wondered how the woman could breathe in there, let alone work at her computer.

'Knock then,' Margery said to Clementine, who had raised her hand as a fist, but had not brought it down onto the wood of the door. 'What are you waiting for?'

'Maybe...' Clementine began slowly, 'Maybe this *isn't* the greatest time. It means we'll have to talk to her twice in one day. She is horrible after all—'

'I can hear you out there!' The muffled voice of Mrs Smith sounded through the door, and Margery and Clementine both jumped.

'Well,' Clementine said and stepped back, 'after you then, Margery. This being your idea and all that.'

They stared at each other. Margery admitted defeat and pushed the garish purple door open, not bothering to knock. Mrs Smith was revealed, perched at her desk. She had taken off the suit jacket she was wearing earlier. It was draped casually on the back of her flimsy-looking desk chair, but she did not look much less dignified in just her shiny silk taffeta blouse.

It was obvious that she had not expected to be disturbed. The box of Thorntons chocolates that were designated for next month's summer fete raffle was open at the desk in front of her, raffle ticket still stuck to it. A vape pen also sat to one side of the desk. Margery assumed she had confiscated it from one of the children, and the small room stank dreadfully of artificial strawberries.

'We're sorry to bother you at this time of the evening, Mrs Smith,' Clementine began gingerly. Margery looked at the clock on the wall above Mrs Smith's desk, which read two forty-five. 'We just had something to ask you about.'

Mrs Smith sat back in her chair; it squeaked as she turned to them, smirking. 'I can see what's happening here. And no, we haven't chosen a successor for the kitchen manager post yet.'

'No, no, it's not that, Mrs Smith,' Margery said, shaking her head.

'Well, believe me when I say the right person will be chosen in time.' Mrs Smith eyed them both, folding her arms tightly to her chest.

'When will you decide? Will we need to do a CV?' Clementine said. Margery didn't like the eagerness in her voice.

Mrs Smith sighed loudly, turning back again to give her full attention to her laptop. 'Oh yes, a piece of paper with your many, many accomplishments. Or in your case, a very, very small Post-it note.'

'Well, we don't want it anyway!' Margery spat out, a bit too abruptly even for her own liking. Clementine turned away with a sheepish look on her face.

'Really?' Mrs Smith regarded them both from the corner of one eye as she continued scrolling through pages of shoes on the internet browser. 'So you're both happy, are you? Being second in command, while Mrs Hughes left early every day to make sure her VCR was recording *Countdown*?'

'She only did that if she suspected it would be a particularly good episode,' Margery insisted. 'Most of the time she worked really hard! She wouldn't have died if she hadn't been here late Friday.'

Mrs Smith just smirked at them both, eyebrows raised as if she did not believe a single word of it. 'All I'm saying is that she should have retired years ago. She could barely walk, always pottering about with that stick. No, she should have given the job up to someone younger.'

'Well… what are you saying exactly?' Clementine asked. 'About the job, I mean?'

'I'm saying I'm not above bribery.' Mrs Smith sneered; there was still chocolate on her lip from the stolen Thorntons.

Margery glared at her. 'Honestly, Mrs Smith, our jobs are taxing enough as it is,' she said. 'We need to talk to you about something else.'

Mrs Smith scoffed. 'You've come to my private office,' Margery eyed the old gym mats resting against the brick wall, 'when you know that today of all days I'm very, very busy.' She clicked on the 'add to cart' button on-screen and smiled, obviously very pleased with herself.

'Have you ever bought anything from Ceri-Ann's shop, Mrs Smith?' Margery asked. She thought she saw something flicker across Mrs Smith's face in the glow from the screen, an emotion other than pride, but it was gone no sooner than she had noticed it.

'Who's asking?' Mrs Smith said primly, her lips pursed tightly together.

'We are, obviously! We're trying to investigate a—ouch!' Clementine cried out as Margery stepped firmly on her foot to shut her up. Mrs Smith looked between them both, an amused expression on her face.

'Ladies…' Mrs Smith said. 'If you ever catch me buying one of Ceri-Ann's abominations, you have permission to knock me down dead with your terrible car.'

There was a long, long pause.

'Is that a promise?' Clementine asked, her voice much too hopeful.

Mrs Smith sighed dramatically. 'Why would I, of all people, buy anything from Ceri-Ann when I am obviously a woman of taste?'

'Are you sure? You didn't buy the earrings for Caroline?' Clementine asked. She grabbed Ceri-Ann's book from Margery and waved it in Rose's face. 'When it says in this book that you did!'

Mrs Smith glared at her. 'Why ever would I buy anything for Caroline, of all people? And do you really think a few scraps of paper written by an idiot means I did?' Mrs Smith picked up the nail file on her desk and began polishing her cuticles, avoiding looking up at their faces.

'Now please, I'm very busy.' Mrs Smith blew on her fingernails and held them up to the light to inspect them. 'As if I'd wear anything Ceri-Ann made.' She flicked the right side of her immaculate grey bob behind her ear with a flourish, showing off the earrings she was wearing. 'These are Welsh gold, for God's sake.'

She went back to polishing her nails as Margery stared at the tasteful drop earring in her earlobe. They stood awkwardly as Rose ignored them.

'But how would Caroline have had them then?' Margery said.

'No more questions!' Mrs Smith said, starting on the other hand.

'Can we at least ask where you were on Friday night?' Clementine pleaded.

Mrs Smith let out an exasperated sigh and spun in her chair to face them. 'It really is absolutely none of your business, but I was with the Year Eight drama club in the village hall, of course. We're currently in rehearsal for a dramatic showing of *Moulin Rouge*, to showcase the school's French heritage.'

Dewstow was linked with the small village of Dormond in France. Margery remembered this well, when they visited on a dinner ladies team-building trip during the summer holiday one year. Seren had sat up on the coach, squinted her teeny eyes out at the window and announced loudly that it could not be a twin town because it didn't look anything like Dewstow.

'Well, go on then.' Rose made a shooing motion at them rudely. 'I've answered your strange and obnoxious questions.'

'Just one more thing.' Clementine was on her way to the door, but she spun back around as she spoke as though to try to catch Rose in surprise.

Rose raised an eyebrow. 'For God's sake, what now?'

'Who do we give the CV for the job to?'

Rose stared at Clementine as though she was a slug she had stepped on bare-footed. If looks could hurt, this one would have been particularly acidic. 'Did we not just discuss this? Now, please, please, please get back into that rust-bucket car of yours, go home and leave me alone.'

Chapter Ten

'Well then, that's one crossed off the list,' Clementine said, a proud note in her voice as they walked down the school corridor on their way back to the kitchen. The building was empty now apart from the odd member of staff and the cleaners. Margery always hated being there when no one else was; it always felt like she had entered an alternate universe. She moved quickly in her haste to escape the quiet of the long corridors, but Clementine sauntered along behind her as if they had all the time in the world.

'Did you actually have to write a checklist?' Margery asked. 'It's just one name.'

'Imagine calling *me* a witch,' Clementine said, as she used a highlighter pen to draw through the lone name on her open notepad page, 'when she looks like one of the children's end-of-year self-portraits that's been printed on a tea towel and left in a book bag all summer. Anyway, Margery, she lives up to her name, doesn't she? Rosemary, I mean. She's a smelly, spiky old plant if ever I saw one.'

Margery let her rant as they wandered along steadily, not in a rush to get back to work. Not that there would be much work left to do when they finally got back: Karen and Sharon would have finished most of the cleaning by now, and Gloria had probably forced Ceri-Ann to take the bin bags down the fire escape to the recycling area. If they were lucky, all they would have to do was put their coats on and go home. She was not sure what Clementine was thinking, regarding the kitchen manager's position, and she wondered why she had not immediately scoffed at the prospect like Margery had thought she would.

When Caroline was promoted, her best friend Helen Melon had left her post as a senior 'Education Centre Nourishment Consultant' in protest and started Melon's Greengrocery. That, in turn, had upset things with Doreen Rolley who was supplying their fresh fruit but could not afford to keep up with Helen Melon's prices. In her eyes, Helen Melon was cheating by using a reputable supplier to supply her fruit, and not just relying on the four apple trees and the blackberry bush she happened to have in her back garden.

Doreen had called Helen a terrible cheat and insinuated that, when they had been at school together forty years before, Helen Melon had not even been Helen's real name. She insisted that her surname was really Bevan, and Helen changed it to make herself seem more of a food expert before her job interview at Summerview.

No matter the truth, it had torn a ley line through their happy work environment for years until they found an uneasy peace. To the best of her knowledge, Helen Melon and Caroline had avoided each other entirely since, and in Margery's eyes, a promotion was not an opportunity but a threat to be dealt with.

Clementine was oblivious to these thoughts, and continued as they rounded the corner and entered through the door into the kitchen team's changing room. '…and Sharon was so upset, she cried so hard she couldn't finish her lunch. I mean, she physically couldn't finish it, the tears made her bread all soggy and she had to throw the whole sandwich away because it was too salty. Oh,' Clementine stopped in her tracks, 'did you leave your locker open, Margery?'

Margery was sure she had not, but it was indeed open. Both of their lockers were. She felt her hand go instinctively to the key attached to her work pass by the lanyard. It was still there.

'Oh my,' Margery said, as Clementine rushed forward to assess the damage, pulling her backpack from her locker where it landed on the floor with a thud. Cough drops and two pence pieces rolled all over in her panic to check her belongings.

'My bag is open!' Clementine wailed.

Margery stepped forward to have a look at her own locker. It did not look forced open, there were no signs of struggle or damage to the lock, but it swung open on its hinges all the same. She rifled through her belongings; her coat and bag were still there. Her handbag was open, just as Clementine's was, but her coin purse was still safe inside and Clementine's emergency asthma inhaler, which she insisted she did not need, was still lying at the bottom in its packaging.

'All my things are here,' she said finally, after checking and double-checking. Clementine was still scrambling around in her bag, like a dog trying to uncover a bone it had buried.

'It's gone, Margery!' Clementine looked up at her wide-eyed. 'The earring has gone! I put it in here before lunchtime and it's gone!'

'It can't be!' Margery dropped to her knees on the cold tile floor, and helped Clementine root through her bag again. She was right; it was gone. All that was left in the bag was Clementine's phone, which was currently resting at five per cent battery, and therefore had about as much use as an expensive metal paperweight, and a half-eaten Kit-Kat Crunchy.

Resigned to the realisation that they had lost their only clue, she sat down heavily on the floor.

Clementine shook her head grimly. 'Who? How? How did they open my locker? I don't understand!'

Margery shrugged. She did not understand it either.

'It's as though they had a key, but if they could open the locker then why didn't they just close it after?' Margery asked, more to herself than Clementine, who had stood from her perched position and began pacing the tiny room.

The door swung open, very nearly hitting Margery, as Ceri-Ann entered, her head buried in her phone. Karen and Sharon followed fast behind her.

'Oh, all right, ladies?' Ceri-Ann beamed down at Margery on the floor. 'Did you catch your murderer or not?'

'No, and we never will now!' Clementine wailed, drawing herself up to her full height, which was not all that impressive at five foot, Margery thought. 'We've been burgled!'

'Burgled?' Karen said, pulling her medium-length light hair out of the constrictive bun she wore it in when at work, and pulling it into an equally restricting ponytail. 'What do you mean?'

Clementine threw her hands in the direction of her locker dramatically. 'Burgled!' She drew out the word in a manner that was a touch too melodramatic.

Sharon burst into tears. 'Ooh, Caroline would have loved this. It's so sad she isn't here!'

Karen patted her gingerly on the back, as she grabbed her raincoat from the coat hook with the other hand. 'Now, now Sharon. Absence makes the heart grow fonder after all.'

Sharon nodded back at Karen, blinking away the tears. 'I know, she'd want us to remember all the drama she was alive to see. Not worry about the things she's missing.'

Karen smiled at her. 'Come on. Let's go and get a cup of tea in the Tesco Café and then go for a nice run around the park, shall we?' She handed Sharon her coat and they waved goodbye to the rest of the team and left.

Ceri-Ann was eyeing Clementine's locker with great interest as Margery clambered to her feet and handed her back her folder.

'I don't understand how they opened it,' Margery said.

'I do,' Ceri-Ann said, scrutinising the inside of the open locker door. 'They just opened it with a credit card or something. Makes sense because they might not have had time to shut it after.' She paused and peered closer, her head disappearing inside for a moment, and then pulled something small and square and plastic out and held it up to show them both with a triumphant gleam.

'There you go!' she said victoriously.

Margery took it from her offering hand, and turned it over to look at the logo on the front. 'Oh,' she said, pulling it closer to her face so she could see. 'It's a leisure centre gym pass.'

'Well, whose is it?' Clementine asked impatiently.

Ceri-Ann squinted over at it. 'Dunno, doesn't say. I bet the leisure centre would know though! It's got a number on it, and you should probably tell Security you've had something nicked anyway. What did you say was taken?'

'A priceless earring!' Clementine wailed.

'Oh, that.' Ceri-Ann looked like she was trying to hide a smile, Margery thought. 'I'll make you another one. It cost me basically nothing to make anyway, and I like you two.'

Clementine rolled her eyes. 'Of *course* you like us, who doesn't? But that doesn't help us. The earring we had contained Caroline's killer's DNA!'

Ceri-Ann was definitely smirking at least a little bit now.

'Yeah, well. I'm not sure if it being flung about in your handbag all day has done that any good has it? Security are probably closed now as well, to be honest, but you should talk to them tomorrow. You sure nothing else has gone missing?'

'Not a thing,' Margery said, 'but you're right. We'll go and see Gary tomorrow and report it.'

Ceri-Ann opened her own locker and started collecting her things. She nodded at Margery. 'Yeah, good idea. I'll tell Gloria if I see her before you tomorrow. She left before me today. Before any of us actually, because her husband rang. He got bitten by one of Caroline's snakes and wanted her to come home.'

'Ceri-Ann,' Margery said, a thought suddenly coming into her head. 'We asked Mrs Smith about her buying one of your earrings, but she said she didn't. She said you must have made it up.'

Ceri-Ann scoffed and pulled a face. 'Yeah well, you know what Rose is like. Anyway, I've got to be off.' She pulled on her coat and hefted the oversized holdall, full of what looked like yoga mats and extra-long acupuncture needles, out of her locker and over her shoulder, turning to beam at them before she left. 'See you later, ladies. God it's been a long week already, hasn't it?'

—

It really had been a long week, Margery thought as they approached the car. And a terrible week to rival all the awful weeks she had had in her life. Even worse than the week Clementine accepted a free massage from Ceri-Ann, which had hurt her back. Margery had had to do everything for her, whilst Clementine had lain on the hard flooring in their kitchen, constantly shouting for Margery to bring her more biscuits.

She was looking forward to getting home. Asking the leisure centre about the card and contacting Security could wait until tomorrow. Especially as the object that was stolen did not really belong to either of them. She was secretly glad to be rid of it, in all honesty. Now they could go home, watch an episode of *MasterChef*, put it all behind them and they might be able to put Caroline's memory to rest.

Clementine helped her attach their bags to the luggage rack on the back of the car and they clambered in. Margery did sometimes wish that they had bought a car with more functional storage space. The luggage rack certainly looked pretty, but they had been confined to the purchasing of only waterproof baggage for the last twenty years or so, and that had got old after about six months. Margery dreamed of owning a silk taffeta bag that she could throw into a ginormous enclosed car boot; the tiny storage space on the back of the Figaro was only big enough to house their canvas shopping bags and a spare umbrella.

She started the engine. It rumbled obediently into life with a start, and they rolled backwards from the parking space as she took her foot off the brake.

'Clem, before I forget, the last time I popped into town I got us a new CD in the charity shop. "Sounds of the Eighties". Shall we pop it on? Cheer ourselves up a bit?'

Clementine looked at her as though Margery had just asked her to drink a pint glass full of liquidised spiders. 'Really, Margery? You know I don't listen to contemporary music. You should have saved your fifty pence for something meaningful.'

'Like what?' Margery said, as they chugged out of the school car park and onto the main road. 'Lord knows we've bought enough Royal Family memorabilia to last a lifetime. What else could fifty pence possibly buy you? And anyway, Caroline didn't get to take all her fifty pence pieces with her, did she?'

They slipped into an unusual and uncomfortable silence. Margery watched carefully to see whether the young couple pushing the pram along the pavement would want to cross at the zebra crossing, but they carried on walking and she did not need to slow the car.

'Clem,' Margery said softly, over the noise of the car engine, 'you aren't thinking of applying for the kitchen manager job, are you?' The approaching traffic light was green, and they rolled through it easily.

'Well...' Clementine said, rubbing her chin, deep in thought, 'it would be a bit more money. Lord knows the boiler won't last another winter, and we've needed a new shed roof for years. Every time it rains, my Argos catalogue collection gets wet.'

Margery sighed as she manoeuvred the car out onto Dewstow Hill and they began the decline. Clementine's soggy catalogue collection had been the cause of one too many arguments in their relationship. 'Yes, but it's not all about the money, is it?' she pleaded with Clementine.

'Well, of course not!' Clementine said stubbornly. 'But it's a definite perk. We should at least consider it—'

'You're being absolutely ridiculous. There's no need to consider anything at all,' Margery snapped at her.

'Margery, there really is no need to swear!' Clementine said back. 'And slow down, this road is a twenty limit.'

Margery checked the speedometer and realised with horror that, while they were arguing, the car had reached twenty-two miles an hour. She put her foot to the brake to slow the car down but the pedal gave no resistance as it flopped to the floor uselessly. She tried again and again, but it was no good. Nothing happened and they continued to roll uncontrollably, picking up the pace as she hammered her foot down again and again.

'The brake isn't working!' she said to Clementine, her fingers white on the steering wheel, foot still trying the pedal in the hope that it would suddenly jump back into service. 'I'm trying to slow down!' Margery cried, stamping down on the brake to no avail.

'Okay,' Clementine said, 'well... um... try not to panic!'

'But I am panicking!' Margery shouted back at her.

'Yes. Well. That's perfectly normal, to feel panicky. Um... have you tried putting it into a higher gear?'

'I can't, Clem. It's an automatic!'

'Well then, what are all these letters for?' Clementine said exasperated, gesturing at the gear selector.

'I'm not sure,' Margery said, desperately wishing she had taken more than two driving lessons. 'I only ever use "1" and "P".'

The car was fast approaching thirty miles an hour now, and time seemed to go into slow motion. Margery could see their estate a short distance away at the bottom of the steep hill. They were going to career straight into it.

'My phone!' Clementine shouted to her. 'I can ask the phone!'

The car's speedometer showed that they had reached thirty-five miles an hour. Margery's hands were so sweaty they almost slipped off the wheel. She had never driven the car this fast before, not even on the motorway. Clementine searched through her coat pockets and came up empty each time, she reached for her bag but it was not there. 'Margery, my bag is in the back of the car!'

Margery cursed the luggage rack for the second time today and the phone for the fiftieth time this year. 'What did we say the other day about phones!' she wailed.

'Well, you won't get to lecture me anymore because we'll be dead soon!' Clementine said.

They careened down to the bottom of the hill and the road evened out onto a flat plane. Margery steered wildly off the main road and they hit the first speed bump as they entered their street, flying over it with a bang. Margery's thoughts came in rapid bursts. They were going to die. She knew it instinctively; could feel it in her bones. They were going to die, and they would never fix the shed roof, or finally get married, or even enjoy another Sunday in front of the television. And who would look after Pumpkin when they were gone? She suddenly found herself remembering the washing up she had not put away the night before. It was funny the things that came to a person at a time like this.

She tried to think of something, anything that could help them. Clementine was gripping the dashboard for dear life, and Margery suddenly realised that there was only one thing left to try. She quickly reached out and pulled the handbrake up with all her might. It crunched upwards and the car began to spin as the wheels locked, Margery realised her mistake as she nearly lost control of it completely.

'Clem, what do I do?' she screamed.

'Aim for the hedge!' Clementine shouted back, gesticulating wildly at the long row of hedges separating the street and the pavement from number forty-four Seymour Road's garden.

Margery swore that if they survived she would never, ever complain about the unsightly nature of next door's hedge again, or Clementine's lack of phone, or Ceri-Ann's blatant disregard for the school's nose-ring policy. She checked that her seatbelt was still buckled, grimacing as they swerved desperately.

The tyres of the car bounced hard off the pavement as they careered haphazardly into the hedge, through the fence and landed in number forty-four's back garden with a terrific crunch.

Chapter Eleven

Margery opened one eye and was astounded to find that they were both still alive. Her hands hurt from gripping the steering wheel so tightly, and there was going to be a big bruise where the seat belt had dug into her shoulder, stopping her from propelling out of the windshield. Nevertheless, it was an overwhelming relief not to be dead. Even the pond water seeping through the floor and into her shoes was not much of an upset. She felt ever so lucky in that moment as she stared through the broken windscreen and out to number forty-four's neatly trimmed grass. The fact that her once pride and joy of a car was in the water was currently irrelevant. She turned and smiled broadly at Clementine, who returned her grin, and they both started to chuckle.

'Oh, no,' Clementine said, her attention drawn to something in the distance. 'Dawn Simmonds is coming, and she looks absolutely livid!'

Dawn Simmonds had indeed slid open her patio doors and was making her way over to them, wearing a flour-covered apron and brandishing a rolling pin, a sour look on her face. On her feet she had on what must have been the closest footwear to her back door – a pair of large men's slippers on the wrong feet. Dawn must have seen them arrive gracefully into the pond through her kitchen window, Margery thought in amusement, the high of escaping the Grim Reaper not yet worn off.

'What the hell are you doing?' Dawn Simmonds said, red-faced and waving the rolling pin around in fervour. 'You've ruined my hedge! Look at the state of it! Do you know how much topiary work that was? I'm going to ring the police!'

'Well, ring an ambulance too!' Margery shouted back through the glassless windscreen, eyeing the bruise on Clementine's forehead from where she had hit the dashboard.

'I will!' Dawn Simmonds said, spitting the words at them, 'And then they can lock you both away, you loonies!' She pointed the rolling pin in her hand in Clementine's direction menacingly. 'I always knew you hated my hedge!'

Clementine's eyes opened wide at that. 'Loony! You're one to talk!'

Margery watched as Clementine unclipped her seatbelt and opened the passenger door with great difficulty. She finally managed it and hauled herself from the car and into the waist-height water, pieces of glass and algae dropping off her as she went. 'Who the hell needs a hedge this big anyway? Who do you think you are? The Queen?'

'You're in the middle of *my* garden!' Dawn Simmonds blustered back.

'Well, I'm sure you would have invited us over at some point!' Margery said, unclipping her seat belt and clambering after Clementine.

Dawn Simmonds was not quite as brave now that Clementine was dragging herself through the pond towards her, like a badly costumed creature in a 1950s B-movie. As Clementine reached the edge of the pond, Mrs Simmonds reluctantly stretched her arms out to help her clamber up. Margery followed. She could not wait to get home and put on a fresh pair of socks and a new cardigan. The koi carp swimming around in the water kept gently brushing her bare legs, making her feel sick, and she wished she had put on anything else but a skirt that morning. She struggled out after Clementine and then, once back on dry ground, she turned and surveyed the scene.

'Oh God, Margery,' Clementine said. 'Look at your poor car.'

They had tumbled through the hedge with enough force to create a big hole in it and bring down a large panel of the fence. They had then careened across the garden, ruining the nicely lined grass with tyre marks, and finally came to rest in Mrs Simmonds's koi carp pond. In a way it was lucky that the large cherub-shaped fountain in the middle of the pond had stopped them, Margery supposed, but looking at the car bonnet wrapped around it was still upsetting.

'Oh, Margery,' Clementine said, squelching over in her wet trousers and patting Margery's shoulder gently, 'I'm sure once we get it out of the water that will buff right out, you'll see.'

The three of them fell silent for a moment, in what Margery felt was a solemn minute of silence for the memory of the car. Even Dawn Simmonds had stopped gesticulating wildly with the rolling pin for a second. Margery would never be able to fix it; it was thirty years old for one, and they did not even make them anymore.

'If I'm being honest though,' Clementine said quietly, 'it didn't have airbags and we aren't both dead so this did go quite well, by all accounts.'

Dawn Simmonds raised the rolling pin again, the spell broken. 'Get out of my garden!'

–

Not long after Dawn Simmonds had threatened them with all number of unspeakable things and thrown them off her property, the police did in fact arrive joined by paramedics and they had to re-enact the entire shambles again. Margery understood it was for the policeman to understand what had happened, but Clementine whispered suspiciously that it was for their own entertainment.

After they were thoroughly checked out by the ambulance crew, the tow truck finally turned up, what felt like days later, and they were finally allowed to go back home and change into dry things. The mechanic who came to pull the car out of the pond had nearly laughed himself sick at the sight of it, and Margery was glad to get away from his constant sniggering.

The young policeman, Symon, was waiting for them, sat in the pink crinoline chair in the living room along with the older Officer Thomas who had arrested them only a few days before. The officers both had a look of bemusement on their faces, and Margery wished she could wipe it off. Clementine wheeled the tea things in, looking none the worse for their ordeal; Margery was always awed and envious of her ability to still look put together in a dressing gown and with towel-dried hair.

'Please help yourselves to a toffee penny, Officers,' Clementine said, playing the graceful host. She had even put the clotted cream and jam in the best china alongside the homemade scones. The china they would use for their wedding if they had ever had one, Margery thought somewhat bitterly. Not that she had not suggested it to Clementine when civil ceremonies had been announced, but Clementine had said, 'Let's see how we get on, shall we?' and then there'd been no more talk of it. She had not wanted to push Clementine, though she did think that forty years together might be enough to "see how it goes".

Clementine reached over the trolley to pick up the teapot, but Officer Thomas motioned for her to sit down and he proceeded to do it for them. Margery could see young Officer Symon looking at the photographs on the mantelpiece above their £49.99 Argos imitation coal electric fire. Most of them were of her and Clementine. The biggest one was of the time they had won Dewstow Town's Cherry Bakewell Bake Off in 1987; both of them were laughing, pointing happily at their winning entry.

Margery had hated that photo when they first got the film developed, but now she could see she was neither as fat nor as ugly as she had thought she was. In fact, she would give anything to go back and do it all again and actually enjoy her healthy younger body and unbroken teeth; to really relish being able to read in a dimly lit room at night time without straining her eyes. She smiled at the memory, though she did now wish she could have lived her youth without worrying about it all so much. 'Worrying gives small things big shadows,' Margery's mother used to say, after she had had a few too many sherries for an evening.

Margery accepted the cup gratefully as Officer Thomas passed it over. She was sure there was something they had meant to ask him, but it had slipped away in all the drama of the day. It came back to her as she watched Clementine add five spoons of sugar to her tea – Caroline's beneficiary had been a Seth Thomas. It seemed a long shot that the officer would be the same one, and she did not think Caroline would have ever seriously dated a policeman. Caroline had always said... well it was probably best not to think about what Caroline called police officers when she was alive. There had been a lot of off-colour jokes.

'Officer Thomas?' she said. 'Lovely name... ah... your name, um.' She stumbled over the words. 'Well, is your first name... err, is your first name also Thomas?'

Everyone stared at her for a long time, and she could feel her face flush. Even Clementine had stopped ladling sugar into her cup, teaspoon paused in the air as if in second-hand embarrassment for her.

'No,' Officer Thomas said, the tiny teacup looking ginormous in his oversized hands. 'Of course, it isn't.' He pointed to the badge on his chest, tapping it gently with his index finger, very slowly as though he thought her very stupid. 'It's Nigel.'

'Right, yes, of course,' Margery said, and pretended to take a sip of tea.

Clementine shook her head. 'Will we have to pay for the fence? Only it's obvious someone was trying to kill us,' she said bluntly. 'First, a priceless kitchen family heirloom is stolen from our lockers,' she waved in Margery's direction, 'and then our brakes fail! And let us not forget about the freezer door incident the other day. I don't need a policing degree, or whatever it is, to know that someone's probably ordered a hit on us to steal our fortune!'

Officer Symon continued to look around the room at the tatty, old furniture.

'Ms Butcher,' Officer Thomas said gently and lowered his cup, 'Let's just wait to see what the mechanic says, shall we? Because, as Ms Baker has just told us, the car is twenty-five years old and she's never had it serviced!' He turned to Margery. 'I'm amazed it passed the last MOT!'

'Oh.' Margery blushed. 'Yes… well. I suppose there were a few faults that needed sorting out.'

The truth was that the number of things that needed 'sorting out' were considerable at the car's last MOT and had cost them a small fortune. She wished she had not mentioned the lack of servicing to the policeman. She did occasionally open the car bonnet and peer inside, but she very rarely did more than refill the windscreen wash.

The only garage in town was nearly always fully booked. So she would often book the date of the next MOT at the same time as paying for the one the car was having done. She worried about it all sometimes, but Clementine always reminded her that they did not do many miles and she nearly always managed to forget about it.

Officer Thomas smiled at her and put his china cup down with a clunk onto the coffee table so he could brush the biscuit crumbs from his moustache. Clementine winced at the mark the cup left on the table top.

'Well, ladies,' he said. 'We won't take up too much more of your time. I would count yourselves lucky that Mrs Simmonds isn't pressing charges on behalf of her fence.' He paused. 'And you're very lucky she had recently insured her pond.'

'Pfft!' Clementine almost spat out her tea. 'I wouldn't give her a penny for that monstrosity to be rebuilt.' She rolled her eyes dramatically. 'Though having said that, I do think we should send her a thank you card. It did save our lives, after all.'

'My grandfather always said to take it all with a pinch of salt,' Officer Symon piped up cheerily.

'Yes,' Officer Thomas said. 'Lovely man, your grandfather. Made horrible tea.'

They all sipped in silence. Margery watched young Symon peering around at the rest of their décor, the look of bewilderment still on his face. He had been extremely helpful bringing their bags in from the back of the car, Margery thought. Practically ruined his nice, smart policing trousers in the process of wading through the pond.

They were lucky the bags had not got too wet to be salvageable but that was the joy of waterproof luggage. Anyway, it had been more of a Titanic situation, the front half of the car submerged and the back exposed to the elements. Well, Dawn's garden. Margery suspected that a good spin in the tumble dryer would sort out her backpack, though her supermarket coupons might not have fared as well.

'My brakes were fine this morning,' Margery said, helping herself to a custard cream. 'Honestly, we went all the way up Dewstow Hill, no issues.'

Clementine looked at her, eyes wide, and Margery silently begged her not to mention how she had stalled as they hill-started through the traffic lights on the high street.

'Well, we'll have to see what the mechanic says,' Officer Thomas said kindly, writing something in his notebook and flipping it closed with a flourish. 'But we've breathalysed both of you and we don't expect foul play.' He took off his round spectacles and gave them a clean with his handkerchief.

'But what about our stolen property?' Clementine snapped.

'Now that I might be able to help with!' Officer Thomas smiled at them. 'What was taken?'

'Caroline's earring,' Clementine said.

'Okay… earring.' Officer Thomas jotted that down in his notepad. 'And where was the earring?'

'In my locker,' Margery said.

'Someone broke into your locker?' he asked, smoothing his moustache with his free hand.

Margery paused. 'Well, we're not entirely sure.'

'We have evidence! The thief left their leisure centre pass card,' Clementine said smugly. She stood and started rooting through her slightly sodden knapsack. 'Oh.'

Her face fell as she pulled out bits of soggy paper from the self-serve sugar sachets she had stolen from the school, all the sugar in them had disintegrated. She tipped the contents of the bag onto the floor and rummaged through them, but there was no leisure centre gym card to be found. 'Oh, no! Someone must have stolen it!'

Young Officer Symon coughed from the armchair he'd been watching this spectacle in. 'I don't mean to sound rude, Mrs Butcher, but the bag was hanging upside down off the car when I got it out of the water for you. Could it have fallen in there?'

'If I'm honest with you ladies, this is an open-and-shut case and a bit of a waste of police time,' Officer Thomas said, replacing his glasses and smoothing his moustache with his fingers. Officer Symon mirrored him, stroking the teeny caterpillar lodged on his upper lip.

'But what about Caroline's death? Surely that was suspicious. Some would say it looked like a murder!' Clementine said, waving her hands around.

'Ms Butcher, the last murder we investigated in Dewstow was of crows!' Officer Thomas said, snapping his notepad shut and slipping it into his front pocket. 'Now, you know that I've written a report for the freezer incident, and I'm going to write a report about this and we will investigate. But from what we can see there's no evidence of wrongdoing, for all we know you drove that car into the hedge on purpose. Mrs Simmonds was very clear on where you stand with it.'

Clementine started to rebuke him. 'But have you considered—'

'Accident!'

'What about the—'

'Accident!'

'But the freezer—'

'I'm sorry, Ms Baker, Ms Butcher. But unless you would like us to start questioning Ms Baker's driving capability, we'd better be off. I've a lovely bit of cheese and some doorstop bread waiting for me at home for tea.'

Officer Thomas paused suddenly, his brow furrowed in thought. 'Gosh,' he said and looked at them wide-eyed. 'How could I be so stupid?'

He desperately grasped for the radio attached to his police vest. 'Mary, are you there? Urgent call. This is Thomas, over.' The radio crackled for a moment, and Margery and Clementine waited with bated breath to see what Mary, whoever she was, had to say. Margery was glad Officer Thomas was finally taking the matter as seriously as they were.

'This is Mary, go ahead Officer Thomas. Over,' came the fuzzy reply through the radio.

'Oh, thank God.' Officer Thomas gasped, sinking into the chair in relief and pressing the button on the radio to reply. 'I'm just checking whether you got the chutney, Mary? Over.'

'Affirmative,' Mary said over the radio. 'I wasn't sure which you wanted, so I did get Branston, but I also got mango. Also, I picked up a small quiche for Lorraine. Over.'

Clementine looked over at Margery in disbelief, her hands still holding the soggy paper sachets.

'Sorry about that, ladies,' Officer Thomas apologised, after he had said his goodbyes to Mary. 'Just had to check in with the wife.'

Clementine shook her head, red-faced with rage. 'Are you kidding? We're down a dinner lady and we've had an earring stolen, and you're using police radio to talk to your wife! Have you never heard of using a phone?'

Margery rubbed her eyes and tried to fade Clem's voice out for a moment, slumping back in her seat as she argued with Officer Thomas. The police were not going to help them, that much was clear, and solving this was going to take more experience than having *Midsomer Murders* on in the background while they played cards. Margery never thought she would dare say it out loud, most definitely not in front of the ladies on the bus, but she found herself suddenly wishing they lived somewhere that cared less about shoplifting and more about solving murders.

-

Later that evening, after Officer Thomas had forced his way past Clementine and out of their home, young Symon at his heels, Margery was glad to finally sit down at the kitchen table. Clementine made them both a cup of tea and a few cheese crackers each for supper.

Clementine had flumped the very recently delivered local version of the Yellow Pages down on the table before she had put the kettle on, and Margery was flicking through it in earnest. There were plenty of Thomases in the ginormous tome of a book, but only one Seth that she could see. She leaned over and grabbed the landline from the Welsh dresser, dialling the number eagerly. To her dismay it did not even ring before the horrid error tone sounded over the line and a robotic voice told her that the number she had dialled was not recognised. She tried again twice, but it was no good. Margery stared at the name in the phone book, willing it to give her an answer.

'No luck?' Clementine asked from her place at the kitchen counter. 'Probably a problem at the exchange, Margery. Someone's off sick so someone else is just plugging everyone in willy-nilly. You're lucky you didn't get transferred to Australia!'

'I don't think that's how it works anymore, Clem, it's all automatic now.' Margery shook her head, still staring at the phone book. 'I think it's more likely the number has been disconnected, or he's changed it. Why would he do that?'

'I don't know,' Clementine said, cutting slices from the big wedge of cheese. 'It does make me wonder if he has something to do with it. It all seems very suspicious.'

Margery nodded in agreement. 'I feel the same. I've been wondering if he knew he was in her will and killed her to get her money; maybe that's too simple, though.'

'Maybe.' It was Clementine's turn to nod. 'No one else would have, everyone else loved her, didn't they?'

Margery smiled at that; she could think of plenty of people who did not love Caroline in the slightest. She could not think of anyone who hated her enough to kill her, though.

'You know, Margery,' Clementine said, finally sitting down at the kitchen table with the cheese and a few slices of toast. 'I took a bit of paper off the car earlier and put it in my pocket. I thought it was another parking fine. I don't know why, why would we even get a parking fine at our own workplace?' She chuckled to herself, shaking her head. 'It got a bit wet but here.'

Margery gasped as she neatened out the wet paper and laid it out on the table. The ink had seeped out into the paper a bit, but the original message was clear enough.

It read, G A R D E N B U S K E R C A T.

'Mystery solved!' Clementine said proudly. 'Though I, err, well, I'm not really sure what that means, a warning perhaps? To not let any cats busk in the garden? I mean, we've never allowed any cat to do that.' She pointed at the fat ball of fur sitting in the rocking chair in the kitchen corner. 'Not even Pumpkin!' Pumpkin mewed softly at the mention of her name, and then went back to sleep. She was so old now that her soft sleeping purrs sounded like a kettle boiling most of the time.

Margery shook her head, completely bemused. 'Especially not Pumpkin.'

Clementine leaned over the table and added a dangerous amount of jam onto her toast. 'It'll all turn out to be nonsense. Like that stupid earring.'

Margery pondered the note, desperately searching it for clues. She was sure she had seen the handwriting before but she could not place where, and it was starting to frustrate her. She wished she could understand what it all meant. The note seemed to have been deliberately placed for them to find. The fact that the car was destroyed in the process was neither here nor there.

'Clem,' Margery said gently. 'You don't think I'm a bad driver, do you?'

Clementine quickly stuffed the bread into her mouth and pointed at her face as though to say her mouth was full. Margery sighed. They went back to quietly chewing their food. At least they were in here, Margery thought. Clementine liked to eat in front of the television in the front room so it was a rare treat to eat in the kitchen, which was Margery's favourite room of their small two-bedroom terrace. It was warm and cosy, and adorned with various knick-knacks from long-forgotten camping holidays and charity shops. Margery's '1977 Silver Jubilee' crockery sat pride of place on the top of the shelving unit, next to Clementine's collection of 'interesting bells'.

Clementine finally broke the silence that had loomed over them. 'What are the chances, Margery?' She set aside her empty toast plate and spread margarine on a cracker.

'I know!' Margery said. 'First getting trapped in the fridge, then the earring gone, my brakes failing like that, and then this weird note! If I didn't know any better, I'd say someone had it in for us. We've got to be the unluckiest dinner ladies alive! I bet the ladies over at Ittonvale never have any problems.'

Ittonvale Secondary was the neighbouring comprehensive and, in Margery and Clementine's views, a far, far less superior school. The rivalry began fifteen years ago when the Ittonvale Educational Centre Nourishment Consultants had cheated at the yearly netball tournament by bringing the children performance-enhancing drugs at half-time. The children of Summerview school's light snack of an orange segment would never have been able to compete with the off-brand energy drinks the Ittonvale staff were ladling out. Margery and Clementine had never forgiven, nor forgotten, and neither had anyone else from Summerview Secondary school. The betrayal would live on, long after they were all gone, Margery knew.

Margery eyed the bump on Clementine's forehead that was rapidly turning purple. 'Clem, will you start carrying your phone with you on your person?' she asked. 'It would have really helped us today. That's twice this week now it could have saved us.'

Clementine scoffed, spraying the table in crumbs. 'Why don't *you* keep your phone "on *you*"!' She air-quoted the last part, and Margery reminded herself to record less American television programmes on their VCR player.

'Because when you got the bloody thing you said what was yours was mine and we were always together, so I didn't need one!' Margery said back, startling herself at the force of her own words.

'There's no need to swear, Margery!' But Clementine seemed to be considering it as she topped the crackers on her plate with cheese. 'It would have been useful today, though, if I'm honest. I asked the phone earlier what we should have done and it said to put the car in reverse! Isn't that funny?'

'Hilarious,' Margery said, flashing her a wry smile. 'Maybe we can ask the phone who took the earring and where the gym pass is.'

Clementine paused halfway through bringing a cracker to her mouth, deep in thought. 'Margery... didn't Seren say she'd been at the leisure centre the day she came to tell us Caroline died?'

She had, Margery thought. She nodded at Clem. What could Seren be doing at the leisure centre on a Sunday? Seren was the least fit person Margery had ever met. If she was not chain-smoking, she was adding eleven spoons of sugar to her sixth coffee of the morning, or trying to cure her indigestion with a mint Aero.

'She did, but what would Seren be doing going into our lockers? She doesn't seem the type,' Margery said.

Clementine nodded in agreement. 'No. She's annoyingly honest if anything. Remember the day she thought she'd forgotten to pay Karen for her charity run and kept trying to put money into her coat when she wasn't looking? Sixteen pounds she managed to sneak in there.'

'Yes, exactly, and she'd only pledged to give her two pounds in the first place,' Margery said. 'It's a shame we lost that leisure centre card. I really wish we'd gone to the leisure centre after work. All this might have been cleared up by now.'

They slumped back into silence. Margery could almost hear the cogs in Clementine's head turning, and quickly regretted ever saying anything.

'Rose was a bit strange today, though,' Clementine said, fiddling with the rings on her fingers.

'Mrs Smith?' Margery paused, chewing her cracker thoughtfully, 'I suppose a bit, maybe? What makes you say that?'

Clementine rubbed her chin thoughtfully. 'She was just so cagey about it all, you know? And thinking about it, she's the only other person I can think of that hated Caroline enough to kill her.'

Margery had thought that, too. 'Rose said she never would have bought anything like that for herself, but why was she in Ceri-Ann's book? I know there's got to be more to it than she let on.'

Clementine paused halfway through a cheese cracker, as though in deep thought, and then suddenly said, 'Get your coat, Margery. We're going out.' Crumbs and crackers fell everywhere in her hurry to get up.

'We can't go out,' Margery said aghast, trying to sweep up the mess with her hands. 'It's five thirty in the evening and you probably have a concussion.'

Clementine had already escaped into the living room. 'We're going out!'

Chapter Twelve

The school's long corridors seemed much more threat-ening in the darkness of the early evening, with the chill still hanging in the air, not quite summer, despite what the sunshine during the daytime would have someone believe. During working hours, the corridors were bright and bustling with pupils and teachers alike, as everyone went about their lives. Margery found the juxtaposition of silence slightly jarring.

Despite Margery's protests, and the inordinate amount of time it had taken Clementine to find her shoes, she had found herself accompanying her back up to the school. It had taken much longer to get there than usual because the buses had all finished for the day and the car was no longer an option. Neither of these facts had deterred Clementine in the slightest, and they had snuck their way back through the grounds after hours. Margery dreaded to think what Mr Barrow would do if he found them trespassing again, it had not even been a week since they were caught the last time.

They wandered through the hallways almost by memory, as the only light came from the small emer-gency torch they usually kept under their kitchen sink.

The comfortable plimsolls Margery usually wore around the house squeaked unsettlingly on the linoleum flooring. If she was being honest with herself, she *had* been on edge since they had climbed through the window in the school's kitchen. It was perfectly easy, as the short set of stairs to the kitchen fire escape meant they did not even really have to climb. Margery wished she had never complained to Clementine about the broken latch on the window during the winter, when she had tried to shut it to keep out the draughts. Not that it was ever truly closed anyway with the amount of time Ceri-Ann spent smoking out of it.

'Shhh!' Clementine hissed at her loudly. 'For God's sake, Margery, do you want us to get caught?'

'It's my shoes, Clem, not me!' Margery hissed back. 'And of course I don't! I don't even want to be here. Stop waving that torch around. You might as well be doing Morse code out of all the windows. Someone will see!'

Clementine scoffed loudly at that. 'As if I know Morse code, Margery! What kind of idiot do you take me for? Please!' But Margery noticed she did lower the torch significantly. 'Now, all we've got to do, Margery, is get into Mrs Smith's office, look for a few clues, and then once we've solved this entire mess, then we can pop back home in time for an episode of *Coronation Street* before bed.'

Although Margery could not help but think that this was one of Clementine's worst plans yet, an episode of *Coronation Street* was something to look forward to indeed. The ladies were not always home to watch it. Bingo and after-school netball matches often got in the way, and so they used their Freeview TV recording box to tape it. They were currently about a year's worth of episodes behind, and Margery was always keen to catch up before she accidentally saw a spoiler on the front of a ladies' magazine when at the supermarket. Really what she wanted to do though was start poring through the tapes Caroline had left them in her will. They had not yet managed to find time to have a proper sort through. She was sure there were at least a few good episodes of *Neighbours* on one of them, and she was relishing the downtime.

'I still don't know what you're expecting to find here,' Margery said, as they continued through the darkness, 'You just don't like her, so you're anticipating the worst.'

'I'll know what I'm looking for when I see it, Margery.'

They finally arrived at Mrs Smith's office door, the garish purple paint a much nicer hue in the dark, Margery noted. Clementine turned the handle and it creaked as it slid downwards.

'Shh!' Clementine whispered, as much to the door as anyone else, Margery thought. The door did not budge at all.

'It's locked, Margery!' Clementine said, yanking the handle down again.

Back to square one once more. Margery sighed in relief internally. They would have time to watch *Coronation Street* after all. If she was honest with herself, the twenty-minute walk up to the school had really worn her out after the commotion of the day. She was sure Clem felt the same underneath it all.

She was wrong. Margery grimaced as Clementine turned to her with a gleam.

'Don't worry, Margery. I've got an idea!'

Margery could feel her time in front of the television set slipping away rapidly, as Clementine started to root around in her handbag.

'What are you going to do, Clem?' Margery said, wringing her hands together as Clementine pulled out her purse and opened it.

'Well, we saw how that thief got into our lockers. Let's get them at their own game, Margery!' Clementine slid her Tesco Club Card from the plastic card compartment of her purse and held it up in triumph. Margery nodded, half convinced.

'Okay,' Margery said. 'Are you completely sure you know how to do that?'

Clementine scoffed dramatically. 'Come on, Margery, how hard can it be? Now, hold the light steady so I can open the door.'

Margery took the torch from her and held it as steadily as she could. Her hands still shaking, the adrenaline from trespassing had still not worn off as Clementine slid the card into the gap between the door and the doorframe and dragged it down past the latch.

'Oh,' Clementine said, as she struggled with the card.

'Have you done it?' Margery asked.

'Well,' Clementine said, turning to look at her haughtily, 'you know, Margery, it's actually much, much,

much more difficult than it looks on television, but I think I'll get there in the end… oh no.'

The card slipped through the doorframe and disappeared into Mrs Smith's office with a soft clack.

Margery and Clementine stood and stared at the office door for a long moment in disbelief.

'Okay,' Clementine finally said, rubbing her chin thoughtfully with her fingertips. 'New plan! Um, Margery, what is the new plan?'

Margery stared back at her. This was a disaster, and as soon as Mrs Smith entered her office tomorrow morning and saw the Club Card with 'C. Butcher' printed on it, she would know what they had tried to do. Desperation, however, caused inspiration. 'What about the cleaner's keys? Surely there's a spare?'

Clementine shook her head. 'No, Margery. I mean I'm sure there is a spare, but Barbara keeps them in the security office and Gary will definitely be there.' It was Clementine's turn to wring her hands in anxiety for once. 'Oh lord, what time is it? He'll be doing his rounds soon.'

Margery looked at her watch. 'You're right, Clem. It's nearly seven.'

Gary Matthews, the school security guard, would indeed soon be lazily hefting out of his chair to drag himself around the building for his on-the-hour walk-around check, wearing the too-small knitted jumper that his mother had sewed on his official title, 'Education Centre Security and Perimeter Patrol Person'. She gazed around the corridor, her eyes landing on a particularly wonky ceiling tile.

'We could go up through the ceiling, I suppose.' She said it half-jokingly but regretted it the moment she saw Clementine's face light up.

'Margery, you are a genius!' Clementine gasped, her eyes widening.

–

A few minutes later and they were back in front of the door armed with a few useful items from the canteen. Margery was standing on a chair slightly off-balance and was hitting the big polyester ceiling tile in front of Mrs Smith's office door as hard as she could with a mop handle, trying not to make too much noise.

'This is a dreadful idea! What if I fall?' Margery hissed down to where Clementine was holding the chair steady. Why did she always have to be the one doing the most dangerous part of the plan? Her arms ached with the exertion of pushing the tile upwards.

'Well, it was *your* idea, Margery. Now get up there and get that door open!' Clementine seemed to have forgotten the need to keep their voices down in her excitement.

'Please, Clem, can you be quiet and hold the stupid chair still so we can get on with the stupid plan?' Margery said as Clementine's grip on the chair became anything but steady.

'Stupid? I'll remind you that I was top of the class at catering college...' Clementine began, and Margery had no doubt that Clementine would begin another rant, had the tile finally wiggling its way out of place not silenced her first.

'Yes!' Margery hissed, as she slid it over the other ceiling tiles and out of the way, throwing the mop to the ground in triumph. 'Come on now, Clem, give me a lift!'

Clementine went quiet for once and did as she was told, allowing Margery to clamber up onto her shoulders from the chair. It was very dark inside the ceiling, Margery thought, as she pulled herself upwards. Thank God she still did her weekly exercise class with the women of the W.I. and had kept all her Jane Fonda video tapes. She allowed herself a moment to worry about asbestos poisoning, and then shook the thought off.

'How are you getting on?' Clementine's muffled voice came through the cheap ceiling tiles. Margery often wondered what the school did actually spend money on. It definitely was not on the building's maintenance. Or on the food budget.

'I'm fine, Clem,' Margery said, as she tried to push herself up further. Getting her head into the ceiling cavity was easy. It would be the next bit that was hard. In one motion, she dragged her top half up and onto the inside of the ceiling as Clementine helped by pushing her feet. She gave one last big shove and Margery tugged herself into a seated position inside the ceiling, with only her legs still dangling. She looked down through the gap in the tiles and smiled at Clementine.

'Yes, Margery, you did it!' Clementine beamed back up at her. 'You know, Margery, this is quite good practice for when you re-felt the shed roof!'

Margery laughed to herself at that, but her mirth was short-lived. Now that she was up in the suspended ceiling, the logistics of the rest of her plan were starting to fall out of place. She knew vaguely that she had to somehow remove a tile above Mrs Smith's office and then climb down into the room, but she was a bit concerned how she would actually manage that without breaking any furniture, or a leg. Worse still, she could see nothing in the darkness of the ceiling.

'Pass me the torch, Clem,' she called.

Clementine threw the torch up at the ceiling and missed completely, smashing a hole into the ceiling tile next to Margery, who nearly lost her balance, and the torch narrowly avoided hitting Clementine in her own face as it clattered back down.

'Shhh!' Clementine shushed the torch as it rolled down the corridor. 'I'm sorry, Margery, I just can't throw it that high. It's too heavy. Ooh, hang on, I've actually got my phone here. It's got a torch on!'

Clementine rummaged around in her handbag again, and Margery breathed a sigh of relief. At least Clementine had started carrying the phone now.

'Here you go, Margery!' she said, and Margery watched as Clementine threw the phone up towards her. Clementine missed both the hole in the ceiling Margery had sat in and the new hole she had made with the torch completely, and there was a dull thud as it hit a tile and bounced back down. Margery was sure she heard Clementine swear under her breath, but thought better than to call her out on it.

'Well.' Clementine looked up at her defeated as Margery continued to squint down. 'You're on your own, Margery. Good luck up there.'

Margery looked out into the darkness of the ceiling. She was sure it was very dusty, and even worse than that, there were probably hundreds and thousands of spiders living up here. She shuddered at the thought, and for the millionth time that evening wished she were at home listening to a Patricia Cornwell audiobook in the bath. Bravely, she reached her arms out and started to drag herself through the ceiling and into the darkness. A cobweb touched her hand and she tried not to scream, brushing it off and going forward. The dust inside the ceiling felt thick and heavy as she crawled through, trying not to put too much pressure on her old knees and trying not to think about the spiders that were probably climbing into her shoes. She pulled herself along for a few feet, which was as far as she could bear and then decided that she must be at a far enough distance into the office. She felt around for the edges of the tiles, pushing down on the one that she hoped would lead her directly into Mrs Smith's office. She struggled for a moment, thinking it would never budge, but years of kneading dough by hand for the school's weekly Thursday pizza lunchtime, and the inherent cheapness of the materials used in the building, finally won out. The tile crumbled and popped down into the room below. Margery called back to Clementine.

'I did it, I'm in!'

'Did you do it, Margery? Oh, well done!' Margery heard Clementine say, though her voice was very muffled,

'How are you going to get in there, though, without the chair?'

Margery had not thought that far ahead. She leaned over to peer into the office and squinted through the darkness, she could not see much in the gloom.

'I think there's a desk in there somewhere isn't there, Clem?' she called back to Clementine.

'Oh, yes!' Clementine said, much too enthusiastically for someone who was watching their elderly long-term partner scramble around inside a ceiling, Margery thought. 'Just pop yourself down onto it!'

'Well.' Margery thought to herself, 'I've come this far' and she swung her legs around and into the new hole in the ceiling. As she was contemplating how she would jump, somehow land on the relative safe harbour of the desk and nimbly skip across the office and open the door, there was a sudden, and very loud, cracking noise.

Before she had even the slightest second to feel alarmed, she suddenly found herself falling headfirst, six feet down into the room as the cheap polyester ceiling gave way, crashing down on her backside with a thump as it all tumbled down in a big plume of dust and spiders.

'Margery!' Clementine called through the door. 'Are you all right?'

Margery groaned and dragged herself up, feeling her way to the door for the handle, coughing as the dust cloud enveloped her. The door miraculously opened inwards, knocking her over again onto her back with the force with which it opened. She rolled over, grimacing as she went and managed to slump forward onto her knees as Clementine rushed to her aid.

'Oh, my God, Margery! We are stupid! The door wasn't even locked! It just opened the other way. This stupid school with its terrible building regulations!' Clementine said, peering past Margery into the office, 'God, that's a lot of dust!' She dramatically rummaged through her bag and brought out her own asthma inhaler, thrusting it into Margery's face.

Margery sat up, flapping Clementine away. 'What do you mean, the door wasn't locked?'

'No, not locked at all. Silly old me!' Clementine said, chuckling nervously in way of apology. 'Well, at least we can get my Club Card back now, I suppose.'

'Yes. I'm not sure what we're supposed to do about the mess we've made, though,' Margery said gloomily, looking down at all the dust in her lap.

'We'll use the kitchen vacuum cleaner, and then we'll just stick the tiles back up with a bit of strong Sellotape,' Clementine said brightly, her face falling as she glanced over Margery's dust-covered pyjamas. 'I'm more worried about you, did you hurt yourself falling?'

'Not really...' Margery was surprised by how little it had hurt; she supposed the tiles and the gym mats that were now all over the place had cushioned her fall. Though she would probably have a few bruises after today. If someone had told her that morning that she would crash the car and be flung through a ceiling, she would have laughed in their face. Clementine offered her hand and helped drag her to her feet. Margery took a few cautious steps to test herself. Nothing seemed to hurt or be broken. 'No, I feel fine. Honestly.'

'Well then, let's have a look for some clues! If Mrs Smith isn't involved in this somehow, I'll be amazed,' Clementine said. 'I'll just take the canteen chair back before that idiot Gary comes around on his rounds. You can't even see what happened from out there.' She paused, surveying the scene outside the office door again. 'Well, apart from a few barely noticeable little holes. Try and find my Club Card, will you?' She closed the office door, and Margery could hear her shuffling away with the chair.

Margery surveyed the scene in front of the door. There was such a mess of broken tiles she could not possibly hope to find the card without moving it all, let alone any clues that would help them. A bit of strong Sellotape indeed. They would need a barrel of it. Sighing, she stepped over to the side and flipped the light switch by the doorframe.

The strip bulb above her dinged on and the office was flooded in harsh white light. From somewhere behind her came a wheezing gasp. Margery froze. She slowly gathered the courage to turn around and see where the noise was coming from. Over in the corner of the room, slumped back in her desk chair was Mrs Smith. She was still in the smart skirt suit she had been wearing when they spoke to her earlier, though it now had a fine covering of the dust from the ceiling debris. Her skin was so pale it was almost blue, and Margery would have thought she were dead if it were not for the harsh rattling breaths she could hear the woman struggling to draw in through her gaping mouth. Margery was just as startled by her ghastly appearance as she was to see that the woman was still sitting in the exact same place she had been before.

'Mrs Smith?' Margery stepped towards the woman in the chair. Mrs Smith grabbed her by the wrist and pulled her closer, 'Rose?'

'Help... me...' she wheezed out, almost inaudible to Margery's old ears; their eyes met, and she could see that Mrs Smith's were wide with terror.

Chapter Thirteen

The ambulance had taken an age to get to the school, it seemed. Gary, the security guard, was as useless and wet behind the ears as a pair of shoes made from kitchen towel when they had finally found him snoring in the security office. Once the paramedics had arrived, there was not enough room for them all to stay, and the headmaster had demanded that Margery and Clementine wait for him in his office.

They had been waiting for him dutifully ever since, sat nervously in the special guest chairs in front of his nice Oak Furniture Land desk. It felt like hours, but Margery was concerned that the clock on the wall showed only twenty minutes had passed. This had to be it, she thought. They were definitely going to be fired now, there was no saving them. Their meddling had finally ruined everything. Thirty-odd years of hard work. She could see it running down the drain in her mind's eye. How would they ever earn enough money to replace the shed roof now?

The headmaster finally arrived. When Gary had called him to tell him what was happening, he had obviously been getting ready to go to bed. He took off his overcoat, revealing the Deep Purple 2004 tour T-shirt and navy pyjama bottoms he was wearing underneath, slumping down heavily into his desk chair. Margery felt Clementine tense up in the chair next to her, and readied herself for the dressing-down of a lifetime.

Instead, Mr Barrow sighed deeply with his eyes closed for a moment, idly running his fingers through his messy red hair. Margery had never seen it when it was not slicked back and perfect. He reached down to grapple with something in his desk drawer, and pulled out a bottle of red wine and a ream of the plastic cups they usually kept in the canteen for the children to help themselves to cheap, watery orange squash at lunchtime. Margery and Clementine looked at each other in confusion.

'I don't suppose either of you have a corkscrew?' he asked, when they shook their heads, he said, 'No matter.' He eased the cork out of the bottle with no great trouble and a flourish, using only the school's front door key. The show of someone who had done that plenty of times before.

'Thought we'd better put it in these glasses, though it is technically already in a glass!' He chuckled weakly, as he poured each of them and then himself a plastic cup of wine.

'Good God,' Clementine said, as she stared wide-eyed at the bottle. 'That's a very expensive bottle of wine.'

'Yes. Good eye, Miss Butcher. It's a 1978 Chateau Lafite Rothschild.' Mr Barrow picked it up and smiled at the label. 'Given to me by Ceri-Ann yesterday. She said most of the wine from Caroline's wine cellar is disgusting, and she's going to stick to pink gin and tonic from now on. Her ignorance is our gain, I suppose.' He chuckled to himself. 'I hope you ladies won't mind that I haven't let it breathe, but I've no decanter in the office.'

Margery took the plastic cup and took a sip, nervously wondering where this was going. The headmaster did not seem angry at all. She had been expecting to be frog-marched out of the building with a bill for the ceiling tiles. They sat in an awkward quiet for a while.

'How is Mrs Smith?' Clementine eventually blurted out. Margery could not blame her for breaking the silence, the stillness was becoming unbearable. Mr Barrow drained his cup and turned to consider them properly.

'Rosemary is on her way to Ittonvale Hospital. Hope-fully we'll know something soon,' he said grimly, looking at Clementine with his eyebrows raised. 'What in God's name happened to your head, Ms Butcher? I didn't know the kitchen was hosting a fight club.'

Clementine raised her hand to her face, as though just remembering the huge, purple bruise on her forehead. 'Oh, this old thing?' she said, as though she was showing off a new pair of glasses. 'Just a small car accident.'

'Oh...' Mr Barrow stared at her a beat longer, then turned to Margery for confirmation.

'We crashed my car into a pond,' she said, nodding at him. His eyes widened.

They sat in silence again. The headmaster twiddled with the plastic cup in his hands, before pouring them all another small cup of wine. He cleared his throat. 'Ladies, I feel like I really should thank you.'

Margery was sure she heard Clementine mutter, 'Mr Barrow, please do not swear,' under her breath.

'I mean, you shouldn't have been on the property after hours, as you know after the other day, and I should really reprimand you for that, there is absolutely no doubt about it. But… but…' He sighed and leaned back in his chair, considering the plastic cup and suddenly looking like a much smaller man. 'But also, I feel like I owe you a debt.'

'Whatever do you mean?' Clementine asked, exchanging a look with Margery.

Mr Barrow sighed again and sat up to pour himself another cup. 'There's little doubt that if you hadn't been here, doing whatever bizarre, meddling thing you were doing, that Rose would be dead. And she is, well…' He fiddled with the cup, seemingly anxious.

'She's…' Margery and Clementine leaned forward in anticipation. 'Well, she's rather important to me.'

The silence was back, and even more forceful than before.

'In fact,' the headmaster continued, 'she's much more than that, she's…' Margery prayed silently that he would not use the word 'lover'. 'She's my lover.'

It was true then. Margery's brain went blank at the very idea of it. Mr Barrow and Mrs Smith conducting an affair right under the rest of the faculty's very noses. Clementine's shocked and slightly disgusted expression mirrored Margery's feelings.

'Oh my,' Clementine said suddenly, like a light bulb had turned on finally in a house whose owners had been on holiday.

Mr Barrow chuckled nervously. 'I've been waiting for Rose to leave her husband, but,' he shook his head, 'there just never seems to be a right time.'

'What's wrong with her?' Margery asked, hoping not to have to hear any more of his infatuation with Mrs Smith.

'Oh, you know, divorce can be so tricky, and they have a dog together and—'

'No, health-wise, in the office, I mean,' Margery interrupted him.

'Oh, right! A collapsed lung, the ambulance crew seem to think,' Mr Barrow said. 'They wouldn't tell me much more.' He hung his head, and Margery hoped he would not start crying.

That was some injury, Margery thought. Though none of it explained how their car brakes failed. Or how they ended up trapped in the freezer. Or why anyone would hurt Mrs Smith in the first place. She shook the thoughts away.

'A collapsed lung!' Clementine exclaimed. 'How does that even happen?'

'No idea. I mean I'm sure it can, but, of course, Rose has always been in fantastic health as long as I've known her. An athlete, really,' Mr Barrow said confidently.

Margery remembered all the times she had seen Mrs Smith chain-smoking in her car.

'Do you not suspect anything a bit more sinister, Mr Barrow? What with what's happened in the last few days?' Margery asked him. If his face was anything to go by, he had not considered that at all.

'Listen, ladies, if this is going to turn into another of your conspiracy theories, then I'm going to reconsider not investigating why you were here trespassing again!' he said, seemingly bright, but there was a menace behind it.

'Oh, no. We weren't going to start all that again, were we, Margery?' Clementine chuckled in a very forced manner and grabbed Margery by the wrist. 'In fact, we'd better get home. What an evening. I'm absolutely shattered. We both are!' She stood, pulling Margery up out of the nice guest chair as she went, and miming the fakest yawn Margery had ever seen.

Mr Barrow nodded and stood to see them out. 'Well, good. I will see you both tomorrow, ladies. Bright and early. Hopefully, we will have some good news from the hospital too.' He smiled at them both. 'It's a good thing you heard her cries and broke through the ceiling to save her. I can't thank you enough.'

Margery let Clementine drag her down the dark hallway and away from the office, nearly stumbling in their rush to escape.

'She was dying, Margery! Dying!' Clementine hissed into Margery's ear. 'Dying in her office, for God's sake, and he's pretending it's all fine!'

'I know, Clem, but what can we do?' Margery said, as they finally reached the kitchen fire escape and slammed it open, almost sliding down the first step as they did so, forgetting, in their haste, that the metal steps became slippery when wet.

'Careful, Margery! It's been raining. These stairs are a death trap.' Clementine reached for her hand and Margery took it. 'Fire escape indeed, pfft!'

'Come on, Clem. Let's just get out of here, please. This has been way too much drama for today,' Margery begged. Clementine nodded in agreement, and they set off down the fire escape and into the rain. By the time they had made it around to the front of the building, they were both soaked through. Margery's canvas plimsolls had filled with water already, and the backs of them were rubbing her heels. She could feel the blisters developing as they walked. 'Clem, should we wait out the storm?'

'Storm, Margery. Pfft!' Clementine shouted over the noise of the rain, pulling her sodden cardigan closer around her as water dripped from her nose in a heavy stream. 'It's just a slight shower!' There was a flash of lightning that suddenly flooded the sky with light. 'Oh well, if you insist, Margery.'

They ducked into the enclosed entrance to the leisure centre and huddled together in the corner. Margery noted that Clementine was shivering just as much as she was, and wished they had not been so reckless as to leave the house without proper raincoats.

'Why would our ancestors build a town here in this Godforsaken hellhole, Margery?' Clementine screeched dramatically, over the pounding of rain. 'Didn't they know all their garden chairs would blow over?'

The rain was drumming off the entrance roof and cascading down in front of them.

It reminded Margery of the time Ceri-Ann had accidentally broken the hose to the pot-wash sink, and it had flung water all over the walls and ceiling until maintenance had been in to turn it off. Margery's fingers were so icy it was almost painful, and she stamped her feet and blew into her hands but it was no help in the chill of the air the wind had whipped up.

'You know, Clem,' Margery had to yell over the sheer force of the rain, 'you say that about the headmaster but you're acting like nothing's happened, too. We could have died earlier and last week in the freezer.'

'Yes, but we didn't, did we, Margery?' Clementine yelled back, wrapping her soggy cardigan around herself. 'We need to look forward not back.'

'I hope this is all over soon, Clem.'

'What?' Clementine peered at her through the storm.

'I said, I hope this is all over soon!'

For a moment, the rain seemed incessant to Margery. They would be trapped here until they both froze to death or drowned, swept away into the leisure centre car park to lie at rest with all the cigarette butts and empty crisp packets. She need not have worried. As quickly as the rain had started, it began to stop. Like some unseen force was turning a bath tap on and off for the fun of it. Margery turned to Clementine, who was trying to adjust her sodden grey fringe from where it was plastered to her forehead.

'Should we go, Clem?'

Clementine seemed to consider it, tugging at the sleeves of her wet cardigan. 'Let's give it five minutes,

Margery, just to be sure. We've still got to walk all the way home. Oh, actually,' her face had brightened, and she began scrabbling around in her bag, 'I can call us a taxi!'

'Oh, fantastic idea, Clem!' Margery smiled at her. A taxi would be a splendid thing indeed.

Clementine smiled back, finally pulling out her phone, which did not seem any worse for wear seeing as it had hit the ceiling, and a few minutes later, they had the assurance that someone would be with them shortly.

They leaned back against the wall and waited. Now that the storm had passed overhead and they knew help was on the way, it was much less horrible ordeal, and Margery enjoyed watching the streams of water still pouring down the car park as they stood in the entrance. The orange glow of the car park's lamp posts looked surprisingly pretty under the newly revealed moonlight, reflecting from the many puddles like a kaleidoscope.

'Look, Margery,' Clementine said, pointing out into the car park. 'Someone else must have got caught out in it.'

Margery looked over to where she was pointing. There was indeed a figure rushing through the car park through the puddles, weighed down under the heft of the several canvas shopping bags they had in each hand. The figure stopped a few feet from the entrance to the leisure centre to put the bags down and pull the hood of their anorak up further over their head and face, huffing and puffing all the while. Margery could tell who they were easily from their gait as they approached.

'Seren! Hello, Seren!' she called out to the woman. 'Do you want to get in our taxi with us?'

Seren looked up with a start, as if seeing them both for the first time, her face pale, her eyes darting between them both, and she dropped the bags in surprise. The shopping rolled all over as she scrabbled to shove it all back in, tin cans and tomatoes tumbling everywhere. She looked up again, and Margery thought she might be about to say something, but then she turned her back to them and ran off in the direction that she had appeared from.

'Seren!' Clementine shouted after her. 'Where are you going? You've left your satsumas!'

Seren dashed past the taxi as it pulled into the car park, and the headlights briefly lit her up before she disappeared into the darkness again. The wheels of the car squashed Seren's satsumas to pulp as it passed over the string bag.

'What was that all about?' Clementine asked, scratching her wet head.

'I've no idea,' Margery replied, waving the taxi over to them. 'But it was very odd.'

The car stopped in front of them and they clambered in. Margery kept an eye out for Seren as Clementine greeted the driver, but it seemed she had disappeared without a trace.

–

Margery found herself in the graveyard where Rose was buried and it was freezing cold, and very, very dark. The rain hammered through her clothes until she was soaked through and they weighed her down as she walked through the darkness, feeling her way over the tomb-stones, the water sloshing out of her wellington boots.

It was silent, except for the tapping that was coming from inside Rose's freshly covered grave, and Margery stopped to stare at it. The soil was moving up and down slightly, as though the thing were breathing on its own. Lurching forward, she dug and dug with her bare hands, scooping up the freezing-cold earth and throwing it aside desperately, scraping at the dirt with her fingernails and digging and digging and digging until she reached the coffin lid. She was sure the wood had been a different colour when she had watched them lower it into the ground, but before she could question much further, the lid started to rise from the coffin of its own accord. She tried to back away and pull herself out of the grave, but her hands and feet kept losing their grip on the wet earth and she slid back in, again and again.

In horror she saw that the name on the coffin's embossed gold sign had changed from Caroline's to her own and she opened her mouth to scream, but there was no sound except the gentle tapping still coming from inside the wooden box. Resigned to her fate, she pulled the coffin lid to the side and stared down, but it was Rose's face that was revealed, full of maggots and rotting. Rose's skull opened its half-decayed jaw and Margery wanted to scream and run, but she could not move, could not even blink as it screeched at her. She inhaled as hard as she could, but no air would go in or out of her lungs as the creature from the coffin rose upward and grasped for her with its skeletal fingers...

Margery woke with a start in a cold sweat, gasping for air. Clementine was still snoring from her side of the bed and the alarm clock read half past four. She stared at it grumpily for a moment, thinking about trying to go back to sleep, but she knew it would be fruitless to try. When they had gotten home last night, they had immediately changed into dry clothes and gone to bed, and she did not feel they had really had a chance to process what had happened.

She had not mentioned it to Clementine, but she was truly unnerved by yesterday's events. The brakes failing was one thing, but then for a teacher to be found with a collapsed lung, the two together were very odd and very bothersome indeed. Margery could not help but feel they were connected, no matter how much Mr Barrow tried to brush it under the rug.

She was worried that they might be in real danger, and the next time there might not be a pond to break their fall. Recent events had finally become strange enough for her to buy into Clementine's murder theory. The brakes, the earring, Caroline's mystery boyfriend... and what had Seren been doing last night? Not to mention the terrified look in Mrs Smith's rolled-back eyes as her semi-conscious body had been put on oxygen by the paramedics. Who could have done such a thing, surely a punctured lung didn't happen naturally?

Margery managed to drag herself out of bed and down the stairs, with the intent to fill the kettle and get it going for her first coffee of the day. It was going to be a long one, and Mr Barrow *had* said bright and early.

As she reached the bottom of the stairs Pumpkin greeted her at the front door. The cat twirled herself around Margery's legs, and then jumped up at the front door mewing at her softly. She opened the front door dutifully, and the cat left to go about her busy day.

Margery pondered the bright morning sunshine, letting it warm her face for a moment, the pleasant cooling breeze blowing through her light summer dressing gown. She watched Pumpkin waddle through the big new doorway they had accidentally made for her, in the hedge across the road. The sunlight reflected off the wing mirrors of her sad-looking car from where it had been dumped on their driveway, and Margery barely recognised the stranger it showed her in them, with the dark circles under her eyes.

There was a cigarette butt on the doorstep. Margery noticed it immediately as she turned around to go back inside the house, in the way that something can sometimes feel alien when you see it somewhere you are not expecting to. She was sure she had cleaned up the cigarette Seren had left in her potted plant that fateful Sunday night a few weeks ago, but now she was unsure of herself. Margery bent to pick it up and, as she did, she saw something else stuffed under one of the terracotta pot plants. To her great surprise it was a folded-up piece of paper. She turned it over in her hands to see what it said, in the same badly penned scrawl as the scrap of paper that had been left on the car, the kind that had to have been done in a hurry.

Chapter Fourteen

If nothing else, it was going to be an incredibly long day. Clementine had done her usual dramatic over-telling of the story about the car, and everyone had oohed and ahhed and said how brave they were, whilst Clementine had paraded about like a prize pig. If she was not showing off her bruised forehead and making Gloria look at the photos of Margery's ruined car which she had taken on her phone, she was saying, 'Made quite a splash didn't we, Margery!' and nudging her every five minutes.

Before they had even arrived at the school gates, Margery had made Clementine promise her that she would not tell anyone that they were the ones that found Mrs Smith, but she need not have worried. By the time they had made it into the kitchen, the headmaster had already been through, sadly telling the story of Mrs Smith's injury and omitting them from it entirely. He did not yet know if she was going to be okay, the hospital would not tell him anything as he was not next of kin, though he had rung and rung, he said. The dinner lady team had started a collection; Gloria said she would pop to the shop as soon as they heard any news, and get some flowers with the six pounds fifty they had gathered for a 'get well soon' gift.

Sharon had suggested they send Seren to get them from the supermarket as a nasty joke, but they all shushed her. Margery was glad that Seren had not been there to hear the sly dig about what had happened after she had been caught shoplifting last year, not least because it would have probably made her leave the kitchen in a strop again.

It had taken them all forever to settle down after the excitement and get back to work, and even then nothing was getting done particularly quickly. Karen and Sharon were back on usual form now that Sharon had stopped weeping at the mention of Caroline's name. It was only half past ten, and they had already spent an hour arguing about what could and could not be recycled.

'It used to have cans of Coke in it!' Karen wailed, brandishing the plastic wrapper at Sharon menacingly, while Gloria tried to intervene. 'So, it must go in the can recycling!'

Margery groaned, closing her eyes and drawing in a deep breath, rather than doing what she wanted to do, which was leap across the kitchen and grab the wrapper out of Karen's flailing hands and shove it into the waste bin. To make matters worse, none of the dinner ladies seemed to be doing their job at all today. Instead of peeling the carrots ready for lunchtime, Ceri-Ann had taken it upon herself to make everyone an unsolicited hot drink, and was standing completely in the way of where Margery wanted to wash the salad leaves. To her left, Clementine would not stop talking about what she kept referring to as, 'the mysterious doorway note'.

'Phlegm?' Clementine said, for the thirtieth time that day. 'Phlegm! What on earth could that mean?'

'Not phlegm, Clem!' Margery snapped at Clementine, who was supposed to be cutting the rest of the salad but was instead writing Ceri-Ann a list of instructions of how to make the perfect cup of tea on the kitchen notepad. She may have well been writing on the very last fragment of Margery's nerves. 'It was spelt, P-H-E-L-M-E. Not phlegm.'

The note that was under the plant pot had been bizarre enough, and Margery had been racking her brains all day over what it could mean. It had contained a single word, all capitals and badly spelt. 'PHELME' certainly had not meant anything when she had read it that morning, and it certainly did not mean anything now. She had, for a moment, supposed that maybe the mechanic had left it there when he had dropped her car off, but Clementine reminded her that he had posted the paperwork through their front door.

'Well…' Clementine said haughtily, underlining the sentence 'only a minuscule drop of milk' several times. 'I'm sure that's how Ceri-Ann spells it. Isn't that right, Ceri-Ann?'

'What?' Ceri-Ann shouted with her back still turned to them at the food wash sink. 'How many sugars do you want, Clem? I don't drink tea, so I don't know how many to put.'

Clementine paused her tea scribbles and thought about it carefully, tapping the pen she was holding against her mouth as she pondered. 'Well,' she said, as if the fate of the entire world rested on her answer, 'that entirely depends on if you are using a teaspoon or a tablespoon to measure it?'

Ceri-Ann wheeled around holding the sugar tub and a ladle.

'Hmmm…' Clementine rubbed her chin in thought. 'I'm going to say… probably just the one.'

Margery's eyes rolled so far back into her head she was sure she had done some permanent damage to them. This was becoming all too much, as if it were not enough to have weird handwritten notes, or car brakes failing, or teachers nearly dying in their own offices, she also had to contend with the odd catering team on top of it all. Something inside her finally snapped and she threw the lettuce she was chopping down onto the cutting board hard. It rolled off the counter and hit the ground with a thud, its layers unravelling as it did so.

'Right, that's it!' she said, pointing her finger dramatically at Clementine. 'You! You will stop writing that and start cutting that cucumber, and you,' she whipped around to point at Ceri-Ann, who dropped the ladle of sugar all over the floor in terror at the sight of her, 'nobody in the history of the universe has ever used such an inappropriate utensil for anything, ever! Get away from that sink and start washing the potatoes that came in this morning. They are still in the sack and they're filthy. And clean up that sugar!' Ceri-Ann jumped to attention and scuttled off to get the dustpan and brush; the rest of the team were staring at her open-mouthed, and even Margery was feeling a bit taken aback by her newfound bossiness, but she could not stop now. 'Gloria, where the hell is Seren? She was supposed to be making the treacle tart today!'

Gloria looked up from where she had been trying to explain what should and what should not go into the food waste bin to Sharon and Karen. 'I haven't seen her at all today to be honest, not even at the newsagents getting her fags.'

'Well, she's not allowed in the supermarket yet, is she?' Sharon said, smirking nastily. 'She's still banned from all Tescos, isn't she?' Gloria shushed her for the second time that day.

Margery wondered if maybe Seren was still getting lifts to work with Mrs Smith and had not known about her sudden illness. She had been in the car with her yesterday morning after all. But surely, she would have rung into work if she knew she was going to be late? It was not like the woman at all. Margery shook the thoughts away; they had too much to do to worry about Seren right now. There was still a treacle tart to defrost and custard to make and it was nearly eleven.

'Gosh, Margery,' Clementine said, staring at her boggle-eyed as she finally started cutting up the cucumber, 'Maybe you should let Ceri-Ann try her hot rock massage out on you, might calm you down a bit.' Margery glared at her. Ceri-Ann had been trying to convince Clementine to let her practise some of her newfound healing skills she had learned on the internet and Margery was terrified Clem might take her up on it.

They had managed lunchtime by the skin of their teeth, pulling everything together at the very last minute, but it meant that they ran over their usual working time and were still tidying the kitchen when the cleaning team came to start their shift.

'Hello, Anita. How are you?' Clementine asked the dowdy woman as she appeared through the kitchen door. Her hair did not look as neat as usual. It looked greasy and unwashed, though it was always harder to tell with blonde hair, and there were dark circles under the woman's eyes. She looked as though she could do with a bath and a nap. She had taken a cigarette from the pack she kept in her apron, but her hands were shaking so violently that Margery was amazed she was still able to hold it between her fingers.

Anita opened her mouth to speak, but then closed it again as Barbara stepped in front of her.

'We're all fine, thank you, Clem,' Barbara said, taking her cigarettes out of her apron pocket, and turning to Anita, she said, 'Go and get our coffee will you love? Thanks.'

Anita scuttled off without even saying goodbye, quite rudely Margery noted, but then neither Anita nor Cheryl were ever particularly talkative when headstrong Barbara was around. Barbara tended to lead all their conversations for them, Cheryl less so as Barbara's right-hand woman, but Margery had rarely heard a peep from Anita in all their years of knowing each other.

'Hello ladies,' Barbara smiled at them, 'Bad news about Mrs Smith, did you hear?'

Clementine smiled a big false grin at her and Margery internally begged her not to mention that they had been the ones to save her. It would only lead to questions about why they had been here at night, and they did not need any more trouble with the headmaster.

'Hello, Barbara, yes we did. Terrible news. Terrible, terrible.' Clementine's voice petered off. Barbara nodded, fiddling with the cigarette she had taken out of the pack.

'Good thing she was found so soon,' Barbara said, as she pushed the fire escape door open and peered out. 'Be a bit of a concern if another one died, wouldn't it? Though Caroline was about nine hundred years old.'

Margery was exhausted when they finally left the kitchen to get their things. She could not wait to get home to watch the television, or maybe read one of her true crime stories. She had bought a few new books from the charity shop recently, but there had been no time to read them. She could picture the warmth of the fire, in the comfort of her favourite chair already, slippers on, feet up on the stool – bliss. She smiled at the thought of it, as she turned the key in her locker and opened the door.

A small piece of paper slid out of it, and she watched as it fluttered down towards her feet. Margery bent to pick it up. 'Clem?' she said, turning it over in her hands. 'Is this yours?'

'What's that?' Clementine asked; she stopped pulling on her coat and bent forward to squint at the piece of paper.

Margery looked at it closely. It seemed remarkably similar to the weird message she had found that morning.

How peculiar. She wished she had brought the other note to compare them, but she was sure it was the same handwriting. At the very least, it was written in all capitals and in the same black marker pen. The kind the teachers used on the whiteboards in the classrooms without electronic boards, she thought as she peered at it.

The note read, 'RECOILED UNDERARM' in short, smudged letters.

Margery could not make heads or tails of it. Why would anyone make such effort to put it in her locker? The words seemed to have purpose, but together she could see nothing about them that was not nonsensical.

'What on earth could it mean?' she wondered aloud.

Clementine, who had been rummaging around in her bag, finally found her reading glasses and shoved them onto her face, snatching the note from her to look at it. Laughing out loud as she did, at the word 'underarm', Margery supposed.

'Margery...' Clementine said, patting her on the shoulder gently with her free hand. 'We, as you know, work in a school, and unfortunately, that means we have to live with the fact that there are disgusting children everywhere.' She folded up the note and handed it back to her. 'It'll be a prank or some horrible new trend, you'll see! Put it in the bin and let's move on, or we'll end up as one of the horrible children's videos on a website, or on the internet.'

Margery grimaced at the thought but was not willing to let it go that easily. School pupils did not have access to their small changing room in the hallway next to the school kitchens, and even if they did, they would have had to somehow get through the kitchen without any of the kitchen staff seeing them.

'Come on,' Clementine said gently, patting her on the arm, 'Let's stick to the original plan, and go to the leisure centre before it closes. If we find out who that card belongs to then we'll have solved who broke into our lockers, and probably a whole host of other mysteries at the same time!'

Margery popped the note into her bag, sliding it carefully into the inside compartment she used to carry her Polo mints.

Clementine nodded in approval. 'Oh yes, good idea, Margery, we'll recycle it at home,' she said, as she opened the changing room door. 'It's lucky Gloria did that speech about paper and plastic recycling earlier. I feel like I've learned an awful lot today.'

–

The leisure centre was located right next to the school, attached to it by a connecting corridor and a big heavy set of double doors. They were locked at night, but during the day access to the leisure centre allowed the schoolchildren to participate in all sorts of exciting events in the pool and gymnasium. There was badminton, freestyle dance classes and precarious games of bench ball to be had. If all of that was not of interest, a person could just buy sweets and chocolate from one of the many, many vending machines. Occasionally, before her death, Caroline would host a water aerobics class set to the music of the early 2000s. The turnout was usually fantastic, as it was mandatory, or at least it had been for the dinner lady team.

Clementine often wondered aloud to Margery about which had come first, was it the school or the leisure centre? A real chicken and egg conundrum, she said. Margery suspected that the mystery could be solved by a remarkably simple Google search, or maybe just asking the headmaster, but Clementine seemed satisfied to leave it an unknown, and so Margery was too.

They walked through the open double doors and down the stairs into the leisure centre corridor. Clementine gasped when she saw the set of vending machines along the wall.

'Margery! They've got white chocolate and banana flavoured Curly Wurlys!' She exclaimed, nearly breaking the zip off her handbag in her haste to get her purse out.

Margery smiled at the commotion, and then gasped as well. 'Gosh, Clem, get me a bag of prawn cocktail Wotsits while you're there. I haven't had them for ages.'

Clementine gleefully rummaged around in her purse and started jamming one and two pence pieces into the machine. It was an arduous process, as the vending machine kept rejecting them, but Clementine would never give up on such an important mission. Margery's gaze drew to the far side of the corridor and the double automatic doors that comprised the entrance, where they had sheltered themselves from the rain last night, though it seemed an age ago. But more concerning to Margery was the presence of Seren, who was standing in front of the reception desk and talking to the man sat behind the till.

Margery noted with alarm that she did not look at all well. Her coat was even dirtier than usual, and her ponytailed hair was flattened to her head with a thick layer of grease. Her face was drawn, with the look of someone who has not slept well, or at all, for days, and she had a wild look in her eyes as she gesticulated madly to the receptionist who looked terribly bored. Margery could not hear what they were saying from this distance, she damned herself for not bringing her ear horn, but Seren looked like she was pleading with the young man behind the cashier's desk.

Seren turned slightly and she froze as she recognised Margery, their eyes meeting for a long moment. As Margery raised a hand in greeting, she turned abruptly on her heels and raced out through the automatic doors into the daylight. Without thinking, and with all thoughts of crisps forgotten, Margery started after her as fast as her old legs would manage, but by the time she reached the concrete steps of the main entrance, Seren was long gone. She scanned the car park, but she could not see any sign of the woman, just schoolchildren arriving for their after-school swimming lessons.

'Margery, yoo-hoo!' Clementine called through the electric doors from inside, and Margery reluctantly turned around and went back into the leisure centre at the sight of Clementine waving a bag of crisps dramatically at her.

'As I was saying,' Clementine said, leaning on the reception desk jauntily, holding the half-eaten Curly

Wurly in her fist. 'It's imperative we find out who broke into our lockers. If you tell us who's lost a card key recently then we can be on our way.'

The receptionist looked even more bored by this conversation than by the one he had been having with Seren.

'Look, like I told the last lady, I can't replace any cards without identification. If you want a new card, then it's five pounds fifty, and I'll need to see a driving licence or passport. Or anyone could come waltzing in,' he said turning back to scrolling through social media on his phone. Margery wondered if he knew Ceri-Ann at all; they would surely get on like a house on fire.

'Do we look like we want cards?' Clementine said, handing Margery her Wotsits. 'Do we look like we do any form of unnecessary exercise?'

The receptionist sat up properly and looked over the counter at them, and at Clementine's slight pot belly nastily. 'I can't tell you any confidential information. Please don't make me ring security.' He did not seem displeased by the idea of ringing security, though, in fact he looked extremely excited. It would probably be the most thrilling thing to happen all year at the leisure centre.

'It's not really confidential is it, though?' Clementine said haughtily. 'How many members can you actually have? Five? Six?' She squinted at his name tag and scoffed. '*Brain*. If that even is your real name.'

'It's Brian, and it's more like sixty members,' Brian said, adjusting the name tag pinned to his shirt and glaring at them, 'and everyone's always losing their cards. So even if

I was willing to help you, and I'm not, you still wouldn't know exactly who's lost the card as you haven't even brought one here. In fact...' he eyed them both suspiciously, 'how can I be sure that you've even found a card without the card? Buy a swimming pass or leave.'

Clementine scoffed loudly. 'We're not leaving till we find out the truth, Brain!' She slammed the chocolate bar she was holding down onto the counter, smearing bits of chocolate and toffee onto the desk.

Brian rolled his eyes. 'Then buy a swimming pass.'

'Fine!' Clementine snapped and reached into her bag for her purse. 'How much are they?'

'Like I said before, five pounds fifty,' he said, not even bothering to look up from his phone this time.

Clementine peered into her coin purse at the bronze coins, and then zipped it up again, stabbing her finger at him. 'Will you accept one pound seventy?' she said, 'All in pence?'

'No.'

Clementine stormed away from the desk and out of the front door, Margery following, briefly mouthing 'Sorry' at Brian, who merely looked amused.

'What now, Clem?' she said, once they were out of earshot from any children waiting to enter the swimming pool. 'And please don't say, "Let's sneak back at night," because that didn't go very well last time, did it?'

'Let's just go home, Margery,' Clementine said, 'No point hanging around here with those idiots. I just wish we hadn't lost the card!'

Margery did too.

Chapter Fifteen

They missed the bus by seconds and watched it careen past them down Dewstow Hill. They had no choice but to walk. Tired as she was, Margery enjoyed the easy stroll down the hill as she followed Clementine's lead. It was a beautiful late spring day, the rain of the night before was long forgotten, and the scenery was green and pleasant as they made their way down the road and through the high street. After a long while Margery noticed, with a start, that they had been unknowingly walking towards Caroline's house.

Caroline had lived in an enormous, and incredibly old, stone terrace. The kind that looks tiny from the outside but seems to go on forever once you get inside. In fact, it was probably one of the oldest and largest houses in town, Margery had always thought, and yet also one of the most impractical. It had no parking other than a small pay-and-display car park a five-minute walk away, and it was a colossal size with way too many stairs and windows to clean for an older lady. But it was one of the original buildings in Dewstow, and Mrs Hughes's parents and grandparents and great-great-grandparents had all lived there. Generation after generation of Hugheses had resided there, until now that is.

Caroline's passing meant the end of the lineage, as she had never been one for children. She always said she would only have a baby when she wanted to double her laundry and halve her wages. Margery found herself smiling at the memory, though Caroline's flippancy had once hurt her soul a bit.

For obvious reasons, there had never been any children at number twenty-two Seymour Road, though she had always longed for some small person to fill the empty space. They had briefly looked into it when same-sex adoption had become legal, but it had not really been 'the done thing' when they were in their mid-forties and nowadays Margery did not think she would have the strength to run after a child. Especially if the children at the school were anything to go by. She looked over at Clementine, enjoying their walk in the sun. They had been lucky, though, luckier than most to find and fill the years with each other. Especially growing up as young women in a time when their relationship had been frowned upon and having children together was out of the question.

Margery knew that was most likely why Clementine was still hesitant to get married, even though they had lived together for decades, and it had been legal for years now. She was still afraid they would end up on some list of public enemies as a threat to society. She supposed that the people who felt like that about their relationship did obviously still exist, of course they did, but there were also many others who would stand by and support them and their love for each other. In Margery's opinion, that was something worth celebrating indeed. She hoped that one day Clementine might be able to see it that way, too.

The row of stone houses did not fit in with the town anymore. Progress and population rise had brought even bigger new buildings, if that was possible, all glass and towering metal. The houses surrounding Caroline's had been fields once when it was new, but one by one they had been sold off to build large family homes. The only window into what the town had once been was the cobbled street, hardly changed at all over the years, and leading you around the bank of the dirty brown river by footpath. Sometimes, if you were incredibly lucky and it was a nice day, you could sit out on a picnic blanket with a few cold cans of something and watch seals swimming up the estuary helped along by the tidal current.

As luck would have it, today was one of those days, and they bought an ice cream and a can of fizzy drink each from the van by the bandstand and sat on the bench on the green grass opposite the house. The mix of the sweet and refreshing treats was a flawless accompaniment to the warm afternoon, and Margery found herself relaxing for the first time in weeks, sinking back into the bench as she leisurely looked across at Caroline's perfectly preserved oak front door. Caroline never would have had to lie about who had made her office desk, she thought mildly, she would bet her next wage packet on all of Caroline's furniture being antique. They sat in silence for a piece, enjoying the pleasant waterside breeze and the saccharine artificialness of the ice cream. Margery could not believe how much had happened in such a short space of time, and none of it good at that. She closed her eyes and lay her head back, enjoying a moment without car crashes and bizarre notes, no teachers dying in offices.

'This week has been like sitting in a paddling pool of misery,' Clementine said finally. 'Drinking a warm Pina Colada and wearing an uncomfortable swimming costume in hell.'

Margery sighed. 'I agree. Clem?'

'Yes, Margery?'

'Do you… do you think we're in danger?' Margery turned to look at Clementine for her reaction. She had her eyes half closed against the brightness of the sun.

'Maybe. Lots of bad things seem to be happening all at once.'

Margery sighed deeply again and closed her eyes. 'That's what I was afraid of.'

'Margery?' Clementine said. 'I need to tell you something, but I don't want you to be annoyed until you've heard me out.'

'What is it?' Margery opened her eyes and turned to look at her. Clementine took a deep breath and turned towards her, but abruptly her attention was drawn back across the street to Caroline's house.

'Margery. Look!' she exclaimed, pointing upwards towards the house. 'Someone's in there!'

Margery snapped her head around to look as well. 'You can't be serious, Clem!' But sure enough, there was a silhouette of a person moving around through the curtains of the upstairs window.

'What should we do?' She turned back to Clementine, but Clementine had already leapt up from the bench with the sprightliness of someone twenty years younger, and was power-walking across the street to Caroline's front door, rummaging around in her bag as she went.

'Come on, Margery!' Clementine called over her shoulder. 'I still have her key!'

'Why on earth do you have her key?' Margery asked, surprised as she rushed after her.

'From when she went to Cornwall at Christmas and I fed the snakes!' Clementine panted as she pulled her key ring out of her bag with a triumphant flourish.

–

Caroline's hallway was cool and dark, and so quiet compared to outside that Margery was afraid she had gone deaf for a second. Photographs littered the walls in a variety of different sized and shaped frames. The majority of them from charity shops, Margery supposed, as there was an Oxfam sticker still sat on the one of Caroline shaking Gordon Ramsay's hand. Off to the left of the long hallway, Margery could see the entrance to Caroline's sitting room.

She peered inside nosily; it looked even more chaotic than it had when she had recorded her will. In fact, the half-finished jigsaw puzzle on the coffee table was most unsettling now Margery knew Caroline would never complete it. It looked like a good one too, Margery thought, as she stared into the room. A lovely floral table scene with an old-fashioned blue vase just like her mother had displayed flowers in. She was sure Caroline did not buy her jigsaws from the charity shop, there was no way she would never risk a missing piece. She probably ordered them in from WHSmith or John Lewis. A second brand-new-looking jigsaw sat next to the coffee table on the floor proved her correct, the box did not even have any storage wear. Margery thought of her old jigsaws at home, all the boxes with their crumpled corners. She exhaled, turning away from the room, and joined Clementine in the hallway just as Clementine shouted up the stairs.

'Hello!' The noise echoed and bounced around the stone-floored hall. There was no reply, and Margery strained her ears for any kind of noise, the silence in the empty house a hideous vacuum. Clementine called again and they waited nervously.

There was something wrong. She had been here a few times, always on much worse occasions, like mandatory kitchen team Christmas choir practices, and the house had never felt like this. But she could not put a finger on what it was.

'Maybe they just can't hear us upstairs,' Clementine said. 'These old houses were built in a sturdier time.' She chuckled nervously and rapped on the nearest wall with her knuckles. A photograph fell to the floor, taking a piece of plaster with it with a crash, and they both winced.

Clementine stepped over the broken glass from the frame, and took the first step of the wooden staircase at the end of the hallway. It creaked loudly like it was alive and upset about being stepped on, and she stepped back down again uneasily.

'Hello, Mr Thomas?' she said again. 'We know you're here!'

'We don't know it's Mr Thomas, Clem,' Margery hissed from where she had backed herself in the sitting room doorway.

'Shh, Margery!' Clementine hissed loudly. 'Say we're window cleaners or something. We can't get arrested again.'

'What kind of window cleaner lets themselves into your house?' Margery whispered back.

Clementine shushed her again and then bellowed up the stairs. 'Hello! Dewstow Window Cleaning! Erm... we're here to erm... err... clean the inside of your windows!'

There was a smash from upstairs and then silence again.

'Oh, sod it!' Clementine said and thumped up the stairs, using the banister to propel herself up faster than Margery could stop her. She disappeared round the corner at the top of the stairs, and Margery stayed put, wringing her hands together nervously. Clementine's head popped back around, and she hooted down the stairs. 'Margery, come on!'

Margery gathered all her fears together and tried to put them in the box in her head she usually kept reserved for the nasty things Mrs Smith would say. She shook her head in resignation and followed in Clementine's footsteps. Her feet clattered on the wooden steps. If the person did not know anyone was here before, then he most definitely did now, she thought grimly to herself as she panted upwards.

Reaching the top, she found herself in another hallway. This one was bereft of photographs, though; in fact the landing was practically nude in contrast with the downstairs. Either Caroline had decided to decorate this space more tastefully or something was missing, Margery thought to herself. She knew immediately that it was the latter; the last time Caroline had forced them around her house on a tour she had proudly pointed out her floor-to-ceiling, wall-mounted spoon collection. There was nothing on that wall now, except dark, spoon-shaped shadows where the paint had faded and changed colour over decades sat in the sunlight from the hallway window.

Margery called for Clementine, and heard her muffled reply come from one of the bedrooms. She slowly crept her way across the landing, and peeked around the doorway to look inside the first one on her right.

The room, which at any other time would have seemingly been a very cosy bedroom judging by the comfortable looking bed linen and striking antique furniture, was a wreck. All the drawers in Caroline's cabinets were hanging out and the contents were strewn all over the place. Margery's shoes crunched over broken glass as she entered the room slowly, all the perfume bottles that she supposed usually lived on Caroline's dressing table, were now in pieces on the floor. The air was rank with the smell of it. Clementine was standing with her back to her, looking down out of the open bay window, the curtains swaying gently in the breeze.

Clementine turned to look at her, her mouth wide and her eyebrows raised, waving at her wildly. Margery felt rooted to the spot again. But then Clementine started to laugh.

'Quick, Margery, look! Oh my, God look, Margery, the idiots got themselves stuck!' She was practically barking with laughter, and Margery could do nothing but shake her head at her like an idiot.

'They did what?'

'They jumped out of the window!' Clementine spun around again, pointing at the open window frame with the hand she was holding her phone in. 'There was someone here and they jumped! I just caught them on their way out!'

'What? Are they hurt?' Margery said, stumbling forward to look at where Clementine was pointing.

'No, they're there. Look!' Clementine exclaimed, waving the phone around as if she had forgotten its existence. 'A true feat of athletic ability. Well, it would be if they weren't stuck on the fence. Get your glasses on quick!'

'Calm down, Clem!' Margery said, peering out of the window. There was indeed a short drop to the extended roof of Caroline's kitchen, and then the long thin garden stretching on for quite a way. The garden had not been kept in quite as immaculate shape as the house and the weeds were starting to take it over, yet there was still a clear path through it, past the greenhouse and the decking, to a tall wall at the end where she could just make out the figure hefting themselves over the fence and out of sight. An athletic feat indeed, Margery thought. She was not sure whether to commend the strange behaviour or condemn it, and eventually she settled for the middle ground.

'Quite athletic. Do you think that was Mr Thomas?' The idea was puzzling. 'Why would he do that?'

Clementine practically beamed at her. 'I knew I wouldn't be able to get down there in time to see them, but I did get a photo of him climbing over that wall in the garden!' She paused again, looking far too smug for Margery's liking. 'On my phone!'

She thrust the smartphone in Margery's direction, and Margery squinted down at the blurry picture. Whatever talents Clementine possessed for breaking and entering, she did not have a budding photography career awaiting. For one, the picture was taken from much too far a distance and Clementine had not thought to zoom in. Mr Thomas, if that is who the subject was, was a small blob against the backdrop of the garden and the photo had a slight motion blur, thanks to Clementine's shaky arthritic hands. The only thing Margery could say about the person for certain is that they were wearing a brown gentlemen's anorak. It was truly a terrible portrait, and yet Margery supposed she might recognise the subject somehow, though she was not quite sure why.

'Why didn't you do it as a video, Clem?' Margery said. 'Might have given us a bit more to go off.'

'It's definitely him,' Clementine said, nodding in the furious manner of someone who has been wrong many times and is determined never to be again. 'And I definitely would have if I could've remembered how to do a video.'

Margery gasped as she finally turned from the phone and the window and took in the destroyed room again.

Clementine looked just as miserable. 'Look at this place. This can't have been a social call can it?'

'Well, no, Clem,' Margery said. 'I don't think so, seeing as Caroline's long dead. This can't have been Mr Thomas.'

'No,' Clementine shook her head, 'You'd have thought he'd have come downstairs and thrown us out of his new house, not brought a big bag so he can nick stuff.'

Margery shook her head. 'I just can't see it being him, Clem.'

'Well, who else would it have been?'

'Well if it was him why would he have smashed everything and ran off?' Margery scoffed, 'And he wouldn't need to steal any of it, would he? He owns it all!'

As she was talking, she became very aware that they were still standing in the bedroom of a deceased woman's home. Surrounded by all the things she had worked so hard to pay for when she was alive, now broken or in disarray. 'We should go, Clem.'

But Clementine was standing frozen next to her, her eyes bugging out of her skull and her mouth open, as though she had just been struck by lightning. She bent down and picked up something from the mess on the bedroom floor. It was a puzzle book. Caroline had had a great fondness for them.

'Clem?'

Clementine dropped the book as if it had stung her. She reached over to Margery and began to frantically rummage through Margery's bag, crochet hooks and Polo mints flying everywhere in her hurry.

'What in God's name has got into you, Clem?' Margery said, trying to snatch her bag back. Clementine shushed her, and finally dragged out the piece of paper they had dismissed only an hour before, pointing at it in a fervour, too excited to get the words out fast enough without shouting them.

'Margery! Look!' She tapped the page sharply with her index finger in Margery's face. 'I can't believe we didn't notice before!'

'What, Clem?' Margery said, as Clementine started to laugh hysterically.

'It's an anagram!'

'What?'

'An anagram is a word jumbled up to make another word!'

'Yes, I'm aware of what an anagram is. I just don't understand what you mean. What does it say?'

Clementine shoved the note back into her bag and took her by the hand smiling. 'I'm not sure yet Margery, but I intend to find out!'

Margery let her drag her down the stairs in her excitement, but she forced her to stop so Margery could quickly run into the living room and swipe the half-done jigsaw pieces back into the box. She also picked up the one of Vincent Van Gogh's 'Sunflowers' on the floor next to the coffee table. It seemed a shame for them to go to waste.

Chapter Sixteen

Once they had known what to look for, the answers came very quickly, Margery marvelled. Remarkably, Clementine was an excellent anagram solver, and by the next morning they had a series of short sentences written in front of them on a notepad at their kitchen table, though the kitchen table was also covered in crumpled balls of paper. Clementine had insisted on bringing the corkboard she had stolen from the school down from their rarely used study, and had busily arranged all their 'clues' as though they were in an episode of *CSI*, complete with photographs cut from the school newsletter.

'Wow,' Clementine said smugly, pinning up a picture of Gloria's face to the board and joining it to the rest of the dinner ladies and the anagrams she had pinned up with a piece of Margery's good crochet yarn. 'Well, this at least proves that someone was trying to hurt us!' She pointed at the transcription of the Post-it that was put on their car windshield. 'Garden busker cat' made a lot more sense now that it actually read, 'Danger brakes cut.' Margery would have laughed if the whole situation were not so absurd.

'So, have we got the order right?' she said, though she knew that they had. 'Badly spelled phlegm. Well that was "help me", and it was the first one, I suppose?'

'No, the brakes one was first! We just didn't look at it for ages, because we were busy crashing the car and destroying that disgusting fence!' Clementine said, a little too proudly.

'Yes…' Margery said slowly, 'Okay, so that was first and then "help me!" and then this new one…'

'Yes, "recoiled underarm",' Clementine ran her finger over the words, 'Hmmm, this one isn't as straightforward.' She took a piece of toast and began adding what Margery thought was a disturbing amount of Marmite. 'I get it to work out as "Caroline murdered" which, really we already knew.'

'Actually, I'd say that was the most straightforward and the most worrying. Caroline was murdered, at least someone else agrees she was killed,' Margery said, 'What more could they say?'

Clementine spat toast crumbs everywhere as she snorted. 'Well, for one they could just tell us who murdered her rather than this nonsense. It's all going to end in a bust, like the earring.' She exhaled deeply and sat down at the kitchen table to examine the board closer.

'So, you really think that someone we know could be involved in all this, Clem?'

Clementine paused. Her brow furrowed. Margery watched her face. Her grey hair was almost luminescent in the soft, morning light from the kitchen window.

'What do you mean, Margery?' Clementine finally said. 'It wasn't you, was it?'

Margery shook her head, astounded. 'No, of course not! I was with you that Friday night!'

'Oh, yeah!' Clementine said; she laughed and brought her hand to Margery's with a grin. 'Then who? It wasn't Gloria. She always goes to church on Friday night, so she can have a lie-in on Sundays.'

Margery nodded in agreement. 'I just think that whoever climbed that fence must have been quite fit. Karen is the only person we know who actually does any exercise.'

Clementine shook her head. 'Nah, she does Zumba with Sharon on Wednesdays at the town hall so she wouldn't have been there last night, I bet we could confirm that with them if we needed to. And anyway, I just can't see either of them bothering to go to Caroline's. I'm still saying that it was the boyfriend, and we just startled him.'

They sat for a moment, pondering, until Margery noticed the clock. 'Gosh, Clem, is that the time? We'd better get up to the school!'

By the time she had found her shoes and Clementine had finally decided whether she should take a raincoat, they were just about to head off when there was a sharp rap at the door. Clementine turned to Margery, panic etched onto her features.

'Who the devil could that be? We aren't expecting a milk delivery, are we?' she said, wringing her hands.

Margery stepped forward bravely and opened the door, regretting it as soon as she had. On their front doorstep, wearing frayed dungarees, a dirty pair of wellington boots and an angry glare was their across road neighbour, Dawn Simmonds. Her lips pursed tightly together as she stared at Margery. She was holding a Tesco carrier bag that was dripping with water and what looked like some form of pond plant.

'Oh, hello, Dawn.' Margery tried to sound cheerful, but her voice betrayed her. 'How can we help you on this fine Dewstow day?'

Dawn rolled her eyes and scowled at her. 'This is not a fine Dewstow day actually, Margery, because I spent all of yesterday draining my beautiful pond of bits of car and whatever other dinner lady crap you left in it.'

Margery was sure she heard Clementine mumble, 'Education Centre Nourishment Consultants' under her breath, but she ignored her. 'Well...' She was not sure what to say to that. 'Our drive has a few bits of car on it, too!' She tried to laugh, but it came out as a kind of forced guffaw.

Dawn Simmonds turned to eye the ruined car that was still sat in their driveway.

'Yes, well... it would have been good if they had stuck around to help me with the pond, not just dragged your rust-mobile out.'

Margery felt her smile becoming more and more forced, and harder to keep on her face. She had loved that car only slightly less than Clementine, and walking past its shell on the way to the bus stop every day was proving unbelievably depressing.

'Anyway,' Dawn continued, thrusting the carrier bag at her. 'I won't keep you. I have fish to replace after all.'

Margery nodded and took the bag. Dawn turned immediately and left, stomping up their driveway in her wellies.

Clementine glared at her as she walked down the garden path, shaking her head. 'I'm glad we destroyed her pond, miserable woman. She acts like she lives at a National Trust country estate for crying out loud.'

Margery opened the bag to have a look at the contents. Inside were several pens, Margery's soaked-through year diary, which she had only used to note when her line dancing classes were, and unbelievably... 'Clem, look! The card!' Margery held it aloft in triumph.

Clementine turned and gasped in shock at the sight of it. 'Yes, Margery!' She snatched it from her and smiled wildly at it, holding it up in the air like a trophy. 'Let's go back to the leisure centre and give that idiot receptionist a piece of our minds!'

'I don't think we need to. I think we can see whose card it is,' Margery said, pointing towards it again. As Clementine was holding it, she had noticed something that they had not seen before. A small piece of white sticker had started to peel from the card where it had got wet. Margery took it back from her and scratched at the sticker gently with her nail; it stripped off revealing where it had covered up its owner's name. This kind of oversight is what happens when you never carry your correct prescription glasses around, Margery groaned to herself. They really must go back to the optician and have varifocals made.

'Oh, it's Caroline's. Really?' Clementine said, her expression turning glum for the second time that day, 'But how?'

'Who had her card?' Margery said, 'Why would they break into our lockers?'

'I don't know.'

They looked at each other for a moment. Clementine patted Margery on the shoulder gently, and leant forward to give her forehead a gentle kiss. 'Come on. Let's get to work and have a nice cup of coffee and one of the special biscuits from the tea trolley.'

–

They arrived in the kitchen in good time, and Clementine immediately started on the coffee she had promised. Margery leant against the worktop feeling quite glum, by all accounts, and becoming more worried by the moment. It was stressful not understanding the circumstances of events, especially when they seemed to be happening to you without your approval. Sharon was in the dry store with the sweeping brush, Karen was washing up, and Ceri-Ann was peeling potatoes under Gloria's watchful eye, but Margery noted with alarm that Seren had still not made an appearance. She watched the rest of the team going about their jobs for a time, until Clementine was handing her a coffee and an apron with a smile. Margery forced a smile back.

'Are you okay, Margery?' Gloria said kindly, she stopped putting away the delivery and turned to look at her in concern. 'You don't seem yourself today. Is everything all right?'

'Oh, I don't know really,' Margery said, taking a sip from the mug. She was not sure where this blue feeling had come from, but she had never been one to hide her feelings from her colleagues, not the ones who were friends anyway. 'It's all just a bit strange, isn't it?'

'Are you still upset about Caroline?' Ceri-Ann said, coming over to lean against the counter with her. 'Don't be upset about her. She was a bit of an idiot anyway, wasn't she?' They all shushed her, but Margery thought that maybe she had a point.

'Well, yes. I'm still upset about Caroline,' Margery said, sighing, 'and Mrs Smith. Mr Barrow said she'd been really ill. She had to have an operation on her lung.'

Ceri-Ann went white at that and stood up straight from the counter, teeth bared in a grimace. 'Well. Yeah, you know I may know something about that.'

'What do you mean?' Gloria said, her brow furrowed in curiosity.

Ceri-Ann flicked her long ponytail back. 'I can't say.'

'Why not?'

Ceri-Ann stood from where she had been slouching against the counter and drew in a breath. 'She made me promise not to tell anyone, but I gave her one of my free health treatment vouchers when she bought the earrings from me. I just offered to do a little bit of acupuncture to help her out... and well... I'd never done it before, and the YouTube video must have been wrong! But I didn't know there was a problem till the next day when we all found out about her being in hospital.' They all turned to stare at her. Margery could feel her jaw dropping of its own accord. Ceri-Ann looked close to tears.

'You nearly killed her!' Margery said, aghast. 'If we hadn't found her, she'd be dead!'

'So, she did buy the earrings!' Clementine shrieked in triumph.

'You found her?' Gloria said, her eyes narrowing at Clementine suspiciously. 'What were you doing here after school hours? I thought Mr Barrow told you to stop sneaking around?'

'He did!' Clementine said, nodding vigorously. 'But we didn't listen and it's lucky we didn't because we saved that miserable witch's life!'

'Don't speak ill of the dead!' Sharon wailed from where she was tidying the dry store in the corner, bursting into tears.

'She's not dead!' Ceri-Ann and Gloria yelled back in unison.

Karen glared at them all as she went to comfort Sharon, muttering platitudes about angels.

'Yeah, and I said I was sorry, like, a million times when I took her the get-well-soon card, so it's fine,' Ceri-Ann said, though to Margery's ears she did not sound entirely convinced. 'She told me not to tell anyone what happened because she was embarrassed.'

'For Christ's sake, as soon as she's better she'll rain hell down on this department. You stupid fool, Ceri.'

Gloria sighed and rolled her eyes. Ceri-Ann started to say something, but Margery turned and gave her a look that stopped her in her tracks.

'Gloria's right, she'll get that idiot headmaster to cut our budget completely, and we're struggling as it is. I've cut the ordering in half already.' Margery had found herself taking over the kitchen ordering and finances in the last few weeks. She had gravitated to the job quite naturally. 'Honestly, the children will be lucky if their Christmas dinners this year actually contain turkey. I'm considering just ordering in turkey dinosaurs and being done with it.'

There was a pause.

'So… you're saying I should have actually killed her?' Ceri-Ann said.

'No!' They all cried in unison.

'Why did she tell us she didn't buy the earrings, though?' Clementine said, her brow furrowed.

'I dunno.' Ceri-Ann shrugged her shoulders. 'She wouldn't tell me.'

The conversation rattled off, and Margery put her coffee cup in the sink ready to face the rest of their shift.

'So… what else has got you all upset this morning then, if it isn't just Caroline and Mrs Smith?' Gloria said finally, as Margery walked over to her workstation to start preparing the onions.

'Well, for one thing we found the card that someone opened our lockers with!' Clementine said, running from the room and emerging a few minutes later, rummaging around in her bag for it. Everyone oohed at the news, Sharon even stopped crying for a beat, as Clementine presented the leisure centre card with Caroline's name on with a flourish.

'Ooh!' Karen practically leapt across the kitchen at them to grab the card, 'Is that mine? I've been looking for that for ages! I had to get a new one from that tosser who works at the reception!'

'Brain? He *is* a stupid-named tosser, isn't he!' Clementine smiled broadly at her in agreement, but then her face soured as she realised what it meant. 'But this says Caroline's name on it?'

Karen smiled as she took the card from Clementine's outstretched fingers. 'Yeah, they all say Caroline on them, don't they? Thank God you found it, I'm training for another 5K charity event and I hate running outside.'

'Why in God's name would it say Caroline's name on it?' Margery said.

'Margery, please do not swear,' Clementine mumbled, but she looked as confused as Margery felt.

'No, she's right,' Gloria said, taking her purse from her apron pocket and presenting them with her gym card, which had a white sticker where the name should be. 'Caroline went and applied for all our passes so we could do her synchronised swimming class, but she said she couldn't remember any of our surnames.' Gloria peeled the sticker off with her nail and held it up to show that it too said 'Caroline Hughes'. 'So, she got herself five passes, and then just stuck a sticker over her name.' Gloria rolled her eyes at the memory.

'Mate, I don't remember that!' Ceri-Ann bellowed. 'Where's mine?'

Gloria turned to her and laughed. 'You probably weren't even born then. I'm surprised you don't remember, though, Margery.'

'Ah well,' Clementine said, rubbing her neck with her palm sheepishly, 'I sort of may have told Caroline to... ah... and I had you in mind, Margery... well just my thoughts on being forced to do exercise and she might have rescinded her offer of gym passes.' Margery shook her head and laughed. 'Well, at least we didn't have to do any swimming, Margery!'

Margery's eyes met Clementine's and she smiled at her. 'I am glad about that, Clem, thank you.' She paused for a moment in thought, eyeing the other members of the dinner lady team. They had known them all for years, and they had been there through thick and thin for her and Clementine. Maybe it was time to ask for help from someone who would take them seriously, unlike the police. 'Maybe we should tell the rest of the team what's going on.'

Clementine nodded in agreement.

'Tell us what?' Gloria said.

'Yeah, what?' Ceri-Ann said, leaning closer to them in anticipation.

The kitchen door banged open and Seren entered, red-faced and panting. Margery noticed immediately that she was limping.

'Sorry... I'm... late...' she wheezed, pulling off her oversized coat as she rushed into the staff changing room; she threw it on a hook and tottered back out, wincing as she put the weight on her foot to walk. 'I had to come all the way from the bottom of Dewstow Hill, and I forgot to do my shoelaces last night and I fell over them, can you believe that?' She laughed, but there was no humour in it and her eyes looked wide and manic.

'Come and sit down, Seren,' Gloria said, her eyes widening at the sight of Seren grimacing as she limped through the room towards them. 'Let's put some ice on that foot.'

Margery noticed the clock in the corner as Gloria escorted Seren softly by the arm out into the canteen to sit at one of the tables. 'Good God, it's nearly ten o clock! We've got to get going if the children are going to have lasagne for lunch. Sharon! Karen! Start getting those onions peeled.'

Seren did not come back into the kitchen for lunch. Gloria fetched her coat and took it out to her.

'I sent her home, Margery. I hope you don't mind? I just can't see how she'll get anything done with her foot like that.'

Margery did not mind. Though she found it odd that Seren would not say where she had been the past few days when she went out into the canteen briefly before lunch service. She had just shaken her head and mumbled something about a private matter, and Margery had been too busy to question her any further.

Chapter Seventeen

It was a beautiful afternoon by the time they were leaving work; Margery had let Clementine coerce her into walking home instead of getting the bus. Margery did not pretend to fight too hard about it. It made a nice change from Clementine trying to convince her to get the car out of the garage, though she supposed that was a nonstarter now that the car was in bits on their driveway.

They strolled arm in arm down Dewstow Hill, another rarity. It was a lovely walk that Margery would never tire of, and the late afternoon sunshine made it all the better. There was a delightful breeze whipping through the trees on either side of the road. The sky was a delicious shade of blue and Margery could not help but admire it, the clouds skimming past wispy and fragile against the backdrop. It reminded her of the sea on a particularly calm day and she daydreamed to herself of the long summer holiday and the lovely day trips that they would take.

'If we did get married,' Clementine said, as they strode together in an easy rhythm, 'it would be nice to do it on a day like today, when the weather is good. Then we could all sit outside after, have a barbecue or whatever.'

'You wouldn't think it was too hot?' Margery asked, smiling at her. 'Wearing a ginormous white dress?'

Clementine scoffed. 'I'm way too old for all that, Margery! You do your Princess Diana frock or whatever, I'll be wearing a nice comfortable cardigan and sensible shoes.'

Margery laughed at that. 'I couldn't imagine it any other way, Clem.'

They fell into a comfortable silence and Margery enjoyed the peace. The only disturbance were the cyclists whizzing past them on the road as they sauntered along the pavement beside it. She felt more relaxed than she had since they had found out Caroline had died. It gave her brain the time to think with more clarity than she had had the privilege of recently and she could properly piece together the events of the past few days.

It really did seem as though someone was trying to stop her and Clementine, if not kill them both, and she could not imagine anyone they knew who would fit the bill for that. If she were being honest with herself, she could never have imagined Caroline dying in the way she had either, or who could have done such a thing, though she must know them if they knew her well enough to tamper with her car. The notes were another strange addition to the puzzle she could not get her head around.

'If it wasn't Caroline's boyfriend in her house last night, Clem, then who do you think it was?' she asked Clementine gingerly. 'And who do you think is sending us the notes?'

'I really don't know, Margery.' Clementine sighed miserably. 'I don't think anyone else would have the keys, and anyway they obviously didn't use a key, did they?

Breaking straight in. I wonder where he is anyway. The boyfriend, I mean.'

'Do you think we should ring the police?' Margery asked earnestly. 'Go down to the station and make a statement at least?'

Clementine shook her head. 'I think they think we're mad enough as it is, I don't fancy a charge for breaking and entering on top of the caution, do you?'

Margery shook her head; she did not. Mr Barrow would have no choice but to take disciplinary action if anything else happened and she did not intend for him to ever find out about the snooping Clementine had dragged her into.

'Bit strange today, wasn't it?' Clementine said. 'Seren turning up like that.'

'Yes, it was,' Margery agreed. 'And she was limping. Clem, you don't think...'

'That she was the one who was climbing Caroline's fence? Of course I do!' She unlinked her arm from Margery's and fetched her phone out of her pocket. She unlocked it so she could wave the terrible, pixelated photo in Margery's face again. 'The proof is in the pudding.'

They paused, both staring at the phone. The photograph was so poor quality that it could have been of anyone. It could even have been a photo of her own face and Margery still thought she would still struggle with working out the features.

'So,' she finally said, 'we can't go to the police. What do we do?'

'I don't know.' Clementine shook her head again, then took a deep breath. 'Look Margery, I just wanted to say, I'm sorry.'

'Whatever for?' Margery asked.

Clementine put her phone away and took her arm again. 'Just, I know sometimes my ideas don't work out quite as I plan them to.' Margery smiled at the understatement. 'I've got you in trouble with the police and the headmaster, and we still aren't any closer to working out what the hell is going on.'

They arrived at the bottom of the hill, and they automatically turned towards the high street, making the decision wordlessly. It was these moments that Margery realised how in tune they really were. She supposed that was only natural after the length of time they had been together, though she was surprised when Clementine dropped her arm suddenly.

'Margery!' Clementine cried. 'I've had a fantastic idea!'

Margery shook her head and looked up at the beautiful blue sky for a moment, wishing for no more fantastic ideas. By the time she turned her head back to where Clementine had been standing, the woman was already grabbing her hand and rushing them down the high street as fast as their old legs would carry them – which was at best a very slow power-walk.

'Come on, Margery!' she shouted back to her, and Margery reluctantly followed, being jolted along as she was in Clementine's vice-like grip.

'Where are we going, Clem?' she hissed, as Clementine dragged her through the crowds of people pottering up and down past the shops. They narrowly avoided being garrotted by a gentleman with an umbrella under his arm. Clementine suddenly slowed down to their usual gait.

'Try to act normal, Margery, Mrs Mugglethwaite can see us,' she hissed through clenched teeth, as they passed the big glass front of the town's small post office. She waved her free hand in a very odd way as though she were the Queen. Clementine's face was pulled into a forced smile that showed way too many teeth. She obviously thought it was very natural but reminded Margery of a hideous ventriloquist dummy her aunt had owned that had terrified her as a child. Mrs Mugglethwaite waved at them, her face a picture of confusion through the window. Margery waved back, as Clementine sped up again and pulled them down a side street.

'Look!' Clementine said, pointing to one of the buildings in front of them. 'It's Mr Tamble's office.'

Margery stared up at the big stone entrance to the solicitor's office and wondered why on earth Clementine would drag her here. 'So?'

Clementine gestured again at the building as though Margery had lost her marbles. 'He'll know where Seth Thomas lives, he'll have his address!'

Margery's mouth opened of its own accord and then closed again as she thought about it; as far as Clementine's ideas went it was not a horrific one. Who better to know who Caroline's boyfriend was than the man sorting out her estate?

They entered the building and clambered up the stairs to the first floor. An awfully familiar and sour-faced receptionist sat behind the desk in the well-dressed room.

'Brain!' Clementine cried in delight. 'What are you doing here? Margery, look, it's Brain from yesterday!'

Brian looked as pleased to see them as if they had burst in and announced they had sold his dog to a circus. The young man looked even more annoyed by their presence than he had the day before. 'I work here,' he said with a sigh.

Clementine leaned on the desk casually, as though she had forgotten she had declared him her worst nemesis the day before. 'I thought you worked at the leisure centre?'

Brian rolled his eyes so dramatically Margery worried about his future ocular health. 'The leisure centre's my main job. I work here on my days off sometimes to help my uncle.'

'Mr Tamble?' Margery asked, and Brian nodded. 'Can we see him?'

'Sure. You can see him...' Brian made a big show of tapping at the computer in front of him; Clementine took her diary out of her bag and flicked through it earnestly. 'On the twenty-third of...'

'Yes...?' Clementine said, leaning forwards over the desk in anticipation.

'On the twenty-third of never!' Brian said, then he started to laugh. Clementine glared at him.

'What? Why not?' Clementine demanded, banging her diary down on the desk in front of him.

'Because he's really busy and if you couldn't afford a swimming pass yesterday then you definitely can't afford an appointment.' Brian scoffed and picked up his mobile phone, ignoring them.

'Isn't there anything you can do?' Margery inquired. 'It's important, or we wouldn't be here.'

Brian looked up at her and shook his head. 'Nah, nothing I can do, sorry.'

Clementine was almost purple with rage. 'Is he here? Just call him out to see us and we'll leave.'

'I won't.' Brian did not even look up from his phone.

'That's his door, isn't it?' Margery said, pointing behind the desk to the slightly open office door, which had 'E. Tamble' written on the gold plaque.

'Fine!' Clementine shoved her diary back into her bag. 'But you asked for this.' She drew her hands around her mouth in a makeshift noise amplifier.

'Mr Tamble!' Clementine screeched. 'Mr Tamble, we're here about Caroline Hughes!'

Brian slammed his phone down on the desk and stood as though to shoo them from the office, but as he did so the door behind him opened fully and Ethan Tamble wandered into the entryway. Brian spun around to see what Margery and Clementine were looking at.

'Sorry, I'm just getting these two to leave now,' he said through gritted teeth.

'No need.' Mr Tamble smiled at him. 'Let them come through. You know ladies, I did give you my card for a reason. You could have called.'

Margery had forgotten all about the business card he had slipped into her fingers on the day of the funeral and suddenly felt annoyed at herself. Some things were meant to be a phone call, not a meeting.

Much to Brian's annoyance, Mr Tamble ushered them into his office and shut the door behind them. His office was much, much nicer than Mr Barrow's, and Mrs Smith's might as well have been a hole in the ground in comparison. The building had obviously not been intended as a solicitor's initially, judging from the high ceilings and original features. The entire wall behind the imposing desk was formed of large, attractive bookshelves; there must have been hundreds of books. The other wall held a cast iron Victorian fireplace that looked as though it must still be in use, judging by the coal bucket sat next to it. Enormous bay windows flooded the room with light and offered a lovely, picturesque view of the town centre. Margery admired the room for a moment before she sat in down one of the comfortable chairs Mr Tamble gestured for them to sit in.

'What can I do for you, ladies?' he said, striding to the other side of his desk and adjusting his tie before sitting down opposite them. His dark hair was streaked back tidily today, and he looked much better than he had done on the day of the funeral. 'You said it was about Mrs Hughes?'

'We did.' Margery nodded. 'Well, it kind of is.'

'We won't bore you with pleasantries, Mr Tamble.' Clementine cut straight to the chase. 'Is Caroline's boyfriend in her house yet or not? We tried to call him, but the number was disconnected.'

Mr Tamble looked at her, eyebrows raised for a moment before answering. 'If I'm honest with you both, he isn't.'

'He isn't?' Margery asked. So, it was definitely not him in the house the day before. Unfortunately, that did not answer any of their questions.

He shook his head. 'I haven't been able to get hold of Mr Thomas yet. Caroline gave me an address, but he doesn't live there anymore it seems. You did better than me just by finding his phone number.' He opened his desk drawer and pulled out a bundle of envelopes, putting it down in front of them. Margery could see just from the top of the pile that they all had 'Return to sender' written on them.

'So, I have no idea.' He shrugged. 'I left a message with the desk at the address, it was a retirement complex you see, and they said they'd try and find out. No luck so far, though.'

Margery sat back in the chair. Clementine picked up the letters and flicked through them, finally throwing them down on the desk with a sigh.

'Well back to square one then,' she said, as Margery reached over and patted her on the shoulder.

'I did go round there the day after the funeral but honestly it wasn't a lot of good,' Mr Tamble said, taking the letters back and putting them back in his drawer. 'He didn't leave a next of kin or a moving address, and they are bound by confidentiality laws you see. It's one of those retirement complexes with the apartments you can buy after you turn fifty-five, you know? I couldn't get much out of them but from what I understand he didn't need medical care or the like so I don't think he had much to do with the onsite staff there.'

'I suppose we could go and ask his neighbours if they know anything,' Clementine said. 'Find out if they know where he went.'

Mr Tamble shook his head. 'I already did and no one knew. I don't think he had many friends. They all seemed to know Caroline, though.' He said the last few words bitterly and Margery suddenly remembered his relationship with Caroline.

'Well.' Clementine seemed lost for words for once. 'I'm not sure what else to do then.'

'I'm sorry I can't help you further ladies,' Mr Tamble said; he looked as upset as Margery felt. 'If you find anything else out, please don't hesitate to give me a call or stop in again, don't worry about my nephew.' He handed Margery his fountain pen and a piece of paper from his desk. 'If you leave your phone number, I'll do you the same courtesy.'

–

Back at home that evening, Margery stared up at the board Clementine had put together and pondered it again and again till she felt she might go mad if she stared at it any longer. She sighed and pushed away her plate of half-eaten crumpets. Clementine pulled the plate towards herself and began to eat Margery's leftover supper.

'So, what do we do now?' Margery asked.

'I don't know, Margery.'

Clementine swallowed and looked at her for a moment, a profoundly serious expression on her face. It startled Margery a little bit. Clementine was usually joking about something or making a bizarre sarcastic comment. Serious was highly unusual. Then she blinked and snapped out of it, going back to her normal self.

'Have you given any more thought to the Kitchen Manager job, Margery?'

'Not that again, Clem. Can't we just leave it? You'd hate it anyway, I know you think you'd like being in charge, but it would be a lot more work. I don't think you understand.'

'Well, you should think about it, you'd be great at it.'

'Let's talk about it another time, Clem.'

Clementine nodded at her, but she did not look happy. They sat quietly for a minute, until Margery felt guilty enough to break the silence.

'Maybe we should actually go to the hospital and visit Mrs Smith tomorrow, Clem. Though she might be out by then.'

Clementine nodded agreeably, finishing the last of Margery's crumpets.

'Sounds like a plan. God, is that the time?' she said, as she noticed the kitchen clock, which read 8:30. 'It's ridiculously late! That's it. I'm off to bed. Will you put the bins out if you're going to stay up fretting over this mess? Oh, and at least have a think about the job, will you?'

It was less a question and more a statement, Margery thought, as she nodded and wished her good night. Clementine kissed her forehead gently and swept away from the room. Margery leaned back in her chair wearily, but she finally managed to drag herself up, and prepare to put the rubbish out bright and early for the bin men.

They no longer took the bin bags through the living room to the front door, after an incident involving a tear in the bag and a large amount of turmeric. The stain had never really come out of the carpet, and Clementine had sent a strongly worded letter to their local MP, presumably to condemn them to hell for getting rid of the traditional wheelie bins the street used to have, and demand they pay for the rug they had bought to cover it. Strangely, she had never received a reply. She dutifully dragged the bin bags from the garden and through the alley behind their house around to the street, dreaming back to the old days where not everything came wrapped in plastic, and the even more joyous, halcyon days of the 1980s where you could just throw all the rubbish in together and let God deal with it.

She wiped her hands on her cardigan and turned back to go and fetch the glass bottle bin, but as she looked up she locked eyes with a figure staring at her from her own front doorstep. They snapped their hand away from the letterbox, a look of complete panic in their eyes, the rest of their face covered by their scarf.

'Stop!' Margery cried, but the person was already in motion. They rushed away from her, down the garden path and bowled past Margery, who tripped backwards off the curb and fell into the street, the bin bags breaking her fall.

'Wait!' she shouted at their retreating back, scrabbling to get up again, sure she could catch the person who was rushing away as fast as they could. 'Wait!'

By the time Margery had extracted herself from the rubbish bags and made her way back onto the garden path, they were long gone. Clementine was already hurrying out of their front door, pulling her dressing gown on over her pyjamas.

'Margery, I heard shouting. What on earth is going on?' she said, as she helped lead Margery by the arm into their hallway.

Margery frantically scrabbled at the inside of their letterbox and pulled out another of the notes. Fresher this time, the ink on it had not even dried; it smudged under Margery's fingers. 'It's the notes, Clem. That was the sender!'

'What? Who was it?' Clementine said, panic rising in her voice, 'Oh God, Margery, you're bleeding!'

Margery was bleeding, she realised as she stared down at her hands. The one clutching the note was indeed badly cut, and the blood was trickling down her arm and onto the carpet by the hallway bookcase.

'And we've only just de-turmericed the floor!' Clementine wailed at the sight.

Margery ignored her as she slumped down to the carpet on her knees and held the note up to read it.

'Who was it? Margery?' Clementine said anxiously, bending down to wrap the cord of her dressing gown around Margery's cut. The pain made her wince and brought Margery back to her senses.

'It was…' Margery was sure she had seen those eyes before, but she could not think who they belonged to. She racked her brain trying to work it out but came up blank again and again. 'I don't know.'

Chapter Eighteen

'We've been doing this for hours. What's that one they left last night say again?'

Margery pointed at it with her non-bandaged hand. 'It said "Hatcheck Pete Gray". Which we think means "Check the gray tape". But we've been wrong before.'

Clementine nodded, her brows knitted in thought. 'Check the tape. Hmmm.'

Clementine had finally stopped trying to take Margery to the doctor's surgery for her hand, which was fine now, Margery hoped. The doctor's receptionist had insisted there were no appointments that day, except for emergencies, and Margery had convinced Clementine to give up in the end. Besides, Margery had had an emergency tetanus jab the year before anyway, after an incident involving Pumpkin and a large rat the cat had brought in completely unharmed. Pumpkin was not a fighter.

Clementine had spent a good hour the night before cleaning the cut and super-gluing it shut, just as she had on the day they had met at Ittonvale Catering College all those years ago. They had been the only women on the course, and she had stepped in when Margery had nicked her hand with her brand-new boning knife trying to fillet a particularly delicate piece of megrim sole. The memory still made Margery smile, even now forty-something years later. 'Stitches are for the weak,' Clem had said then and yesterday, though she had also chastised her at the time for using the wrong knife for the wrong job.

Margery stared at the board and at the unravelling clues, willing them to suddenly start meaning something, anything, to her.

There was, 'Danger Brakes Cut', 'Help Me', 'Caroline Murdered' and the newest addition, 'Check the grey tape'. They had already checked that there was not a Pete Gray in the local Yellow Pages and ruled that out, though Margery had not been surprised when it was not that simple.

She was worried about the note writer, who obviously felt that they were in danger if they were asking for help from the likes of her and Clementine.

'Who do you think is sending them, Clem?' she asked, looking over to Clementine who was staring at the board still and shaking her head.

'I dunno, Margery,' Clementine said. 'Maybe Seren? She seems the most likely person but I don't know whether that's because we just haven't properly seen her for ages.'

'Wouldn't we recognise her handwriting, though?' Margery asked, 'We've worked with her for years, surely we can get a copy of her writing from the fridge temperature sheet or something at work?'

Clementine shook her head. 'She never fills in the paperwork book, does she? Remember how annoyed Caroline used to get about it.'

Margery did remember. Caroline had once glued all the pages from the food safety manual onto the walls of Seren's locker in anger when she had forgotten for the umpteenth time to sign the kitchen's opening procedure form.

Whomever they were, Margery hoped that the puzzle pieces would not fit in a way that ended badly for the sender, though she suspected that this may already be the case.

She eyed the actual jigsaw puzzles from Caroline's house, which she had unceremoniously dumped on the table the night before, smoothing her hands over the lid. They had a good hour before work; neither of them had been able to sleep the night before, and they had got up at an ungodly hour. And then last night's anagram had only taken Clem ten minutes to solve and pin to the investigation board. Maybe she could just start one of the puzzles. She liked jigsaws, and anyway she had not had time to check all the pieces were there last night. She debated which one to start, but eventually the sunflowers won over the vase, and she popped open the box and went to pour it out.

She pulled her hand away as if it had been burned when she saw what else lay amongst the pieces.

'Clem,' she said, her voice rising in shock. 'There's something else in here.'

'A spider?' Clementine flung herself away from the table, nearly toppling herself out of the chair. Margery shook her head. Buried in all the puzzle pieces, laid an unmarked DVD disc in a plastic sleeve. Margery stared down at it in shock.

'The tape!' Clementine announced snatching it from the box, jumping up from her chair and holding it up in jubilation. 'This must be it, Margery!'

'I really doubt that, Clem. That seems much too easy.' But Margery got up too and followed her into the living room, where she watched Clementine waste a good five minutes trying to turn the DVD player on. She finally managed it, down to luck more than anything else, and they sat down to watch after she had slid the disc in.

Bizarrely, it was a copy of Caroline's video will. Margery wondered how it had ended up in the puzzle box. It was possible that Mrs Hughes had not been sure where to put it and had just stuffed it in there out of the way. She was not known for her technological prowess. Margery would be incredibly surprised if she even owned another DVD. Caroline still exclusively used the television and videotape player combo she had had forever. Margery could remember her being so excited about the day she ordered it from the Argos catalogue, which must have been some twenty years ago now. She could never forget Caroline's jubilation that it had a power cord. Until then she had been watching her soaps on a battery-powered, portable television she had got as a free gift for signing up for what turned out to be a pyramid scheme.

They sat and watched silently through the rigmarole of the taped will for a second time until the part with Mr Thomas and the house and the car and the money. Nothing new. No new leads. In fact, it was all the more depressing watching it for a second time, especially now that they were sure something awful had happened to her.

Clementine slumped back in her seat and sighed. 'Well, that's that then. I was so sure that if we watched it again, we would realise something, you know?' she said to Margery. 'You see it all the time in the Agatha Christies! She would have solved this case *and* had a BBC Christmas special about it by now.'

Margery nodded, only half listening, still watching the tiny screen figure of Mrs Hughes struggling to get out of her comfortable chair like they had before. It had gone way past the point where Mr Barrow had turned it off now, and she felt almost cruel for finding the struggle between the chair and the slightly rotund Mrs Hughes amusing.

'For Christ's sake, help me you idiot!' Mrs Hughes cried from on screen, and finally someone did step from behind the camera to help pull her out of her seat, huffing the entire time.

Margery and Clementine gasped as they stared at the screen, transfixed, both entirely lost for words for once. Clementine almost dropped her phone in her hurry to bring up the photograph she had taken on it the day before. They had pored over it all night trying to determine if they knew who it was.

'That's Seren, look! It was definitely her in the house yesterday!' Clementine said, as she thrust the screen in Margery's face.

'I still don't understand why she would be in Caroline's house,' Margery said, batting the phone away.

'Robbing her blind, don't forget!'

'There must be more to it than that. We've missed something here.'

'It is hard to believe. What with them being such firm friends.'

Margery turned to look at Clementine in disbelief. Clementine continued.

'Well, not friends as such… but they had a great kind of banter going on.'

Margery rolled her eyes. 'Seren didn't like her! But I just can't see her murdering her.'

'No, I can't either. Though after all that last year…' Clementine said. 'Well, she hasn't exactly been her old self, has she?'

Seren had not been herself recently, Margery thought darkly. Since she was arrested last year, Seren had changed considerably. She had never been the life and soul, but she had withdrawn significantly even by her standards. She now refused to take the bus anywhere because of the reception she had received from Mrs Mugglethwaite and her ilk. She had even come off all social media and changed her phone number. Well, that was what Ceri-Ann had said anyway; Margery was not one for social media. But she just could not see her hurting Caroline or stealing from her home. There had to be another explanation.

'We need to talk to her, Margery.'

Clementine jumped out of her seat and went careening back into the kitchen, and Margery followed. Clementine pulled her reading glasses on and desperately tried to link the picture of Seren's face from the school newsletter to one of the other clues on her investigation board. She threw the yarn back onto the kitchen table and peered closer to the original note for the thousandth time, shaking her head at it.

'Come on, Margery, there's only one thing for it.'

'And what's that?'

'I think it's about time we paid Seren a visit,' Clementine said, her jaw set in determination.

'Clem, this could be dangerous,' Margery said, fidgeting with the sleeves of her cardigan. 'You can't tell me the car and everything else was an accident! We could be being watched, for all we know going to Seren's house is exactly what they want us to do.'

'Well, we can't just sit here waiting for something else terrible to happen, can we? Do you have any better ideas, Margery?'

Margery shook her head. She did not.

Chapter Nineteen

Clementine had been hammering on Seren's wooden front door for what felt like an age, but must have only been a few minutes. Margery could sense her growing impatience with every knock, but she did not have the heart to tell Clementine that Seren may well have left for work already.

'What's keeping her, Margery?' Clementine said, clearly exasperated at the delay. 'She can't be washing her hair, for Christ's sake.'

'Well… it is nearly eight, Clem.'

Clementine snorted, peering in through the bay window next to the front door, the net curtains obscuring any view inside. 'You can't tell me she's already run off to the school. She hasn't been in all week, except the one time when she was *late*!' Clementine spat the word as though she was the absolute pinnacle of a perfect employee and was not constantly trying to sneak away to the dry store to do crosswords. She turned back to the door to knock again.

'Just a minute!' The muffled shout through the front door made them both jump. Clementine took a big step back off the doorstep. 'Well, after you, Margery. You give her what for.'

Margery shook her head at her and waited patiently as the door swung open. The woman standing before them with the toddler under her arm was not Seren.

'Can I help you?' the woman said, eyeing them both carefully. She was wearing a saggy pair of leggings and had a headband holding her fringe back; Margery could see the vacuum cleaner in the hallway behind her. The toddler was struggling to free himself, waggling his chubby little legs about, and Margery could not help but smile at the scene.

'Oh,' Margery said, 'Hello. Um… is Seren there?'

She shook her head. 'Who? Oh, do you mean Seren Jones? Hang on.'

She closed the door again, shutting it in their faces with a bang. Margery and Clementine looked at each other, eyebrows raised. When she reappeared several moments later it was without the baby, but this time her hands were full of envelopes.

'Can you give these to her? I kept writing 'not known at this address on them' and putting them back in the post box but they keep coming.'

Margery stared at her in surprise as she thrust the letters at them. 'Does she… does she not live here?'

She stepped back to look at the metal number nailed to the side of the building. They were certainly in the right place. Seren had invited them over a few times before and she always hosted a *Great British Bake Off* finale party where they would all cram into the small flat. It had to be here, Margery could remember Karen and Sharon tripping over the empty glass milk bottles on the doorstep, and falling drunk into the geraniums that she could still see growing in the neat and tidy garden bed. Though now that she thought of it, they had not been invited to anything at the flat for a long while and the grass in the front garden was too neatly mowed to have been done by Seren's own hands.

'Nah.' The woman shook her head. 'Me and my husband have been here since October. Can you tell her to change her address on all her stuff, though? It's doing my head in.'

'Certainly,' Margery said, her brow furrowed as Clementine took the post. 'Do you know where she went?'

The woman shook her head. 'No, sorry. If I did, I would have taken them round myself. The post, I mean. I did ask on the Dewstow community page on Facebook, you know? But no one knew.'

They left, after giving their apologies for disturbing the new tenant, stopping to sit at a bench so that Clementine could pass the letters to Margery to look at. It was mostly junk mail, except for a letter about her pension and an envelope with the leisure centre's logo printed on it in black and white that Margery stared at solemnly for a moment, before stuffing into her bag with the rest of it.

'I will give you the rest of the Quality Street if that isn't a replacement leisure centre card,' Clementine said, shaking her head. 'This is a complete swizz. That note said to watch the tape, we did, and this was useless. How did we not know she'd moved out? How did that tape help us in any way at all? I don't get it, Margery.'

'Well…' Margery leaned back against the uncomfortable wooden bench and stroked her chin, pondering, 'They did say "tape". That was rather more of a disc. How would they have known about it anyway? It was at Caroline's house, for God's sake.'

Margery waited for Clementine to chastise her for swearing, but instead Clementine dropped her glasses into her own lap, and turned towards her, mouth agape.

'That other word!' Clementine cried, 'Gray! But no one spells grey like that. What are we, American?' She snorted in disgust.

'It's an anagram too!' Margery said, clarity suddenly flooding her brain.

They had come to the same conclusion. How foolish of them to not rearrange the separate word, she thought. How naïve that it would be so easy!

'Yes, it didn't say Gray!' Clementine yelled, ripping the leisure centre letter from Margery's bag and waving it triumphantly above her head like a flag, in a fervour Margery had not seen since the last royal wedding. 'It said Gary!'

'Gary, of course!' Margery breathed a sigh of relief, of course. 'Gary Matthews, you think?'

'Who else would have access to CCTV tapes but the school security guard? Tapes, Margery!' Clementine was practically frothing at the mouth in her excitement; she had already leapt up from her seat and was waddling away as fast as she could. 'Come on, Margery! We've got to get up to the school!'

With all the excitement of the morning and taking the detour to Seren's former home, they missed the bus by moments again, and Clementine decided that, rather than wait, they should walk. By the time they reached the school's security office they were both completely out of breath and practically purple with exertion. Clementine had used her inhaler six times, and Margery had been tempted to sit down at least twice on the way up, but they had persevered. Whoever would have thought to build the town on such a foolishly steep hill? If she ever met them in the afterlife, she vowed privately that she would punch them straight in their smug, well-exercised face.

'Gary!' Clementine shrieked as they entered, startling Gary from his previously quiet spot reading his book behind the security counter, as she collapsed against it.

'Ms Butcher!' he exclaimed, rising from his seat, putting down the copy of *Dolores Claiborne*, 'You can't need another pass again? I'll have to definitely see some identification this time!'

Clementine dragged herself upwards, so her face was visible over the desk, and Margery passed her inhaler over for what felt like the fortieth time that day.

'Gary,' Margery began, once she had caught her breath a bit. She could feel the sweat dripping down her face. 'Do you know Seren?'

She looked over at Clementine, who was still gasping for air, mouth open like a dying fish, and leaving sweaty finger marks all over the security desk. 'And do you have any paper towels?'

'I do know Miss Jones, yes. We err...' He paused. 'We erm... well, sometimes we have lunch together,' Gary said finally, still taking in the scene in front of him.

Margery could not imagine great hulking gym buff Gary eating Seren's staple lunch of a Toffee Crisp and three cigarettes, but lots of things had surprised her in the past few days.

'What about her? She's not in trouble?' He reached into his desk and handed Margery a single sachet hand wipe from a fast-food restaurant.

'She killed Caroline,' Clementine squeaked from where she was collapsed on the floor before the counter at Margery's feet. Gary gasped.

One of these days, Margery thought, Clementine would say something so frustrating that Margery's eyes would roll all the way back into her head never to be removed.

'We don't know *that* exactly,' Margery said, poking Clementine with her foot to shut her up. 'All we know is that she was in Caroline Hughes's house yesterday, *and* we had a note put through the door telling us to look at a tape. So we watched the will video again and we saw Seren on video in Mrs Hughes's house!'

Gary waved his arms in front of him. 'Well, she lives there, doesn't she? So... maybe she helped Mrs Hughes make the video or something? What's the problem?'

Margery stared at him. 'She doesn't live there?'

'Well, she definitely *was* living there.' Gary scratched his goatee thoughtfully, 'That's where I drop her off.'

'What?' Margery cried.

'You dropped her off there?' Clementine piped quietly from her place on the floor.

'Yeah.' Gary seemed to have finally realised he had revealed something he was not supposed to. 'Well, I didn't this week, though. She wanted me to bring her back here. Dunno why.' He scratched his head again, his eyebrows furrowed in confusion. Margery remembered Seren's pale face as she had run from them in the leisure centre car park on Tuesday evening. 'Wait. How do you know she was there yesterday?'

Margery was not entirely sure how to answer that without admitting that they too had been trespassing inside the deceased woman's house.

'We just know,' she finally settled on, dabbing at her face with the lemon-scented hand wipe.

He sighed and sat back in his chair, the wheels of it squeaking under his mass. 'She didn't kill Mrs Hughes. Trust me, mate.'

'How do you know that?' Margery asked.

'I just do,' he said, but he would not look at either of them.

'Look, maybe we'll believe you if you show us the CCTV tapes,' Margery snapped.

'Yeah, show us the tapes, Gary!' Clementine's shout came muffled from behind Gary in the back room of the office. Margery had not even noticed her move from where she had practically been dying on the floor, but somehow she had managed to sneak behind both of them. Gary spun around sharply on his office chair, as Margery started towards the back room, but Clementine was already pressing buttons rabidly on the school's closed-circuit television system, as the screens flickered on and off.

'Stop that!' he cried, and grabbed at Clementine's hands as Margery tried to stand in his way, but it was like trying to hold back a giant. It culminated in a short scuffle between them, but Clementine was smaller and faster and somehow managed to wriggle away waving a video tape in the air.

'Gary! I'll smash it!' she threatened, holding it above her head. 'I'll do it!'

Gary let Margery go from the loose grip he had on her shoulder in and threw his head back at the heavens in frustration. 'Oh, for God's sake!'

Clementine raised the tape even higher, which seemed an impossible feat to Margery, given that she was only five foot.

'Please don't swear, Gary!' Clementine said.

'Fine!' he cried, slumping back into his office chair in a huff. 'I know Seren didn't do it because I dropped her home that Friday!'

'Oh my.' That stopped Clementine in her tracks, she dropped the tape to arm's length and Gary leapt forward and snatched it back.

'If someone did kill Mrs Hughes, they must have done it in the time I was taking Seren back home. But you can't tell anyone that. I'll lose my job if Mr Barrow finds out I wasn't even here.'

'Really? You and Seren?' Margery said, trying to hide the surprise that she could feel showing on her face. 'Together?'

Gary looked at her red-faced. 'We aren't together like that!' he said, exasperated. 'It's just that she's had a hard time the last year after what happened, and I drive her over to Ittonvale to go to the big ASDA there. It's been really hard for her not being able to go to Tesco.' He twisted the regained video tape around in his hands as he spoke, 'It's nice to have a friend to sit with and just chat sometimes. I'm sure you ladies understand that kind of friendship.'

Margery saw Clementine roll her eyes at that.

'I only gave her a lift home, and then came back for the rest of my shift! I've got a dashcam in my car, I can prove it, you'll hear us talking on it,' he insisted, slightly more sharply than Margery would have expected. He was telling the truth, she realised. It was a very valid alibi. Margery suddenly realised why Seren had run when they had seen her scuttling through the car park with her shopping bags. She must have been ashamed for them to see her.

Seren had been banned from the only supermarket in town last year for shoplifting. Seren had sworn and cried that the cheese had slipped into her Bag for Life accidentally, but it had ruined her in Dewstow. She had been the talk of the town for months after. The local paper had even run a story on it, the headline reading 'NOT SO GOUDA NEWS'. They had used a still from the CCTV footage of Seren being led into the back of the store by a security guard. Margery suddenly felt terribly, awfully guilty for not realising that Seren might have needed help shopping. She hadn't even considered it. She had assumed that Seren enjoyed living on a diet of Pot Noodles and hot dogs from the newsagents at the bottom of Dewstow Hill. How short-sighted they had been, so wrapped up in their own lives. Clementine's shouting brought her back from her daze.

'That's all. Really?' Clementine said, her voice laced with sarcasm and about a thousand decibels too high. 'Then why so cagey, Gary? If that is your real name!'

Gary looked down at his name badge, which read 'Gary Matthews'.

'Fine! We went to McDonalds drive-through on the way to Mrs Hughes, that's all! I have the receipt! We had a McFlurry each!'

'What flavour?' Clementine screamed, pointing her finger at him dramatically.

'Flake, all right. Flake!'

'Okay.' Margery finally breathed out, batting Clementine's accusatory hands down. 'Well, that's that, then.'

Gary nodded stiffly. Clementine eyed him suspiciously. 'But it doesn't explain the message we got to ask you about a tape,' she said.

Gary looked at her for a moment. 'Well, I can't help you with that anyway.' He sat back in his chair again stiffly. 'The only cameras we have are outside ones. It's not like you would have been able to see anything going on in the kitchen. The police took the tapes to look at them, but they obviously didn't find nothing.'

He paused for a long moment, considering them. 'The thing is, though, I was sure I locked the office before I left that evening. I always do. But when I came back...' he trailed off, shaking his head. 'When I came back, the door was open.'

'Do you think someone broke in?' Margery said.

'Yeah, I do. Inside job, though, if they did. But there was something wrong in here. The control panel didn't look like it did when I left it. But I can't even tell the headmaster because he'll fire me.'

'Why not?' Margery asked gently.

'I was supposed to be here. It was my shift and I left early,' Gary said, and for a moment Margery thought he might cry, like he nearly had the other day. 'I blame myself. I really do.'

—

They were the latest they had ever been for work, by the time they finally rushed into the canteen kitchen. The latest anyone had ever been, possibly, Margery thought to herself. Well, except maybe Seren in the past few days. It was nearly ten o'clock by the time they had put their things in the changing room.

Gloria, red-faced, saw them hurrying in and slammed the kitchen door open. 'Oh, thank God you're here. I didn't think you were coming! Come on, quick!'

They grabbed aprons and hairnets and ran immediately to where Sharon and Karen were desperately wrestling an enormous joint of roast beef into the oven. Ceri-Ann was panic-whisking instant gravy powder into a twenty-litre saucepan.

'Where have you been?' Gloria said, as she smothered salt and pepper onto tray after tray of roast potatoes, 'And where the hell is Seren? Not that she'd be any use with her bad ankle!'

'Seren's the one who stole Karen's gym pass. We're convinced of it,' Clementine told her, as she started desperately peeling carrots. 'And she doesn't live at her flat anymore!'

'Doesn't she?' Gloria said, lifting her head from the potatoes to stare at them in surprise. 'She never said she'd moved, or sent a change of address card.'

'I know! I can't believe she's not here. We ought to tell the headmaster.'

'Ha! As if he'd do anything about it. Remember when Helen kept ringing in sick?'

Margery did remember when Helen Melon had rung in sick day after day for three weeks and then returned finally, with bags and bags of duty-free sangria and a suspiciously Spanish glow for someone who was supposed to be suffering from jaundice. Or the time Clementine had rang in sick for both of them so they could go and watch the last Harry Potter film at the cinema. 'Accident with a toffee penny,' she had said. 'Yes, for both of us.' Mr Barrow had bought it all. Hook, line and sinker.

'Hey!' Karen called from across the kitchen, where she was mixing a huge pot of Smash. 'What's this about my card? What could Seren want with it?' Her face darkened. 'She's not training for a half marathon, is she? Because it's hard enough for me to get the charity money off people without any competition.'

'I just hope she's not in trouble,' Margery said quietly. 'It's just not like her.'

They all nodded their heads in agreement.

After they had served lunch and cleaned down the kitchen, Gloria nominated Margery and Clementine to take the still-undelivered sympathy flowers and card to Mrs Smith, who had been discharged from hospital and was making an excellent recovery at home all told. They were not quick enough to think of a way out of it, as they had already told Gloria they had no evening plans when she had sneakily asked them earlier in the day.

'Go on, ladies, it's on your way home, and you were late...' she had said, guilting them into making the journey so she could go straight home after work instead.

It had taken a long time to find Rose's home; the estate was relatively new. All the houses were of a similar design and used the same beige-colour brick. Unless you knew where you were going, it was easy to get hopelessly lost in street after street of townhouses. Like someone had pressed copy and paste too many times. The estate was set up to look like a quaint little neighbourhood, but Margery had always felt like it was not quite right. The houses were too soulless, and the streets were too empty of life.

They eventually found themselves outside Mrs Smith's ginormous, boxy, three-story townhouse, more by recognising her BMW sat outside it on the drive than anything else. Caroline would have hated it, Margery thought to herself, as they walked up the path past the prim, tidy front garden. She had campaigned for years to stop the houses being built, always getting the dinner lady team to sign one petition or another.

Clementine knocked on the door, and they stepped back from the doorway and waited for it to open. Margery looked down at the sad-looking bunch of daffodils in her arms and wished they had splashed out a little bit more.

The door swung open and Margery looked up ready to smile at Mrs Smith, but the person standing in the doorway in front of them was not Mrs Smith at all.

'Seren!' Clementine said, as Margery's jaw dropped to the floor. 'We've been looking for you everywhere.'

Chapter Twenty

Seren had refused to answer any questions initially, but she begrudgingly invited them in and made them take their shoes and coats off before she showed them into the large sitting room, where Mrs Smith was laid out on an enormous grey corner sofa that took up most of the wall. She was wrapped up in a big blanket, her slippered feet sticking out of the ends like she was a chrysalis about to hatch. She did not look at all pleased to see them, as they padded through the plush beige carpet in their socks and perched carefully on the other edge of the sofa. The silence, as they stared at each other, was maddening. The wall-mounted electric fireplace was on and roaring, and Margery felt that they might all boil to death before anyone spoke.

'Hello, Rose,' Clementine began, with what Margery could tell was a false smile. It must have been almost painful for Clementine to contort her face into that shape for so long. 'Erm, you didn't die then. Good… that's good.'

Rose rolled her eyes at them. 'Hello, Ms Butcher. No, obviously I did not die.'

'This is why we turn down the constant offers of holistic therapies from Ceri-Ann,' Clementine said.

Margery nodded in agreement. 'You never know what you're going to get.' Clementine held out one palm and then the other. 'Could be a nice yoga session, could be a near-death experience. You just never know!'

Mrs Smith eyed them beadily from under the blanket, looking like nothing more than a disembodied head. 'I'll keep that in mind.'

Seren carried the droopy flowers they had brought into the room in a crystal vase and put it down gently in front of the marble fireplace, rearranging the many, many other vases of much nicer-looking flowers until Margery and Clementine's were nearly out of sight. The mantelpiece was smothered in 'Get Well Soon' cards already; they were obviously extremely late to the party. If the television hanging above it had not been so enormous, the cards would have obscured it from view. Margery hoped it never fell off the wall, because it would crush whoever was underneath it at the time, and probably take the sofa out with it.

Seren disappeared again and then reappeared pushing a drinks trolley and holding a Le Creuset teapot, that Margery knew, from staring at it longingly in John Lewis, cost well over forty pounds. The matching mugs must have cost a fortune too. Mrs Smith obviously knew how to spend her money.

'Tea, anyone?' Seren piped up, from where she stood awkwardly in the corner of the room. Seren looked a lot better than she had the last time Margery had seen her, she thought. She was not wearing one of her dreadful coats, just a comfortable-looking jumper and jeans, and it looked as though she had even washed her hair.

'Good God, no. We don't want to stay any longer than we have to.' Clementine snorted, then realised what she had said. 'Ah, I mean… no, thank you, Seren, we don't want to keep you long.'

Mrs Smith laughed out loud from where she was wrapped up like a swaddled baby. It was a completely alien sound coming from her mouth. Margery had never heard her laugh for real, only a mocking sort of chuckle if she was making fun of Clementine. Clementine looked just as startled as Margery felt.

'Don't worry, I won't keep you. Thank you for the flowers anyway, girls. It is appreciated.' Mrs Smith was smiling at them. Margery felt Clementine grab and clutch her hand in fear. 'And thank you for calling the ambulance. Much appreciated indeed.'

'You didn't hit your head as well as break your lungs, did you?' Clementine asked, finally letting go of Margery's fingers. 'Accidentally change your entire personality?'

Mrs Smith chortled again. Margery would never get used to the sound, even if she heard it every day for a million years.

'No, I think maybe a near-death experience makes you reconsider some things in your life, though. How you treat people, things you regret.'

Margery nodded. If she could go back in time, she would certainly try to help Seren out more now that they knew the circumstances. She looked over at the woman manning the tea trolley. 'Seren, where have you been? We've been worried.'

Clementine scoffed. 'Yeah, worried about who's been poking around Caroline's, more like. Why were you there, Seren?'

Seren looked at them both, staring like a rabbit in the glow of Margery's car headlights. Mrs Smith sat herself up as much as she could, still inside her self-inflicted straightjacket on the sofa, and stared between them with an interested look on her face.

'I've been here the whole time,' Seren finally said, her cheeks red. 'Mrs Smith let me stay. I haven't been back to Caroline's since the will-reading. Honest.'

'It's true,' Mrs Smith nodded. 'At first I thought she would be annoying, and to be honest, Seren, you are incredibly maddening, but then Barty left me because he found out about James, and your little minion Ceri-Ann nearly killed me, and it's been very useful to have someone around to bring me things.'

'Your husband found out about your affair with the headmaster?' Margery said before she could stop herself.

'Yes,' Mrs Smith said. She did not seem too concerned. 'But we weren't that careful about it in the end. James can be so passionate.' Margery noticed Clementine physically recoil at the words. 'The house, the car, the chateau in Dormond where I summer, they're all in my name. He had much more to lose. Honestly, you'd think I killed someone the way he carried on.' Margery could see some of the old Rose flickering through under the surface of her new, kinder personality. 'Anyway, you were living with my mother, weren't you, Seren? I kind of felt obliged.'

'What do you mean your mother? Who was your mother?' Margery asked, looking between Rose and Seren for clues. 'I thought you were living with Caroline, Seren?'

'I was.' Seren nodded as she finished making Mrs Smith's tea and placed it delicately on the coaster in front of her. 'Caroline was her mum.'

'Don't call her my *mum*, for crying out loud. She was more like an egg donor.'

For once neither Margery nor Clementine had anything to say. They were both completely stunned into silence in surprise. Margery looked at Mrs Smith in the fresh new light drawn from this revelation. They did look alike now that it was mentioned. Though Mrs Hughes had fared rather better in the nose department, and Mrs Smith had a much more expensive haircut. Maybe the same eyes, Margery thought as she scrutinised her face, the same blue, you did not see that shade very often. And they had the same stern-looking jawline. There were definite similarities between them, though it was a case of two apples falling from the same tree and landing in different orchards.

'I don't understand,' Margery said. Her voice felt very small all of a sudden. 'Caroline always said she didn't want children. She always said—'

Mrs Smith sighed loudly. 'She didn't want children. I was an accident. I only found out she was my mother when I was ten. I would have ended up in care if my grandparents hadn't taken me in and brought me up. For a long time, I just thought of her as a strange older aunt.'

'This is just way too many revelations for one day,' Clementine said, shaking her head. Seren gestured to the tea pot again. 'Stop trying to give me tea, Seren, for Christ's sake. Get me gin!'

'Now you're talking!' Mrs Smith said gleefully, reaching her arms out from the blanket and sitting up properly for the first time since they had arrived in the house. 'Get the gin out, Seren! The good stuff, though, the Wye Valley one, none of that English nonsense. And the big ice cubes from the good freezer!'

Once they all had a gin and tonic, with a massive ice cube shaped like a diamond, Margery felt ready to ask questions again.

'So, you haven't been to the house at all, Seren?'

Seren shook her head, squeezing a drop of lemon juice into her glass. 'No, only to get my stuff after the will reading. I don't know why I thought she'd leave it to me. She said she was going to but that was probably another of her jokes.'

Margery nodded back at her.

'But where's the mystery boyfriend, then?' Clementine asked. 'Anyone seen him?'

'He's real.' Seren said nodding. 'I've never met him, but she used to go and stay with him.'

'I can't believe you used to live with Caroline,' Margery said, watching the ice cube float around in her drink, clinking against the glass. 'She never said.'

'I asked her not to.' Seren sat down in the grey quilted armchair in the living room bay window, nearly knocking over the 'LIVE LAUGH LOVE' decorative sign on the windowsill with her elbow as she did so. 'Out of embarrassment more than anything else. You know what happened with the supermarket. Wasn't that bad enough? I couldn't afford to pay my rent because I had to keep getting Ocado orders, you know how expensive they are, and then having to get on that bus every day, everyone thinking I stole that cheese!' She sobbed, wiped her eyes on her sleeve and continued, 'And I didn't! I don't even like cheese. I do Slimming World for Christ's sake!'

Clementine reached over from where she sat and gave Seren an awkward sympathy pat on her arm.

'Then my bus pass ran out and I couldn't even afford to get it anyway.' Seren shook her head, her eyes narrowing at the memory. 'But Caroline caught me crying after school and I ended up telling her everything. I don't know why, it's not like she was ever particularly nice to me, the opposite in fact.' Margery nodded at Seren in what she hoped was an encouraging way. 'But she said I could use her guest room for as long as I wanted, and I did, till she died, that is. Anyway, it really helped me start to get back on my feet. She didn't even charge me any rent. I just did some of the chores she had started to struggle with, what with her legs being the way they were and her arthritis.'

Margery had always thought Caroline was a funny one like that, so generous, but so secretive about it. It was as though she did not want anyone to know she had a heart, like she had to always balance it out with something horrible. She had always been anonymously donating large amounts towards Karen's charity runs and then making up for it by changing the sugar for salt in the staff room.

'I'm just lucky Mrs Smith took me in after my Hello Fresh free trial ran out. I came straight from Caroline's to here once I told her what had happened.'

'What can I say?' Mrs Smith said beaming. 'I'm like Mother Teresa.'

They sat in silence for a moment, sipping their drinks. Margery looked around at the grey textured wallpaper and duck-egg curtains, with the swirled gold and rose-coloured cushions on the sofas and chairs, and rose-gold candlestick holders on the mantelpiece. There was hardly anything of emotional value in this room, not even a photo in a frame. It was the polar opposite of their own house, which was practically drowning under the weight of sentimental trinkets. The framed Matisse on the wall above the sofa was lovely, but Margery found herself much preferring their own messy living room with its hodge-podge of framed photographs.

'Well, maybe not quite a saint,' Mrs Smith began, thoughtfully. 'I did lie to you about the earrings.'

'I knew it!' Clementine stood, stabbing a finger at her and then seemed to realise they were not mortal enemies anymore, sitting down again bashfully on the suede sofa. 'It's just been hard. I know we had little to do with each other, but she was still my mother. I've spent the last forty years trying to make something of myself that maybe she'd be proud of, make her change her mind.' Rose stared into her glass, looking like she might cry, but managed to contain herself.

Margery suddenly felt sorry for her; the feeling was as alien as Mrs Smith's newly found smile.

'I really tried. Towards the end. I...' She swallowed, tears in her eyes. 'I bought her the earrings as... well, a kind of friendship gift, no hard feelings, that kind of thing.' Her eyebrows pulled together and she sneered at them, 'But she threw that back in my face, didn't she? Said she thought the earrings were disgusting! Let me ask you this. If they were so disgusting why did she keep them in her locker?'

Margery shook her head. She did not know why Caroline would keep them. It was possible that she had not hated them as much as she had let on. There was never any telling with her.

'Also,' Mrs Smith looked a bit sheepish now, 'I got Seren to steal the earring you had.' Seren hung her head in shame.

'I do feel bad about taking Karen's gym pass to open your locker, but I didn't have my purse with me,' Seren said, sadly. 'She's been working so hard on her training for the Ittonvale half marathon.'

'Why on earth would you do that?' Clementine asked, looking between them both.

'It's the last thing I had of her. The last thing I gave to her. Why wouldn't I want them back?' She sat back on the sofa heavily, 'Anyway, Ceri-Ann made me some special ones after she nearly killed me.' She beamed at them both, catching Margery off guard again, manoeuvring herself from under the duvet just enough so they could see her ears and gesturing at them with her fingers. 'Lovely, aren't they?'

The earrings were definitely one of Ceri-Ann's creations, Margery thought, and were comically hideous. This pair was a set of green octopuses with gems on each of their legs. Each octopus only had seven legs, though, and Margery could only assume that Ceri-Ann did not know how many 'octo' meant.

'We thought it might have been you in Caroline's house, Seren.' Margery said, ignoring Mrs Smith and turning back to the other woman. 'Since you came to work limping, why were you so late anyway?'

'I really did fall over my shoelaces and hurt my leg, well… I fell over the shoe rack.' Seren said, sadly. 'I'm not used to there being so many pairs all in the same place, I had to go to the doctor and get stitches in it.'

Mrs Smith laughed so hard she began to cough, and some of her drink sloshed down her dressing gown. Seren leapt up and started dabbing at her with a gold-trimmed napkin she grabbed from the tea trolley.

'Jesus, any other secrets we should know about either of you? Has one of you possibly discovered the meaning to life or where Atlantis is, hmmm?' Clementine said sarcastically, slamming her glass down on the rose-gold coffee table.

'You'd better settle down, Clementine Butcher,' Mrs Smith said, managing to look fierce even while batting Seren away with both hands. 'Else I won't be looking at the kitchen manager application you put in.'

It was Margery's turn to be apoplectic with rage. 'What do you mean, kitchen manager application, Clementine? We said you weren't going to do that.'

'Well, she did,' Mrs Smith said, putting her glass down onto the coffee table with a clunk, and obviously enjoying the drama. 'Handed it in the other day, James says. Looking very promising.' She smirked at them both.

Margery had heard enough. 'Right well, I'm going home then. I'm glad you're feeling better, Mrs Smith.' She stood and rushed for the sliding doors to the hallway, only stopping to grasp her coat from the rose-gold coat stand and slip her shoes back on.

'Oh, come on, Margery, hear me out!' she heard Clementine shout after her, but she was already slamming the front door.

—

By the time she got home it was nearly dark, and the house looked very unwelcoming in the dim light. As she let Pumpkin into the house, she briefly had the same feeling she had had the day before at Caroline's and she paused in the downstairs hallway for a moment, just listening. It was much too quiet in the house when Clementine was not there. She shook her head, trying to snap out of it, but the feeling lingered.

She could not believe Clementine had applied for the job. Not after everything they had just been through, and when she had not even spoken to her about it. Margery did not like feeling like a horrible person who was step- ping on Clementine's dreams, but how could she be when

Clementine had never said that this was what she wanted? She felt out of the loop and misled. If this was what Clementine genuinely wanted, why did she put absolutely no effort in at work? Clementine was the new leader of the fun now Caroline was gone, and it was a role that did not include much responsibility. Sighing, she wandered through the living room towards the kitchen, thinking she would make herself a nice soothing pot of tea and perhaps then just have a bath and go to bed.

As she passed through, she noticed the bag of tapes that Caroline had gifted them in her will. It was still sitting in the corner of the living room next to the big wooden cabinet they usually kept things like that in. Clementine had promised to alphabetise them and put them away at the weekend, but it had just never happened. Quelle surprise, Margery sneered to herself. No matter, she thought finally. Maybe she would watch one tonight and relax.

Picking up the bag, she realised that there had not been as many tapes as she had first thought there'd been when Anita the cleaner had kindly dropped them over. Probably only about fifteen all told. Certainly, it was far from the hundreds that Caroline had promised them in her will, but that was to be expected of the late Mrs Hughes. She was a bit of a joker and well, Margery said it out loud, 'She was horrible.'

She sighed and carted the bag over to the coffee table. How had it come to this, she thought to herself. Saying horrible things about a dead woman all alone in her house.

Margery tipped the bag up and all the tapes clattered out onto the table. She started to sort through them.

Again, Caroline's promise had not held out. Rather than the promised episodes of *Coronation Street* and *East-Enders*, they were all labelled things like, 'School Concert 2007 (Gloria forgets words to Good King Wenceslas)' and 'Summer Sports Day 2018 (Ceri-Ann falls over at egg and spoon race)'. All written in Caroline's elderly scrawl, it was a catalogue of her colleagues' failures and darkest moments.

Margery shook her head and sat back heavily on the sofa, feeling like all the weight of the world was on her shoulders. One of the tapes had a slightly different cover, she thought mildly. Maybe it was a nice episode of *Friends* or something. Margery flipped it over to see what it said on the label and dropped it in shock. It bounced off their worn living room carpet and she stared at it open mouthed.

The front door creaked open and Clementine appeared in the living room doorway.

'Margery, I'm...'

'Clem!' Margery said, interrupting her. 'Look!' She pointed to the videotape on the floor.

'Oh, God,' Clementine said. 'It's not another episode of *Friends* is it? Ceri-Ann set it up on the Netflix for us, don't you remember?'

Margery shushed her and jumped up, grabbing the tape from the floor, and rushed over to the VCR recorder they had stopped using years ago, but had never been able to bring themselves to get rid of. She put the tape into the machine with shaking hands.

The television screen flickered for a moment, then came to life. On-screen was the security camera footage of the school kitchen's backdoor fire escape. It was a good view of the wall and the fire escape door with its little flight of steps leading down. Five, then six minutes went past, judging by the time the tape had recorded. They sat and watched quietly for what felt like an age.

'I don't understand,' Clementine breathed. 'What is this?'

'It was in the bag. It had "Caroline" written on it,' Margery whispered, wringing her hands together. She turned to look at her as she spoke, but Clementine's eyes were still drawn to the screen. Suddenly, to Margery's horror, the tape sped up and began to race through, the picture flicking before their eyes.

'Clementine, stop fast-forwarding it!'

'Look, Margery!' Clementine had pressed play again as a familiar set of figures emerged. The abrupt change in the volume of her voice made Margery jump as she turned back to the television. 'Look!'

On-screen the cleaning team poured out of the building through the fire escape door, each holding a cup of coffee. Margery could have picked their hair out of the crowd at a packed parade at Disneyland. The cleaners were obviously mid-shift. Anita was carrying a mop bucket, which she left to hold the fire escape door open on the top step of the stairs as they made their way down, presumably for a smoke break. Then there was nothing again.

'Shall I fast forward it again, Margery?'

'No!'

They need not have worried. No sooner than Clementine had picked up the remote again, there was more movement on the television screen. They waited with bated breath; the only sound in the room was the VCR whirring as Caroline Hughes appeared in the doorframe of the fire escape. She was looking down at a clipboard, the stocktake paperwork, Margery presumed. She watched in horrified slow motion as Caroline, who had always been clumsy, did not notice the mop bucket and careened right over it, water splashing everywhere, falling down each stair and landing in a crumpled heap at the bottom. She did not move again. Margery and Clementine gasped in unison.

There may have been no sound on the tape, but Margery could see the horror in Anita and Cheryl's faces as they screamed when they found her at the bottom of the stairs, minutes later. Barbara swept into the scene again. Margery wished she could hear what they were saying, but she could tell Barbara was yelling at them both, there was a lot of pointing and gesticulating. Eventually, though, they all grabbed one of Mrs Hughes's appendages and hauled her up the fire escape stairs with great difficulty, leaving a trail of blood behind them. Cheryl took the mop bucket back into the kitchen, and then she helped Barbara to drag Caroline's body inside. Anita paced the bottom of the steps, obviously conflicted. Margery could see Barbara screaming at her, and eventually Anita gave in. She ran up the stairs and joined them in moving the body; the fire escape door slammed shut behind them. Moments later Barbara emerged again throwing a bucket of water down the stairs, sluicing away the blood from Caroline's head injury. On the video it had started to rain, washing away any sign that Caroline had ever been there at all.

Margery sat in horror. This had much worse implications than they could have ever imagined. Caroline had not been dead when they shoved her into the walk-in freezer, they knew that from what they had seen inside it. She had fought and struggled and tried to open the door, but must have been too weak from the head injury. They had killed her – Barbara, Anita and Cheryl, whether they had known that she was alive or not, the minute they had put her in there. They could have just rung for an ambulance, and she might have still been with them.

Who better to cover up an accident than a professional cleaning team? Margery thought darkly. It made perfect sense that there had been no evidence of foul play for the police. They would have had time to tidy it all away and clear it all up. It would have looked like a terrible accident involving an elderly member of staff who was not known for being steady on her feet. No wonder they had got away with it until now, it had been the perfect crime.

'What do we do, Clem?'

'I don't know, Margery.'

Chapter Twenty-One

'I met Caroline once, you know. She was her late husband's guest to our Christmas Ball, God... must be decades ago now. She'd brought these doughnuts for the buffet and we were all looking forward to them, but, when we all bit into them, she'd filled them with mayonnaise!' Officer Thomas guffawed loudly and slapped his palm on his desk. He wiped the tears from his eyes, and then seemed to notice that neither Margery nor Clementine had returned his laughter.

It was Monday morning, and they were sitting in his tiny office at Dewstow police station, for what Margery felt was the fiftieth time since they had called the police on the Saturday morning. The room was little more than a cell, the walls were smooth and bare, the entire back wall taken up by filling cabinets, and the only natural light came from the tiny slit of a window high up in the wall. It was the room opposite the one they had been cautioned in, but it was not any more glamorous.

They had spent a long time worrying about what they should do. After they had seen the tape, Margery had wanted to go immediately to the police station but Clementine had convinced her to wait until the morning. They were tired and stressed, she had said. Caroline's murderers were not going anywhere.

Clementine had been wrong about that. It was Monday morning two days later, and although the police had been out searching for the cleaning team, they had only managed to take Cheryl Higgins into custody. Barbara Harvey and Anita Reynolds were still at large, though Officer Thomas had assured her that they would find them. He was taking them a lot more seriously now they had some actual evidence, though he had at first appeared to be a bit annoyed at seeing them for a third time in such a short period, when they had first appeared in his office a few days ago.

Margery found herself unable to look at Clementine without anger rising in her throat, and so she tried not to speak to her at all. She knew that she could not be upset forever, but they had still not spoken about Clementine's betrayal, and the longer the wild goose chase went on with the cleaners the more irritable she became. Whenever Clementine entered a room, Margery would leave it, which meant they spent their lives playing a slow game of tag at the moment. Pumpkin did not know what to make of it, or which lady to go with, and so she spent her time sitting between them in the hallway.

'Don't worry, ladies.' Officer Thomas smiled at them from behind the flimsy desk he sat at, as they sipped the well-sugared tea young Officer Symon had made them. 'We'll find them.'

Only when they left the police station and were once again out in the bright May sunshine did Clementine turn to Margery.

'Are you coming to work, Margery?' she said, twisting her fingers together nervously. 'I mean… you don't have to. Mr Barrow said we could have as much time as we needed, but I think maybe it would be better to get back to normal. There's nothing else we can do now.'

Margery was not sure about that. Finding out who had killed Caroline merely seemed like the tip of the iceberg now. What had happened with their car, surely that had not been an accident? Especially since someone had seemingly written them a bizarre warning letter. If it had not been Seren, and no one else they knew had come forward to confess, then who was it? Margery could see the familiar stranger in her mind's eye, as they ran down the garden path again. She still could not put a finger on who it had been, and her memory of it was growing less and less clear by the day. She wished, for the millionth time over the years, that you could take a photograph of your memories to look at them later, so she could lay them out in front of her and organise them properly.

'No, I don't think I will, Clem,' Margery said, shaking her head. 'I think I'll just have a day to myself.'

'Oh,' Clementine said, the hurt evident in her voice and Margery suddenly felt horribly guilty. 'I understand. I'll see you tonight then?'

After they had parted, Margery found herself wandering aimlessly down the high street, wondering what to do with herself. She was not always sure who she was without Clementine, who was usually a big enough character for them both. She did not want to go home yet. It would be too strange without her there, though Pumpkin would probably be pleased to see her back so early.

As she walked down the high street, she wondered if she was being too harsh on Clementine. They had never fallen out in the thirty years she had known her, not like this anyway. She tried to put her to the back of her mind as she walked, but it was hard work and she looked around for a distraction. Maybe she could pop into Greggs for a nice Belgian bun, and then go to the sewing shop to spend a half hour admiring the knitting patterns? It would not feel right without getting Clementine one of the sugar-strand doughnuts, though, and all the joy had gone out of knitting recently. Perhaps she should just go to work, she thought to herself, make herself useful, stop moping about the place, no use to anybody.

She turned to make her way back up the high street to begin the long walk up to the school, but paused outside Mr Fitzgerald's, curious to see what odd combination of things he would have on display today.

She felt her jaw drop in disbelief. She peered into the glass display window on the storefront, her nose practically pressing against the glass as she stared and stared. Proudly presented pride of place on the display stand was a Welsh love spoon collection. Margery would have bet a million pounds that it was the exact collection she had noticed were missing in the upstairs hallway in Caroline's house. There was still dust collected on them; he had not done

258

a particularly good job of cleaning them up before he desperately tried to get rid of them. Margery tutted at the audacity of the man.

Without thinking, she rushed into the shop, the bell above the door tinkling and startling Mr Fitzgerald, who nearly toppled over as he stood to greet her, sending the dog on his lap flying to the floor. Jason ran at her, yapping like he was a rottweiler, not the tiny ball of fluff he was, and Margery scooped him up instinctively.

'Hello, Margery!' Mr Fitzgerald beamed at her, both his hands on the desk to balance himself. 'No Clementine today?'

'No,' Margery said, putting the dog on the floor, where he ran immediately back to his owner. 'One of us has to work, I suppose!'

'Quite, don't we all? Got to make a living, haven't we?' He smiled again, but it was more of a grimace to Margery's eyes as he lowered himself back into his chair, wincing as he did so.

'Are you hurt, Mr Fitzgerald?' Margery asked carefully, watching for his reaction.

'Yes, bit of an accident I'm afraid.' His smile was gone now, and Margery thought she saw panic cross his face for a fleeting moment before he continued. 'A bit of a fall. No harm done. Could have been worse at my age.'

Margery nodded in agreement. 'Could have been much, much worse. I wouldn't climb a garden fence at my age.' She felt the anger rising inside of her. 'Let alone yours.'

Mr Fitzgerald smiled at her, but it held not even a flicker of warmth. 'It was you, wasn't it? I should have known it wasn't a window cleaner. Who cleans the inside of windows anyway?' He shook his head, staring past her to the shop's front window absently. 'I suppose you'll call the police. I did really only mean to take a few bits, but the allure was just too much. There were just so many great works of art there.' It was only then that Margery noticed the framed photograph of Caroline fixed to the wall behind the counter; she was shaking Ainsley Harriott's hand on the set of *Ready Steady Cook*.

'I'm not going to call the police,' Margery said finally. 'But can you stop stealing things from her house? It's disrespectful. Not just to Caroline but the new owner too. He might want to keep her things.'

Mr Fitzgerald stared at her, wide-eyed, raising his eyebrows. 'You've met him then?'

Margery shook her head. 'No, I haven't.'

'Well, that says it all then, doesn't it?'

Margery sighed and looked around the shop at the old tennis rackets and swimming gala trophies. Maybe it did say everything. He obviously had not cared enough to come to the funeral, had not cared enough to visit her house, had not even cared enough to show his face at all.

'Just promise me you won't take anything else,' Margery begged, 'I know you probably thought it was a great idea, but it isn't.'

'I promise,' Mr Fitzgerald said shiftily. Margery gave him a stern look, and he threw his hands up in surrender. He grinned a genuine smile at her, his mouth opening wide to show his yellowing teeth like a giant rat. 'I mean it! I don't think I could climb that fence again, honestly.'

'Good,' Margery said, eyeing the wall behind the counter again. 'Now, how much for the photograph?'

—

'Knock, knock, Margery,' Clementine said, grabbing one of the big spice containers from the shelf and waving it around. 'Can I cumin?'

Margery had gone to work after her confrontation with Mr Fitzgerald, and had started the kitchen stocktake. Partially because it needed to be done, and partially so she could hide herself away in the kitchen dry store. She ignored Clementine and continued counting the bags of pasta Caroline had over-ordered before she had died.

'Oh, come on, Margery! You can't still be angry.' Clementine slammed the cumin back into its home on the shelving unit and glared at her. 'I said sorry.'

Margery closed her eyes briefly and then snapped them open at the sound of Clementine opening a bag of the expensive dark chocolate callets they used to make Gloria's special chocolate cake recipe and helping herself to a handful.

'Hey! Put that back! They cost ten pounds a kilo!'

'Pfft, Margery. You can't put a price on delicious.'

Margery eyed her partner, whose mouth was very unattractively rolling chocolate around her face like a masticating cow. The sight made her smile, though, in spite of herself.

'Why did you apply for the job, Clem? I thought we were a team.'

Clementine swallowed and looked at her thoughtfully, a rare image that Margery had seen too often the past week or so. 'We are. Of course, we are. But I think you're better than this. Mr Barrow said your application looked great!'

'What? What application?'

'The one I made Ceri-Ann fill in for you on her computer.' Clementine looked extremely pleased with herself. 'Well, who else is going to fill Caroline's shoes? There's a reason she was such a bitch sometimes. Her job was hard! But I believe in you.'

Margery's brain was filled with a fog of confusion. 'You applied for the job for *me*?'

'Well, yeah.' Clementine went to scoop another handful of chocolate out of the bag, and Margery batted her hand away from it with her stocktake clipboard. 'Who else is going to apply for it?' She looked at Margery like she was explaining to a teenager how to use a washing machine.

'I thought you applied for *you*?'

Clementine started to laugh, nearly asphyxiating on the chocolate in her open mouth as she did so. She laughed so hard she had to hold onto the nearest shelf and nearly pulled it down on top of them as it supported her weight.

'Me! We'd all have died of salmonella in a week if I ran this stupid place! No, no, no, Margery!' She poked her head out through the dry store door. 'Hey Ceri-Ann, Margery thinks I'd be a good kitchen manager!'

There was a roar of laughter from the main kitchen, and Margery heard Gloria shout, 'Clementine can't even tell an onion from an apple, Margery!'

Clementine wiped her eyes, still chuckling under breath. 'Oh God, no, not me. You, you silly woman. You're already basically doing the job anyway, you might as well get paid for it!'

Margery thought about it; it made a lot more sense. Clementine may have been overly cocky generally and love a scheme, but she would never do any hard work. That was what she had Margery for. She felt a bit foolish for her anger now. All of it could have been avoided if she had just let Clementine explain.

'So, do you forgive me?' Clementine demanded, reaching over to dip her finger in a bag of caster sugar. Margery was too shocked to stop her this time. Everything seemed to be coming together. She could not be mad at Clementine for putting her forward for the job because she was right, they needed a new kitchen manager, and she was the only one who seemed to be able to keep on top of it all.

'Why didn't you just tell me you applied for it for me?'

'I tried! You always shut the conversation down before we could talk about it. I thought you'd just assume I applied for you not me and you were mad because I applied for you without telling you!' Clementine shrugged, her teeth crunching on the sugar granules in her mouth. Margery shook her head. All this worry and pain could have been avoided if she had just sat down and told her how she felt. She resolved to always speak her mind much more clearly in the future.

'Anyway, you should be glad I applied for you.' Clementine's face turned serious for a moment. 'Because you'd never have applied for it yourself. You don't believe in yourself enough, Margery.'

They got back to work, and Margery told Clementine all about her confrontation with Mr Fitzgerald and showed her the photograph she had purchased from him, which Clementine found hilarious. The day continued as normal as ever; Mr Barrow popped in to have his usual for lunch and to update them on Mrs Smith, as he had taken to doing since the incident. Margery resolved to go to work early the next day and ask him formally about the kitchen manager position. She had nothing to lose.

Later, as they walked home together, she thought about a question she might want Clementine to answer as they enjoyed the afternoon breeze. She could not bring herself to ask it just yet but if the events of the past few weeks had taught her anything, it was that life was short and she should stand up for herself more and ask for what she wanted. They had been living together for an exceedingly long time and they knew everything about each other. Well, Margery thought, nearly everything. Why shouldn't they get married? It was perfectly legal for them to marry now, which had always been Clementine's reason not to until the law was changed. If she got the kitchen manager job they would have the money to do it, which had always been Clementine's second reason, though she knew she should not count all her chickens before the eggs had hatched but Clementine seemed to have softened on the subject lately. The worst thing that would happen, she pondered, was that Clementine would say no and then they would carry on living just as they had before. Best case scenario, Margery would get to be the luckiest woman alive and have the privilege of calling Clementine her wife.

Anyway, now she was really thinking about it, it did not have to cost much at all. They could just have the ceremony at the registry office, and then all go back to their house for sandwiches and scones, and she could make both of their outfits for them with the old curtains she had boxed up and stored away in the attic. The material had been too lovely to throw away at the time, and it would be good to use it for something. She could see it clearly in her mind. It would be a lovely day, and an excuse for a party after the gloomy events of the last few weeks. She just had to pluck up the courage to bring it up, possibly at the weekend after they had had their Sunday roast. She could see them now cosied up by the electric fire watching a nice episode of *The Vicar of Dibley*.

Clementine, who had been yapping away more to herself than to Margery the entire walk home, suddenly stopped dead and grabbed Margery by the arm. 'Did you leave the door open this morning when we left, Margery?'

'No, Clem. I always check it's locked before we leave.'

But their front door was indeed open wide, and home no longer seemed inviting at all.

Chapter Twenty-Two

Of all the evenings she had enjoyed in her life, Margery supposed this was not one of the better ones. She groaned. Her arms being bound behind her was becoming unbearable now, and sitting on the floor against the sofa was doing nothing for her sciatica. To add even more insult to injury, Barbara had taken great pleasure in demanding Anita tie them up with her own knitting. The jumper Margery had been working on for Gloria's youngest was unravelled and ruined now; it had simply not been designed to tie elderly ladies up in their home. What a waste of wool, Margery thought to herself sadly, as she tried to stay deathly still.

She turned her head slightly to look at Clementine, who was squashed up next to her. They were both tied together by the hands with Margery's good wool. She was as stone-faced as Margery felt. Pumpkin was sat above them on the sofa busily washing herself, completely unconcerned with the kidnapping she was an impartial witness to, and Margery found herself wishing they owned a dog, the thought flickering away when she remembered that it would have needed walking over all the years that they had had the cat.

Barbara was pacing the carpet in front of them, still holding the knife she had threatened them with when they arrived home. Her hair did not look as sleek and intimidating as usual; her typical beehive bouffant had been replaced with a backcombed mess. She had obviously not had time to care for it while they had been on the run. Anita was standing in their living room doorway, similarly dishevelled, ashen-faced and shaking. Margery longed to go back in time and call the police instead of wandering straight into the house like idiots.

Barbara finally turned to look at them. 'I'm sorry it's come to this, ladies,' she said. Margery could hear the sincerity in her voice. Barbara sat down heavily in the pink crinoline chair by the bay window, plonking the knife down with a clatter that dented the coffee table as she helped herself to one of the last toffee pennies from the open Quality Street tin.

'Let us go. The police are looking for you! You won't get away with this!' Clementine yelled at Barbara from her powerless place on the floor. Barbara looked like she might scream back at her but then she sighed, her shoulders limping forwards in defeat.

'I suppose you're right about the police. I still can't believe it was you two who shopped us in.' She laughed, but there was no humour to it. 'Well, we'll see if you can talk to the police after this, shall we? An eye for an eye and all that.'

'What are you going to do?' Margery asked. She had been afraid when Barbara had first confronted them, waving the knife around like a lunatic, but she was terrified now. Barbara's demeanour had changed. She was cool and calm and ready to proceed with whatever terrible plan she had formulated.

'Some friend you turned out to be.' Clementine scoffed, wiggling manically to try and free herself. 'I thought you liked us, Barb! We always had such a good laugh.'

Barbara stared at her, radiating anger. If looks could maim, this one would have peeled all the skin off Clementine's face till it slid off in sheets. Margery saw Anita back even further into the hallway, cowering like a frightened child as Barbara dragged herself upright in the chair and stabbed a manicured finger at Clementine.

'Don't talk about friendship to me, you little witch! Friends cover for each other. Friends don't go around asking questions and poking into other people's business. Do they?'

There was a long and awkward silence, the only sound in the house the alternate ticking of the many, many carriage clocks. Finally, Margery broke the silence with a cough.

'What else could we have done, though, Barbara?' Her voice felt much too high-pitched to her own ears and her face felt hot with panic. 'You can't just go around killing people without repercussion.'

'Especially not work colleagues!' Clementine piped up, unhelpfully.

Barbara just shook her head. She searched through her bag and pulled out a carton of cigarettes and a box of matches, lighting one and taking a deep drag. Margery stared in disgust, as she exhaled the smoke all over the curtains and flicked the ash into the Quality Street tin.

'We didn't know she wasn't dead.' Her lips pursed in a grimace as she inhaled and exhaled another long stream of smoke. 'But when we found out that she hadn't been well... that was real work wasn't it, Anita?'

Anita nodded from where she was wringing her hands in the hall doorway.

'We'd convinced the headmaster that Caroline was getting a little bit unsteady on her feet. Her age, you know. And the police could have cared less once the CCTV tape didn't turn anything up. Didn't want to blemish the town's perfect record with anything as sinister as a murder, did they? Couldn't have it affecting the house prices. What a con.'

She smiled a humourless smile at them both. Margery pulled against the knots around her wrists desperately trying to free herself again to no avail.

'I was surprised when you turned up the day after we shut you in the freezer. Wasn't expecting anyone to come and free you. And we were all annoyed that you didn't die when your brakes "failed".' She added air quotations with her fingers to the word, smirking at them.

'It was you!' Clementine yelled at her. Margery could tell she was struggling against their wool bindings desperately.

'It was Cheryl.' Barbara looked down to inspect the nails of the hand not holding the cigarette. 'She's always been good with that kind of thing, car maintenance and that.'

'I can't believe you killed her,' Margery said.

Barbara slammed her fist down hard on the table, her brow furrowed in fury. The Quality Street tin jumped up into the air and fell onto the carpet, ash and toffee pennies rolling everywhere.

'We didn't kill her! It was an accident.' She leered at them nastily. 'She didn't look where she was going, and it ended badly for her.' Barbara shrugged her shoulders. 'That's all there is to it. If I'm guilty of anything it's bad management, because I didn't stop Cheryl from leaving the mop bucket on the stairs.' She scoffed at them both. 'Boo-hoo! Remind me to update the risk assessment.'

'But why wouldn't you call for help? Call an ambulance?' Margery asked frantically. 'Why just shut her in the freezer to die?'

Barbara shrugged again, her cigarette was down to the filter now. 'Hindsight is twenty-twenty, Margery. Everyone makes mistakes.'

'Yeah, but usually a mistake is putting something in the wrong recycling bin, not manslaughter,' Clementine scoffed.

Barbara ignored her; she stood from the chair and rummaged around in her large handbag, finally pulling out a bottle of lighter fluid.

'Here's the thing, though,' Barbara said, nonchalantly. 'This definitely isn't going to be a mistake. We'll get away, and this will have been just another tragedy.'

Margery stared at Anita pleadingly as Barbara popped the cap off the bottle and began sploshing lighter fluid all over the room. Anita stared back, wide-eyed, stepping backwards, before disappearing out of view into the hallway. This was it, she thought as she struggled fruitlessly against their bindings. They were going to die, burnt to a crisp in their own living room. Forget the turmeric bin-bag incident, the carpet would never recover now. She flinched as she felt a hand grasp hers and hold it tightly, but she knew it was Clementine's.

Time seemed to stand still as she turned to stare at the other woman's face, but it could have only been a few seconds at most. From the corner of her eye Margery saw Barbara drop the bottle down on the floor with a clang, and begin fumbling with the box of matches, ready to step from the room and throw in a lit match to start the inferno. She finally managed to shuffle one out of the pack and struck it across the touchpaper, but it went out as she brought it up into the air. She cursed as Margery breathed a very brief sigh of relief, then slid another one from the box. This time it stayed lit as she brought it into the air.

'I'm sorry, ladies. Any last words?' She considered them carefully. 'Like how you managed to get the CCTV footage in the first place?'

Margery opened her mouth to answer, but before she could say a word there was a tremendous crash and Barbara was flung to the floor like a rag doll, where she collapsed, narrowly missing them, crumpling dramatically onto the carpet unconscious.

Across the room stood their saviour, panting heavily. They were still holding the weapon they had hit her with, the terracotta plant pot from their front door step. Margery's favourite succulent had fallen from the pot in the force from the hit and it rolled across the living room and came to a stop in front of her on the floor.

'I gave them the CCTV tape,' Anita said, kicking the matches away from Barbara's body, still panting with adrenaline and exertion. She dropped the pot onto her unconscious back and rushed over to untie them. Margery rubbed her wrists to try and regain some of the feeling in her hands.

'What the hell just happened?' Clementine said, sounding as dazed as Margery felt.

Anita helped Margery up back onto her feet, where she swayed unsteadily for a moment. Margery looked at her, unsure of what to say.

Anita finally broke the silence. 'She had it coming.'

On the floor, Barbara groaned, and Clementine whispered down at her, 'I hope every cup of tea you ever drink is cold.'

—

After a long argument about the best knot to tie up a prisoner with, which Anita won as she already had the most practice, they reconvened to the kitchen to wait for the police. She offered to make them all a cup of tea, and Margery and Clementine agreed but only on the understanding that she did not try to poison them or any other such nonsense. It had taken all three of them to drag Barbara across the room so they could see her from their chairs in the kitchen. It was decidedly not as easy as the movies made it look.

'I knew you'd understand my notes!' Anita beamed with pride from where she was sat across from them at the table. 'Barbara always makes fun of you for doing the cryptic crosswords, so I thought I'd leave you some clues of my own.'

'That isn't what a cryptic crossword is,' Clementine said, aghast. 'And I've never actually finished a cryptic crossword. I just do them because there's always too much time on a Sunday!'

'Oh…' Anita said, looking down sadly and fiddling with the sugar spoon.

'Why didn't you just talk to me when I saw you the other night, Anita? You really scared us.'

Anita shook her head wildly. Her long blonde hair had completely fallen from where it was usually bundled on top of her head and it draped across her shoulders gracefully. Margery could not help but think it suited her much better.

'I couldn't, Barbara's been extra suspicious since the accident; if she'd have found out what I was doing, she would have killed me. It was hard enough to sneak out of the house to post it. I daren't be caught talking to you.'

'What if we hadn't figured it out, though, hmmm?' Clementine looked as though Anita had asked her to eat a big bag of wasps. 'No one would have ever found out the bloody truth, would they? What year is this for Christ's sake? You could have texted or rang or even twittered me!'

'There really is no need to swear at poor Anita, Clem,' Margery said, patting Anita's arm gently. 'She tried her best and we got there in the end, didn't we?'

Anita nodded, looking like she was on the brink of tears. Clementine pointed dramatically to the investigation board still propped up on the kitchen sideboard.

'In what way do any of those notes resemble a cryptic crossword? You did it all in anagram!'

'Well, I've never actually done a cryptic crossword, so I just assumed...'

'Assumed!' Clementine jumped up and snatched one of the notes, ripping off the cork board it had been pinned to, and shook it in Anita's face. 'A cryptic clue is the literal definition of the word, all jumbled up in some horrific way. This is just a mess. Busker cats, what does that even mean?'

'Well, it's hard writing anagrams!' Anita winced as Clementine threw the paper towards the table. It floated down slowly and gently landed in front of Margery, who continued to pat Anita's arm soothingly. This was probably the most she had ever spoken to the woman sat in front of her. It must have been very brave of her to step forward and try to tell them, as shy as she usually came across as, and constantly smothered under Barbara's wing. Without all the hair and make-up, Anita looked much younger than Margery had assumed she was. She had thought her to be in her fifties like Barbara, but Margery would be surprised if she had had her fortieth birthday yet.

Clementine sat down again, red-faced. Anita had gone quiet again and looked like she might burst into tears.

'There, there, Anita,' Margery said, pouring another cup of tea from the pot and sliding the sugar over. 'You did your best. Clementine's very sorry. Aren't you, Clem?' She kicked Clementine under the table. Hard.

'Yes, yes,' Clementine said, poker-faced, rubbing her shin. Patting Margery's hand on the table in apology. 'Very sorry.'

They sat in silence for a while, sipping and nibbling at the Party Rings Margery had got out of the good biscuit tin. She hoped the police would arrive soon; she could not wait for their ordeal to be over.

'So…' Clementine said eventually, never one for silence. 'What happened then? Why did you try and help us anyway?'

'You have to believe me,' Anita pleaded, gravely. 'It was an accident.'

'Caroline died by accident?' Clementine said mockingly, and then winced as Margery kicked her under the table again.

'I shouldn't have left the mop bucket on the stairs, I know that!' Anita burst into tears, Margery jumped up and handed her the kitchen roll from the kitchen counter. 'I didn't think. If I hadn't put it there Caroline wouldn't have fallen, and Barbara wouldn't have made us put her in the freezer, and then she wouldn't have died! It's all my fault.' She broke down into a fresh set of sobs, and Margery could not stop herself from feeling terribly sorry for her. 'Barbara insisted we put her in there or we'd get in trouble. She said we'd be fired!'

'Well, you're probably going to get fired now,' Clementine said, jumping up out of her seat so Margery could not kick her again.

Anita continued, 'I didn't try and ring you because I don't have your number, and I knew Barbara would be suspicious if I tried to get it. She's had it out for you ever since we heard you talking about Caroline's death being suspicious at the funeral. So, I thought I'd just leave you a few clues, especially after she got Cheryl to cut your brakes. That was a step too far.'

She looked between them, earnestly. 'Barbara told me she'd go to the police if I didn't get rid of the CCTV tape she stole from security, so I waited till everyone was at the wake and went to the headmaster's office and slipped it into the bag of them that Caroline gave you in her will. I thought that was the easiest thing to do, I thought you'd find it straight away.'

'We didn't,' Clementine said. Margery shook her head. If they had seen the tape first a lot of the tribulations of the past week would not have happened.

'I'm sorry' Anita sniffed again, wiping her eyes on the kitchen roll. 'I told the policeman I'd heard a noise coming from the freezer that day after Barbara shut you in as well, so that he would go and let you out.'

'Well, we're glad you did.' Margery nudged the woman standing next to her. 'Aren't we, Clem?'

Clementine nodded in agreement, then she sighed and sat down in the chair again. 'We are. It was very brave of you to do that.'

Margery agreed. She was seeing a different side to the usually meek Anita. Normally, the woman could not do or say anything without Barbara's say-so, though it was unfortunate that it had taken a murder to bring out a stronger side to her. She offered her the plate of Party Rings again and Anita took one.

'I wish I could have found some other way to tell you. But between Cheryl and Barbara it's been impossible. My husband must think I've gone mad.' She twirled the biscuit between her fingers. 'I suppose he might not want to stay my husband now. I just wish I'd gone to the police at the beginning. Asked them to protect me from Barbara. Then you wouldn't have crashed your car and Barbara wouldn't have blackmailed me.'

They sat in silence for a long time, listening to the kitchen clock tick and the refrigerator buzzing.

'We'll never get the smell of smoke out of the curtains,' Margery said finally.

'That's okay,' Clementine said, patting her hand kindly. 'We'll have a nice trip to the shopping centre. We can spend that Marks & Spencer voucher we got for Christmas.'

'I'll get you a new plant pot,' Anita said, twisting her hands together nervously. 'Sorry, it was the first thing I could grab.'

'Don't worry about it,' Margery said, 'The pot seems fine, I'll just replant the plant.'

'Good old garden centre,' Clementine beamed. 'They've got a café, you know.'

They lapsed back into silence and Margery made them all another cup of tea.

'We should have looked at the tapes sooner.' Margery sighed deeply as she watched Clementine add sugar to her cup. 'Figured it all out earlier.'

'You can't blame yourself,' Anita said. 'It's my fault for not being clear enough. And for leaving the bucket on the stairs. It's all my fault.'

'This would have all been much easier if the boyfriend had actually killed her,' Clementine groaned, slumping back in her chair in defeat. 'Who is he anyway?'

'No idea,' Anita said. 'But having met Mrs Hughes, he's living proof that love is blind and deaf.'

They laughed at that but then the doorbell rang, and they all jumped out of their skin. Margery looked at Anita one last time, questioningly, and she nodded.

She got up to let the police in, stepping over Barbara's tied-up body as she did so.

Epilogue

It may have been the middle of the long summer holiday, but the kitchen was in full swing. Margery was piping cream into the last batch of profiteroles for Ceri-Ann. She knew a croquembouche with its ginormous tower of choux pastry puffs and caramel wasn't really traditional wedding fayre anymore, but it had been such a long time coming that they'd felt they needed something elaborate for the dessert table. Clementine was over on the other side of the kitchen helping Gloria make quiches, Seren was putting together the toffee penny cheesecake, which no one had asked for or wanted, and Sharon and Karen were busily buttering bread for the sandwiches. They should have started all this a bit sooner, Margery thought privately. The wedding was tomorrow, and they had not even finished decorating the cake yet. Still, the kitchen team had been good enough to come into work on their time off, and she had not even had to ask them; they had offered.

She smiled to herself. When the headmaster had offered her the job, she had been nervous that maybe she would not be up to Caroline's level, but the longer she was Kitchen Manager the more she enjoyed her new role.

And although Margery would sometimes still wake with a start, being assaulted in your own home was one of those things that would easily wake you in the middle of the night, there had been no real harm done.

After Cheryl had admitted to cutting their car brakes, Margery had been able to claim on her car insurance. Although the pay-out would have covered another Figaro, Clementine had persuaded her that perhaps something more modern, and with airbags and safety features, would suffice for the time being. The Nissan Micra was not anywhere near as lovely, but it was a worthy sacrifice for not having to listen to the gossip on the bus. Margery felt like they had had more than enough drama for the time being, thank you very much.

Anita had pleaded guilty and took the punishment for her part in Caroline's death and stealing the CCTV footage bravely. It had not been a pretty court case, and Margery had found giving evidence particularly difficult. Anita wrote to them from prison regularly, and they planned to keep the correspondence going for the next few years until she was out. Sometimes she would write in anagram for a joke, and Clementine would put it straight in the bin in annoyance.

However long Anita's sentence seemed, Barbara Harvey had fared much worse. She had received a life sentence for the harassment and blackmail of Anita, the attempted murder of Margery and Clementine, the breaking and entering and, of course, the manslaughter of Caroline Hughes. Cheryl Higgins had received a similar fate.

It had been a huge source of outrage at the school once the news had broken, and Margery knew how hard it had been for Mr Barrow not to throw a school assembly about it, as wrapped up as he was in his grief and guilt. He had apologised to them both sincerely for not taking them seriously, even letting them use the school kitchen out of term time for their wedding planning. Margery and Clementine had decided that his ongoing relationship with Mrs Smith was enough punishment for anyone, especially now that Seren seemed to go everywhere with them. She was the worst kind of hanger-on; absolutely oblivious to being the third wheel.

Mr Barrow also had the unfortunate job of hiring an entire brand new cleaning team before the end of the summer holidays, and Margery did not envy him in the slightest. Barbara, Cheryl, and Anita may have accidentally killed someone, but no one could manage the school's cleaning schedule like they had, and the new employees would have very big shoes to fill indeed.

Clementine had wanted to send a smug letter to Officer Thomas and his young apprentice Symon, belittling them for being wrong about the car brakes, but Margery had finally managed to coax her out of the idea. Being right about Caroline's death had been enough.

Margery handed Ceri-Ann another profiterole, and then stood back to survey the scene. Yes, there was a lot to do, especially as Mrs Smith had initially refused to come and then swept into their living room yesterday with the RSVP card and a list of her many, many menu-defying dietary needs for the reception, but Margery had great faith in all of them.

'What is this, Margery?' Clementine said, wandering over holding the wedding menu, her brow furrowed. 'What have you picked for the evening? Street food? What the hell is that?'

'Oh… you know,' Margery said, stepping away from the counter to turn to her, wiping her hands clean on her apron as she did so. She was not entirely sure either, but she had been assured by Karen that they would not actually be eating outside on the pavement. 'A few of those cheesy bits and bobs, mozzarella sticks, you know.'

'Gosh,' Clementine said. 'Sounds like a right splosh-up. But if you're sure.'

She fidgeted with the menu a moment, twirling it in her fingers.

'I've umm… well… I've been practising my speech.'

'Oh…'

'Shall I read you a bit of it?'

'You can do!' Margery said, trying to remain stoic, though really there was nothing she wanted more than to hear a declaration of love from Clementine the day before their wedding. 'If you don't want to keep it a secret?'

'No, we've had enough secrets for the rest of our life-time, haven't we?' Clementine chuckled, she took a piece of paper out of the pocket of her chef trousers, and started to read from it. 'Thank you for coming everyone. It's been a very emotional day, even the cake is in tiers!' She paused to look at Margery expectantly, then put the paper away again.

'Obviously, it needs a bit of work, but that's what I've got so far!'

Margery smiled at her. She really could not wait to become Mrs Butcher-Baker tomorrow. Especially since it had taken every piece of her nerve to demand that they finally get on and do it. If it had been up to Clementine, they would have gone to their graves unwed and future historians would have labelled them 'great gal pals'.

'Done!' Ceri-Ann suddenly exclaimed, towering above them on the stepping stool. She triumphantly popped the last profiterole into place at the top of the tower, and immediately reached into her apron pocket to dig out her phone. 'I had to use a bit of glue to get it all to stick but it's all non-toxic.'

Ceri-Ann had recently left her post as an Educational Centre Nutritional Consultant, and was due to start an NVQ level 2 in 'Holistic Health and Beauty Therapy' at Ittonvale College. She had offered to come into work and help anyway, which made Margery's heart sing. They would miss her dreadfully in the kitchen. Although it was an unspoken fact that she *had* recently nearly killed someone with her beautician handiwork, she was finally going to go and do something she loved, and that meant all the world in Margery's eyes. She looked around again at the team preparing the wedding food. It had been quite a year.

As Ceri-Ann finished taking her photos and was making her way back down to the ground, a gentleman stepped through the precipice of the kitchen doorway and cleared his throat loudly enough to draw their attention.

He was wearing a smart, grey three-piece suit and his white hair was carefully slicked back with wax.

'Can we help you?' Margery asked.

Gloria put down the ribbon she was using to tie party bags and stepped behind her. Margery would have laughed at the defensiveness of it, if there had not actually been a murder in this very room.

'I'm ever so sorry, ladies, is this a bad time?' he asked politely, glancing for a second at the Rolex on his wrist. They stared at him. Margery found herself taking a step back subconsciously, nearly bumping into Gloria as she did so.

'I'm Seth Thomas. I was Caroline Hughes's, uh...' he paused, his eyes skyward, gesturing with his hands in an awkward manner, as if to think of how to say the words delicately. '...I was her friend.'

'Oh,' Margery said and turned to look at Clementine, who was gaping at him along with the rest of the team.

'I just found out about...' He sighed and tapped his fingers against the doorframe. 'Well, I received a letter from Caroline's solicitor yesterday. I think I was meant to have it a long time ago, but I've just moved into a new over fifty-fives' complex and I'm afraid he was looking for me at my old address. You know how slow the mail-redirection service can be.'

They all nodded at him in agreement, goggly-eyed.

'Gosh, we couldn't find you at the old address!' Clementine said abruptly. 'We couldn't even get through to you on the phone.'

'I've got a new phone number,' he said, brightly. 'I kept getting nuisance calls on the old one, so I sacked it in. Sorry for any bother.'

He smiled, glancing around the room, rubbing the back of his neck. Margery noticed that although the rest of him was impeccably dressed, his trousers were a little too short for his frame, and he liked his socks the same as his ladies: odd.

'I'm sorry to just barge in on you all like this, but Mr Barrow said you were in today, and I've driven all the way from Shropshire.'

'Oh my,' Margery heard Clementine say beside her. 'How exotic!'

Margery smiled at him. 'I think you'd better come and see the headmaster, and then we'll make you a nice cup of tea and some lunch.'

She stepped forward to take him by the arm gently and then they made their way down the hallway together.

–

After they had finished fitting the last piece of the new shed roof and were settled in for the evening, Clementine brought Margery a round of toast and jam in the living room, whilst Margery was putting the finishing touches to the small crocheted favours she had made for the wedding.

'Have you checked the lottery ticket, Margery?' Clementine said, as she cut the crusts off the toast for her helpfully. 'Someone in the UK won!'

Margery shook her head and they lapsed into a peaceful quiet, bothered only by the sound of the builders across the road, erecting number forty-four's new fence.

Mr Thomas had turned out to be very lovely indeed.

When he had found out what Caroline had left him in the will, he had gone straight to her solicitors to contest it. Mr Barrow had sat him down in his office on his arrival, and they had explained the whole debacle to him. He assured them both that Seren would be able to live in Caroline's house indefinitely. She had seemed unsure, saying that Mrs Smith still needed her, and he had promised her he would maintain the house and the grounds and that the offer stood if she changed her mind. He did not need the money, he had said, and he would prefer to help out one of Caroline's closest friends. Margery and Mr Barrow had exchanged a look at that last bit, but said nothing. Margery had a feeling that if Mrs Smith had her way, Seren would be moving into Caroline's tomorrow.

Suddenly, there was a knock at the door, shattering the peace.

'Who the devil could that be?' Clementine finally said, after what felt like an age. She eventually put down the butter knife and walked to the door to find out who it was.

'Mrs Mugglethwaite! To what do we owe this pleasure? At this time of night, on this very day!' Clementine enthused, beaming at the woman who looked more than a bit surprised.

'Clementine!' Mrs Mugglethwaite looked suspiciously happy to see them both, Margery thought. 'You ladies haven't been on the bus, where have you been?'

'Well...' Clementine started to say, but she was interrupted as Mrs Mugglethwaite rudely pushed past into the hallway, and made herself at home in their living room.

'As I was saying,' Mrs Mugglethwaite said, as she threw her summer raincoat onto the pink crinoline chair and slid off her sensible slip-on shoes, 'you haven't been on the bus and I've very much needed to speak to you both.'

It was only as she squashed herself down into the armchair, which looked very small in the new peach cover Ceri-Ann had ordered them from the internet to match their new peach curtains, that Margery realised what the woman was holding.

It was a copy of the front cover of the 'Dewstow Press' dated two months ago, which had a small picture of Clementine and Margery in their work uniforms next to a much bigger picture of the cleaners from the school's last end-of-year photograph. Clementine scowled at the headline for the five-hundredth time since they had first seen it in print.

'A stupid headline,' She had said. 'I would have put, "Educational Centre Nourishment Consultants Solve Mystery".'

Margery was brought back to the present as Mrs Mugglethwaite grabbed her sleeve in her old, wizened fingers; the small sheep Margery had been crocheting fell to the floor and bounced under the sofa.

'Listen, you've got to help me!' Mrs Mugglethwaite hissed. 'I have a terrible problem that needs solving.'

'What do you mean?' Margery said, her brow furrowed in confusion. 'We can't help you.'

'You can.' Mrs Mugglethwaite let go of Margery's arm to help herself to a green triangle from the new tub of Quality Street on the coffee table; Clementine narrowed her eyes at her. They were her favourite, and there were never enough in the tin.

'We really can't,' Margery said, her eyebrows raising as Mrs Mugglethwaite lifted the paper, and held it up so Margery could see the front cover clearly, tapping it so hard with her index finger Margery thought the page might rip. Mrs Mugglethwaite smiled at her.

'Of course you can,' she said through a mouthful of chocolate. 'After all, you're the Dinner Lady Detectives!'

Acknowledgements

There are far too many people to thank for this book existing, but I am going to try!

Firstly, thank you to the original Mrs Butcher for lending me your name and your Royal Family Wedding memorabilia. I hope the fictional Margery is half as lovely as you were.

To my family, I love you all so much. Thank you for all your love and support in return — special thanks to Dad, Kirstie, Mum and Jim. Thank you for convincing me to continue when I wasn't sure I should.

Thank you to Bethan Watson, I couldn't have done this without your endless WhatsApp messages of support and the many, many plays we wrote as teenagers and filmed on your Dad's VHS camcorder.

Thank you, Natasha Barrett, who suffered through some very early drafts that should probably have never seen the light of day.

Thank you, Tash Macadam, for convincing me to pitch the book on Twitter and for letting me pick your knowledgeable author brain. Also, many thanks for reassuring me that a suspended school ceiling could hold a grown adult's weight.

Thank you, Lauren 'Deadly Knitshade' O'Farrell, for the editing and advice and for your endless support in anything I've done since we met on an app. Vine forever!

A huge thanks to the whole team at Canelo for making my dream come true! Special thanks to cover designer Ami, and of course my editor Siân Heap, who worked so hard on this book with me and truly believed in Margery and Clementine and their story. The ideas you had for the cover and edits were always what I had in mind as well, it was such a fantastic experience.

But the biggest thanks of all must go to my wife, Robyn. Who didn't look at me like I'd lost my marbles too often during this process, laughed in all the right places and told me when what I'd written was stupid. Thank you for thinking I'm as funny as I think I am and thank you for coming on this journey with me. I really couldn't have done it without you or our spoilt cat babies, Cosy and Beau. I love you.